BENJAMIN FORREST AND THE BAY OF PAPER DRAGONS

CHRIS WARD

"Benjamin Forest and the Bay of Paper Dragons"
Copyright © Chris Ward 2018

The right of Chris Ward to be identified as the Author of this Work has been asserted by him in accordance with the Copyright, Designs and Patents Act 1988.

All rights reserved. No part of this publication may be reproduced, stored in a retrieval system, or transmitted, in any form or by any means without the prior written permission of the Author.

This story is a work of fiction and is a product of the Author's imagination. All resemblances to actual locations or to persons living or dead are entirely coincidental.

ABOUT THE AUTHOR

A proud and noble Cornishman (and to a lesser extent British), Chris Ward ran off to live and work in Japan back in 2004. There he got married, got a decent job, and got a cat. He remains pure to his Cornish/British roots while enjoying the inspiration of living in a foreign country.

www.amillionmilesfromanywhere.net

ALSO BY CHRIS WARD

Head of Words
The Man Who Built the World
Saving the Day

The Fire Planets Saga

Fire Fight
Fire Storm
Fire Rage

The Endinfinium series

Benjamin Forrest and the School at the End of the World
Benjamin Forrest and the Bay of Paper Dragons
Benjamin Forrest and the Lost City of the Ghouls

The Tube Riders series

Underground
Exile
Revenge
In the Shadow of London

The Tales of Crow series

The Eyes in the Dark
The Castle of Nightmares
The Puppeteer King
The Circus of Machinations

The Dark Master of Dogs

The Tokyo Lost Mystery Series

Broken

Stolen

Frozen

Also Available

The Tube Riders Complete Series 1-4 Boxed Set

The Tales of Crow 1-5 Complete Series Boxed Set

The Tokyo Lost Complete Series 1-3 Boxed Set

*It is as though, given enough time, anything can turn into anything else.
Who'd have thought it?*

Jeremiah Flowers
An Illustrated Guide to the Flora of Endinfinium
(date unknown)

THE BAY OF PAPER DRAGONS

PART I

NEW ARRIVAL

1

BIRTHDAY CELEBRATIONS

In a land with two suns instead of one, it was not so easy to predict how the seasons might change, but across the rolling hills and forests of Endinfinium, there was definitely a feeling of spring in the air. Flowers that neither Benjamin nor Miranda had ever seen poked their heads out of the spongy turf—wide, orange-headed ones, and big, yellow ones the size of dinner plates. Then there were the ones characteristic of this world, in which everything seemed backward: waist-high flowers with purple leaves and great green heads that swung back and forth—depending on the time of day—as if unsure which sun to charm, the larger yellow one that followed a conventional path across the sky from west to east, or the smaller red one that made a complete circuit of the horizon during the course of the day, never rising high above it, yet never quite dipping beneath it, either.

Today was what the teachers at Endinfinium High referred to as Sunday, because it was the one designated day off during the week. No one was quite sure what day it might have been, but long ago, a routine had been established to keep the school's pupils familiar with what they had known back in their old lives before abruptly waking up in a land where the rules weren't quite as they remembered.

The days, measured on recovered clocks whose trustworthiness depended entirely on the extent of their reanimation, lasted for just over twenty-five hours. For five successive days, classes took up eight of those, followed by clubs for those pupils who wished to join. Saturdays were for trips and excursions, while Sundays were free—provided certain rules were followed.

Even after a history stretching back several hundred known years, the teachers and the pupils weren't sure what to do with themselves on their day off.

Miranda liked to walk on the cliffs, so Benjamin inevitably went with her. Miranda, crimson-haired, athletically built, and pretty enough that both Benjamin and Wilhelm had taken note—although her recent growth spurt meant poor Wilhelm had to take note from below her eyeline—was by regular years thirteen years old. Benjamin was—at least, he thought—still twelve, but birthdays had ceased to exist upon their arrival into Endinfinium, and now they counted additional years by the cycle of four school semesters—because any kind of summer vacation was hardly practical—since the date of their first arrival.

Tomorrow was, therefore, Miranda's birthday, and while loneliness and longing was something all of Endinfinium's inhabitants had needed to come to terms with, for Miranda, it was more acute than most. Unlike Benjamin and Wilhelm, both of whom had left behind some kind of family, Miranda had come from a future neither of them had ever known.

'We used to get a cake in the Growth Centre,' she said. 'It was decorated with the number of candles of your age and red icing, because that was our cloning group.' She smiled, but Benjamin could sense her resentment. 'They always put a message in red icing, and it was always the same message: "Happy birthday, Red-37!"' She shrugged. 'I used to eat it, you know, but I never liked the taste.'

'What was it?'

'Strawberry.' She smiled again. 'I always wished I'd been part of the blonde group, because they got banana. I always liked bananas.'

'What did the brown group get?' Benjamin grinned. 'Potato?'

Miranda sighed. 'Chocolate.'

'Did you get a present?'

She shook her long, crimson hair, and it shimmered in the sunlight. Although he was a boy, Benjamin wished he could grow his hair more than a finger length without it curling up into a matted mess of little whirlpools. If he didn't get it cut at least every four months, it looked almost as bad as Ms. Ito's. Miranda, he remembered, had been created genetically perfect; she could grow her hair down to her feet and it would fall in two neat lines like a waterfall from the top of her head.

'No presents,' she said. 'We had no material possessions at all. I didn't even know what they were until I turned up here and found ... stuff ... everywhere.'

'What about clothes?'

She narrowed her eyes. 'My hair used to be a lot longer,' she said.

'So you all walked around naked? All fifty of you?'

'Don't even go there, Benjamin Forrest.'

They had trekked as far as a lookout point, two headlands down-coast from the towering post-modern mess of walls and buttresses of Endinfinium's only known school, aptly but rarely affectionately nicknamed 'The

School at the End of the World.' It wasn't quite, but a couple of miles offshore, the sea dropped away into nothingness and an empty expanse of sky, so it was certainly close. Benjamin wasn't keen to get any closer.

'What did they do with you after you grew up?' Benjamin asked.

Miranda shrugged again. 'I don't know. Perhaps they sent us off to work. I never got to find out because one day I went to bed, and the next time I woke up I was here.'

'Strange isn't it? What year did you say you came from again?'

'2887.'

'And I came from 2015, yet you got here first.'

Miranda smiled. 'Hanging out with you and Wilhelm is like hanging around with a pair of antiques.' She punched him on the arm, slightly harder than was comfortable. 'Come on, let's go down to the beach and see if we can't find me an early birthday present among all the junk.'

Benjamin shook his head. 'You know we're not allowed. We'll get a thousand cleans if the teachers find out.'

'There's only the two of us here. Who's going to dob us in?'

'But it's dangerous.'

'Everywhere's dangerous. Don't you just like to push the line a little bit?' She winked at him. 'What, are you scared? I bet Wilhelm would come. He'd be halfway down to the beach by now.'

Benjamin scowled. 'All right, race you. Whoever loses has to carry back anything we find.'

He jumped up, but as he turned to the top of the steep path leading down to the beach, Miranda stuck out a foot and he went facedown in the grass. As he got up and brushed himself off, he caught a glimpse of red hair before

Miranda descended out of sight. He groaned. On the steep, treacherous cliff path he had no chance of catching up. It would be just his luck if Miranda found a big, heavy table that she liked, washed up on the shore.

It was her birthday, he supposed, and if he was sneaky about it, he could use a little of his magic to take the weight off of his shoulders.

With Miranda's victory dance already visible in his head, he raced after her, determined that, while losing was inevitable, he could at least be close enough to not embarrass himself.

2

NEW ARRIVAL

Not all beaches were off limits without the presence of a teacher, but after new rules had been agreed upon a few months before when several people—including Benjamin and Miranda—had gotten into trouble after the Dark Man's army had attacked the school, many unsheltered beaches open to the sea or without adequate access paths had been decreed too dangerous. The sand, were it was visible in sparse patches among the shingle, was too soft, allowing for vicious reanimates to hide, and the waters themselves teemed with many creatures that would eat the pupils up without a second thought.

This, of course, only made the beaches more popular. Benjamin had barely had a taste of school life before being thrown into battle with the Dark Man, his giant, reanimated war machines, and his armies of ghouls and wraith-hounds. But now that life had settled down, he had discovered that scavenging cool stuff washed up onto the beaches was a popular pastime. Several of the pupils had secret games consoles, while others collected more mundane items like books and music, or kept tiny robots hidden under their beds. Wilhelm was the owner of a short-wave radio with which he often tried to pick up a signal from the world—or worlds, if some pupils were to be believed—beyond theirs.

As of yet, he'd had no luck, managing to catch only the pre-recorded broadcasts of other radios, still powered by solar panels suddenly inundated by the light of twin suns, as they floated down the great river that split the land in two.

Miranda waited for Benjamin at the bottom of the path, at the back of the foreshore where most of the objects around them were made of rock. Heaps of junk didn't start accumulating until further down the beach, at the highest tide line.

Where they did, though, they were impressive—great mounds of old appliances and furniture, cars and bicycles, even one or two huge industrial objects half-buried in the sand.

Further up the beach, a couple of turtle-cars ambled along the shorefront, wheels half-reformed into stumpy legs, bumpers bent into pincers to snap up food into mouths where their radiator grills had been. While easy to avoid when you could see them, they were a different proposition if you woke up and found one burrowing up out of the sand right beside you.

Miranda climbed up over a pile of junk, pulling away broken toasters and computer printers and other seaweed-choked, water-damaged items Benjamin couldn't identify. He shouted at her to be careful, but she had been on Endinfinium longer than he, of course, and as a Channeller—someone who could use small amounts of animation magic at will—she was well capable of looking after herself.

Benjamin followed her tentatively, picking his way

through the piles of junk, careful to put his hands only on flat, smooth surfaces where reanimated mouths were less likely to snap at him. The first rule of reanimation always applied—if something was warm to the touch, keep away from it. But apart from a few pens and pencils that danced along the sand like little birds, most of the items were from the long-dead depths in the silt at the bottom of the sea, unearthed and washed up in a recent spring storm. They would reanimate eventually, but even then a little bit of heat in their components might be as far as they got.

'Look!'

Miranda held something up, standing right up on top of a pile of junk with the red sun at her back so the circular object in her hands appeared to Benjamin like an eclipsed moon.

'What is it?'

'Fool, it's a clock, what does it look like?'

Before he could reply that it looked very much like a circular black shadow, she had tossed it down toward him. It was about the size of a dinner plate, and he turned it over in his hands, looking at the intricate designs behind the glass face that had been chipped and damaged by the water.

'It'll look great on my dorm room wall when Gubbledon's not looking,' she said with a grin, referring to their housemaster—a reanimated corpse of a racehorse. Gubbledon Longface—a name secret to the pupils—didn't have the greatest of memories, and if Miranda could make a convincing argument that the clock had been on her wall all along, the housemaster would eventually forget about it. She would need to clean it up first, remove the water damage, but the general way among pupils was to keep it somewhere safe and let it reanimate for a while, repairing itself. Then they would secretly sneak it past the Sin

Keeper into the lockers for a clean with the chamomile lotion to keep it from altering its form into something that might cause trouble.

It sounded like a nightmare to pull off, but as Benjamin had found out, pupils were as resourceful in Endinfinium as they were in any other boarding school. Sneaking past the teachers and school staff—human, once-human, and reanimated alike—had been refined into a fine science.

'Oh, and look at this!'

Miranda kicked aside a heap of televisions and held up a square box whose front had once been painted white, with the outline of a hand drawn on the side, like the residue of its former owner.

'What on earth is that?'

'It's a beatbox. Kind of like a drum machine or a tom. You hit it with your hands and it makes a rhythm. We could use it at secret parties so people can dance. You remember that old electric organ that Gus and Melody found? Perhaps we can start a band.' She gave it a solid slap, but it just made a gurgling sound as though full of water. Miranda shrugged. 'I suppose we'll have to let it dry out first.'

She tossed it down to Benjamin, who, right at the last second, realised just how heavy it was and jumped out of the way. It struck the rocks at his feet and the back broke off. He heard Miranda gasp, and he looked up with a guilty grin on his face.

Miranda, though, wasn't looking at him. 'Did you hear that?' she said, peering down into the junk under her feet.

'What?'

'That sound.'

'It wasn't from you? I thought that gasp was from you.'

'What do you think I am, a wuss?'

'No, but—'

'There's someone down there. Trapped, maybe. Quick, we have to get them out. If they're not expected, they might be in danger.'

Benjamin had never really understood how some pupils were expected and some were not. Apparently, Grand Lord Bastien, by way of being not fully human, had one part of his soul still trapped in the Earthly world, and therefore received vivid dreams that told him of the date and arrival of new pupils. Benjamin himself had woken up on a beach not dissimilar to this, and he would have been eaten alive by a turtle-car had Miranda not been waiting for him. For the unannounced—the numbers of which for obvious reasons were unknown—waking up in Endinfinium could be treacherous.

He climbed over the rocks to the other side of the junk pile, while Miranda climbed down. The strange gasp came again. This time, there was no doubt someone was trapped underneath.

'Hello?' Miranda asked, peering into the shadows. 'Is there someone in there?'

'Can't … move,' a voice called back. It sounded like a boy around Benjamin's age, his tone still light and feminine with a hint of a deeper tone soon to come.

'Can you move your feet?' Benjamin asked. 'Try to tap your toes on something.'

To Benjamin's right, a soft rhythm tapped out against an old flatscreen TV, and when he pulled away a soggy cardboard box that had been covering it, he revealed a foot sticking out.

'I see you!' he cried. 'Hold still, we'll pull you out.'

It didn't take them long to locate the boy's other foot, and after checking that he wasn't caught on anything, on the count of three, they took hold of one ankle each and dragged him out onto the sand.

He was about their age, skin slightly silvery as if still wet, hair slicked back against his scalp. He wore a plain linen shirt and linen trousers, and his shoes were simple beige gym shoes. Either his parents didn't like colour very much, or he came from a poor family.

Then he lifted his head to shake water out of his hair, and Benjamin's mouth opened in surprise.

Beside him, Miranda gave a soft gasp, one hand lifting to cover her face.

3

RIVER SOURCE

The boy's hair was a perfect aquamarine blue, a colour so deep and absolute that his hair looked more like water than the sea did, which only accentuated the smooth, perfect features of his face. Benjamin thought he looked like a futuristic teenage pop star, and at first, as he watched Miranda stare at the boy with utter astonishment, he wondered if she felt the same.

'Blue,' she whispered, reaching up to touch her own trailing crimson hair, and Benjamin understood.

The boy climbed stiffly to his feet, then picked a piece of seaweed off of his clothes. 'Thank you,' he said. 'I don't know how long I was stuck under there. I saw those creatures moving and I was too scared to move.'

Miranda grinned. 'They're harmless,' she said.

'Not when they're about to eat you,' Benjamin added, winning him a scowl from Miranda. 'I'm Benjamin Forrest,' he said, sticking out a hand. 'And this is Miranda Butterworth. Welcome to Endinfinium, I suppose.'

'Thanks.' The boy shook Benjamin's hand then turned to Miranda. 'Red—'

'Red-37,' she finished. 'Batch 17, Maturity year 2893. You?'

'Blue-9. Batch 16, Maturity year 2891.'

Benjamin looked from one to the other. Not only did they seem to know each other, but the newcomer was two years older than Miranda, and—it pained Benjamin to admit—quite handsome. Wilhelm would be gutted when he found out.

'Red-37,' the boy said. 'You were famous for disappearing, you know.'

Miranda shrugged. 'Not really my fault. And I go by Miranda these days.'

'How pretty.'

Miranda's cheeks flamed a crimson colour to match her hair. Benjamin, standing between them, felt awkward enough that he almost wished one of the turtle-cars would pop up out of the sand and chomp down on his ankles, just so he had an excuse to get out of their line of sight.

'And you?'

'I've never really thought about it, but I suppose … Cuttlefur.'

'Cuttlefur?' Benjamin snorted. 'You can pick something else, you know. How about Bob?'

'Cuttlefur is the name of my favorite flower,' the boy said, giving Benjamin a sour look. Miranda had tilted her head to one side and now gave a long sigh that made Benjamin feel nauseated.

'I've never heard of it,' he said. 'What kind of flower?'

'Benjamin's not from the same time as us,' Miranda said. 'Times don't work here like they do elsewhere.'

Cuttlefur lifted a manicured eyebrow. 'Oh, really? When are you from?'

'2015.'

'Wow. You're practically a caveman, aren't you? I

suppose it hadn't been developed then. It's a beautiful, dark blue flower that only comes out in moonlight.'

'Sounds lovely.'

'Sounds wonderful.' Miranda was swooning so badly she was practically falling over. Finally, a grinding of metal not far behind them indicated they'd attracted the attention of a turtle-car, which was slowly clacking in their direction.

'Let's get Cuttlefur back to the school,' Benjamin said.

They made their way back up the steep cliff path, stopping every so often for Cuttlefur to catch up. The boy's legs were stiff, as though he had been unmoving for a long time, and Benjamin felt an uncharacteristic desire to berate him, except he remembered that feeling well. Obviously, since Miranda had come from hundreds of years in the future, the laws of time in Endinfinium didn't quite add up with those in the world they had come from, so an indefinite amount of time might have passed between being whisked away from their regular life by a force Benjamin still didn't quite understand, and ending up here in Endinfinium.

'Wow, it's quaint,' Cuttlefur said, when he got his breath back at the top of the cliff. 'What there is of it.'

'You get used to it,' Benjamin said.

'I think it's pretty,' Miranda said. 'At least all this rubbish got used for something useful.'

Endinfinium, as far as they could tell, was made entirely of ancient rubbish that had corroded over time back into soil and rock, or had decided to reanimate into some form of life. The hills and cliffs looked like the hills and cliffs of any other country, while the forests, too, looked just like forests. Living in them, however, were all manner of unusual creatures, while the great river that flowed down from the north, cutting them off from the vast Haunted Forest to the west and the High Mountains—home of the Dark Man—beyond, was filled at times to bulging with rubbish, much of which had reanimated into bizarre sea creatures by the time it reached the ocean.

Benjamin would never forget almost being eaten by a monstrous cruise-shark, a reanimated ocean liner that prowled the outer edges of the known sea.

'Does the sea really just fall over the edge?' Cuttlefur asked as they headed north along the clifftop. 'I mean, where does it go?'

'We're not allowed to go and look,' Benjamin said. 'It's too dangerous.'

Cuttlefur grinned. 'But you want to, don't you?'

Benjamin shrugged. 'I used to. I'm not sure anymore if I do or not.'

As Cuttlefur turned to Miranda and their conversation drifted to a life they once both shared, Benjamin stared westwards, watching the great river as it meandered through the hills from north to south, before abruptly cutting east and widening into the sea. At this time of the year, the waters were low, the surface grey and smooth, the thrown-away treasures it carried hidden below the surface. The ferry, the only way across, had been rebuilt and improved, and was now staffed by a group of cleaners, mindless workers who staffed the school kitchens as well as did odd jobs like cleaning and gardening. All trips across to the Haunted Forest, however, were by express permission of a teacher. Rumours were abound that despite the Dark Man's apparent banishment, ghouls had still been spotted flitting between the trees.

Benjamin's foot caught on a protruding gorse root, and he stumbled, breaking out of his reverie. Miranda and Cuttlefur were some twenty paces out in front, their brightly coloured heads leaning close, talking in excited tones. Benjamin felt a sudden pang of loneliness; after all, he was still relatively new here, too, and whenever he spent too much time alone he got thinking about the past and his old life back in Basingstoke in England before he had one day woken up on a strange beach with a creature that looked like a cross between a turtle and a car trying to eat him.

He peered out at the river again, wondering for the thousandth time not where it was going, but where it came from.

One day, he promised himself, he would find out.

4

RESCUED FRIEND

'This way,' Professor Eaves said, leading the small group down the hill path to the trickling stream in the valley below.

Wilhelm looked up at a cluster of dark clouds that had begun to obscure the yellow sun. This low down, the light of the red sun passed over their heads, creating a line of shadow further up the hillside. Out of the sun it was pretty chilly, and he wished he'd brought an outer jacket like some of the other nine kids in the Rambling Club. Still, it was nearly eleven, and the schedule said they would return to the school at half past in order to get back in time for lunch.

Beside him walked a sullen Snout, the tall boy with the slightly bent-up nose whose real name was Simon Patterson even though the teachers sometimes forgot, looking decidedly miserable. Snout, whose unusual skill of calling ghouls up out of the ground—plans to integrate the term 'Ghoul Caller' into the school's records were still ongoing; they had only stalled because so far Snout was the only one anyone knew of with such a specific skill—meant he had to be careful about concentrating too hard on anything negative. Ghouls, semi-magical creatures created from the broken parts of machines fused with the souls of the dead, were the Dark Man's unofficial fingers. Snout, by his very skill, required another boy to watch him at all times, even though Wilhelm had found him to be perfectly friendly now that his nasty ringleader, Godfrey, was no longer around.

'Over here, we have a *Petroneous Libicus*,' Old Dusty Eaves was saying, pointing to a tall purple flower that resembled a foxglove poking out from between two grey rocks. 'It only flowers once every two years, its bloom lasting just a week, so you're really lucky to see it today.'

Murmurs of agreement rose up that didn't sound all that lucky. Other kids were probably also thinking about lunch. Dusty Eaves squatted down and began to make a cutting from one of the flowers. Wilhelm glared at the bulge just below his shoulders most people thought was a slight hunchback, but what Wilhelm, Benjamin, and Miranda knew were hidden wings. It didn't matter that Grand Lord Bastien claimed Dusty Eaves was on their side; Wilhelm was convinced the old, moth-eared professor was a denizen of the Dark Man, and wherever possible, refused to let him out of sight.

Rambling Club was pleasant enough, but the twice-weekly evening Taxidermy Club was a real chore, particularly when the only other pupil, a fourth-year called Colin Gibbs, hardly ever showed up.

'All right,' Dusty said, as if reading minds, 'let's start heading back. Good job, everybody.'

Wilhelm didn't really understand who had done a good job, since no one had actually done anything other than follow Professor Eaves along a series of dirt trails for the last three hours. But teachers here in Endinfinium, just like in his old school back in England, existed on a different level of what was considered interesting. Teachers were teachers, Wilhelm remembered.

Some of the kids up front were whispering about a game of football out on the front courtyard after lunch, but Wilhelm—who was about as good at sports as he was at taxidermy—edged toward the back to keep an eye on Old Dusty. He wasn't sure what he expected the professor to do, but ever since the Dark Man's attempted destruction of the school, life had been unnaturally quiet. Something bad had to happen soon, and something a lot worse than earning a thousand cleans for being caught spying through Dusty's apartment window at midnight.

'Well, look at that.'

Dusty had stopped to peer into the path-side shrubs, and Wilhelm turned back to look just as the old professor lifted something grey and plastic out of the bushes. Wings the size of the professor's palms and made of white plastic flapped frenetically.

'What is it?'

'A Scatlock. The little blighter was caught on a branch.'

Wilhelm gave a nonchalant shrug. He was going to be late to lunch for this? Scatlocks, the hideous bat-like creatures made from reanimated plastic bags, that knocked pupils off of the cliffs to their deaths…? Nope. As far as Wilhelm was concerned, they should all be incinerated.

'Can you still fly, little friend?'

Professor Eaves tossed the Scatlock up into the air, and for a moment, it was caught on the wind, its wings fluttering wildly, then it spun earthward, with only a sudden updraft stopping it from crashing into the path.

Instead, it bobbed back up on the wind and slammed straight into Wilhelm's midriff.

He was too surprised to cry out. The Scatlock lay flat

across his jacket as thin as the plastic the creature was made of. As the wind gusted, the Scatlock made a couple of brief attempts to lift its wings, then gave up and just held on tight.

'Oh-ho. Looks like he likes you, boy.'

Wilhelm looked up at Professor Eaves, then back down at the Scatlock. He had never seen one up close and still before: they were usually fluttering so fast, it was impossible to make out their features. Now that he looked at it closely, though, he saw that its reanimation had given it a clear form: two wide wings, a body along where the bag's seam had been, and a head made out of the bags handles twisted together.

Two little beady eyes, their ovals made from the faded blue of a long-forgotten supermarket logo, looked up and blinked.

The wind rustled across its wings in a sound reminiscent of a purr.

Professor Eaves stumbled over as Wilhelm carefully detached the Scatlock from his waist and held it up in his hands.

'See there, boy.' The professor pointed. 'Got a tear in his wing. He's done for. Toss him back in that stream, and he might tumble in with something else and reanimate in time.'

Taxidermy Club had some benefits. Their work had been exclusively on reanimated objects, and while it had been rather bizarre to fix up cups and plates twisted and reshaped until they had legs and feet, he had learned from Professor Eaves that, rather like recycling itself, most objects would only reanimate a certain amount of times before they were forever labeled as inanimate rubbish only good for the incinerator that pumped heated water throughout the school on cold nights. Objects made from natural materials such as wood and stone could reanimate dozens of times, but those of synthetic materials would reanimate a number of times seemingly in correlation with their complexity. Something like a computer could be cleaned weekly for years on end, but a simple creature like a Scatlock, reanimated from a single plastic bag, had only one chance at its new life.

Dusty had wandered on up the path, while Wilhelm still stood holding the injured Scatlock. He had never owned a pet before. He remembered always wanting a cat or a rabbit: something he could cuddle. A bat-like creature made out of a plastic bag wasn't quite what he'd dreamed of, but from the way it rustled in a comforted manner, he got the impression that it was quite willing to be a pet in return for a little servicing.

'Hmm ... what to call you?' Wilhelm frowned, trying to come up with a suitable name. He thought back to books he had read in the orphanage, but couldn't think of any, until he remembered the rabbit his primary school class had kept as a pet during term time.

'Rick,' he said, giving the little curl of plastic a pat on the head. 'Your name is Rick. Is that okay with you?'

The Scatlock rustled, seeming satisfied.

Instead of following the others straight to the dining hall, Wilhelm headed up to the school's fifth floor, then out onto the treacherous cliff path that arced around to the pupils' dorms—a rickety, wooden building perched on top of a narrow headland. Along this section of cliff, the flocks of Scatlocks were notoriously dangerous, swooping down at passing pupils as though they had a bone to pick from some past life. In addition to the obvious risk of plummeting to one's demise, Scatlocks inadvertently caught in one's clothing could cause trouble in the dorms either by lodging in one of the fans or squeezing through a window gap and making it large enough for others to get in. For that reason, inside the doors of the school and the dormitory stood a cupboard from which a single-zipping Scatlock-cape should be taken, zipped up over one's body, then used to get across the path before shaking loose onto the porch any caught Scatlocks.

As Wilhelm donned his cape, Rick made an excited rustling noise. He figured few Scatlocks had ever been inside a Scatlock-cape before, and that for something which—outwardly at least—had the mental agility of a mosquito, must have been quite the thrill.

He hurried across to the doors, then got out of his cape. The dorms were empty, of course, with everyone, including the housemaster, over in the dining hall. Wilhelm left Rick sitting on a table in the common room while he ran into the office beside the little dorm kitchen. There, amongst the piles of junk, he hunted out an old cardboard box and a roll of tape.

Upstairs in the room he shared with Benjamin, he fixed up Rick's torn wing with a piece of tape, then used a couple of small towels from his drawer to make the Scatlock a nest inside the box. The creature's wing would take a few days to knit back together, after which the Scatlock would want to be released, he assumed. But for now, it seemed fine to sit among the blankets, its plastic body rustling lightly with contentment.

As Wilhelm watched it, he realised he'd already developed a sense of fondness for the creature. Shame to see it gone so soon, he thought, as he slid the box under his bed and headed off to catch the end of lunch.

5

LIBRARY

'For this year's first-year school excursion, you'll be going up north to the Bay of Paper Dragons,' said Professor Robert Loane, the second highest-ranked of the teachers, after Grand Lord Bastien. 'The bay is thirty miles north of here, and the only place in Endinfinium where the dragons can be observed in their natural habitat.'

Benjamin glanced at Wilhelm standing two places to his left, as Loane droned on about what coursework they would have to do before embarking, and what they would need to take with them. Wilhelm, though, didn't appear to be paying attention; he kept casting furtive glances at Miranda standing further along the line, who, in turn, had her gaze fixed on Cuttlefur standing in the shadows to the right of the stage. Cuttlefur was flanked on one side by the wild Ms. Ito, and on the other by the wide Captain Roche who, even standing near side-on to watch Professor Loane make his speech, made the triumvirate seem lopsided by his sheer width.

The blue-haired boy, for his part, stood calmly with his hands behind his back, looking out at the assembled pupils.

Whenever Benjamin looked up at Cuttlefur, his gaze, more often than not, seemed directed at the left corner of the group, conveniently where Miranda stood.

'And finally,' Professor Loane said, 'we have a new pupil to introduce.' He waved Cuttlefur forward. 'This is, um, Cuttlefur, come to us from the year 2887. Cuttlefur, please say a few words to the pupils.'

The boy approached the front of the stage, leaned over the microphone, and smiled. 'Thanks for accepting me into your school,' he said. 'It was quite a surprise to wake up here, but I'm sure we'll have a lot of fun together. Thanks.'

Bored applause from the boys was drowned out by frantic applause from the girls, none of whose was louder than Miranda's. She turned to glare at two of the fifth-years, whose catcalls had made Cuttlefur blush. Glancing back at Wilhelm, Benjamin saw his friend looking despondently at the floor while pretending to clap.

~

'I wish we were going for a month,' Wilhelm said, holding up the information leaflet for Benjamin to see. 'Anything to get out of this place.'

'What on earth is a paper dragon, anyway?' Benjamin said. The leaflet was tantalisingly vague, talking only about how these 'dragons' were to be found nowhere else on Endinfinium. Having seen plenty of monsters in the few months he had been here, Benjamin wasn't too keen on seeing more.

'Probably nothing to get excited about,' Wilhelm said. 'At least for a few days we'll get to do something other than wander around the school. Plus, Dusty's coming, so I can keep an eye on him.'

'Has he given himself away yet?'

Benjamin still clearly remembered their run-in with Dusty Eaves in the cave of the Haulocks, the large, black, plastic sack-based cousins of the Scatlocks. Despite trying to capture them, Professor James Eaves had later laughed it off as an attempt to keep them out of trouble.

'Not yet, but he will, believe me.' Wilhelm sighed. 'And you know who else I don't trust?'

'Who?'

'That new kid. Cuttle-what's-his-name?'

'Cuttlefur.'

'That's it. I wouldn't trust him as far as Ms. Ito could throw him.'

'Why not?'

'He practically knows Miranda, for starters. All of us here are from years apart, yet they're as good as brother and sister. That's quite some coincidence, isn't it?'

'I suppose, but Endinfinium doesn't exactly follow any rules, does it?' Benjamin grinned, giving Wilhelm a nudge in the ribs. 'You're just jealous.'

'No, I'm not. How could I be jealous of a kid with blue hair?'

'Some people think hair like that is kind of cool.'

'Well, I think it looks stupid. Don't you?'

Benjamin shrugged. While blue hair was certainly more interesting than his own tabletop brown, he had to show solidarity with his friend. 'Of course,' he replied.

'See?'

'Well, at least he won't come on the school trip, since he's a third year.'

'There is that.'

In an attempt to change the subject, Benjamin pulled a map of Endinfinium out from the pile of leaflets and notices from Professor Loane. The school sat in the middle, perched on a line supposedly representing the coastline. It meandered south, past the river estuary, then a little way further on. The Bay of Paper Dragons was indicated right at the top of the map, to the north. Benjamin sighed. It wasn't exactly detailed. Whole areas to the east and west were blanked off, with no river source. The thick blue line just ran off the edge of the paper and disappeared.

'Is this the best they've got?' he wondered aloud.

'Best of what?'

'The best map. There must be a more detailed one somewhere.'

Wilhelm shrugged. 'I suppose the library might have one. Do we really have to go down there?'

'Yeah…' Benjamin shivered. 'It's a shame there aren't any computers we can use to check. If we all go, it won't be so bad.'

'We stick together,' Wilhelm said. 'No wandering off. Say, do you think Miranda would want to come?'

Benjamin shook his head. 'I think she was given the task of showing Cuttlefur around.'

'Oh, the new kid. Right.' Wilhelm nodded. 'Perhaps we could bring him along … and leave him there.'

6

CLEAT

The library was on the third basement level, just one above the locker room and two above the incinerators where all of the rubbish that could no longer reanimate was sent. It was set in a series of groaning, wood-framed rooms that could have once been part of a medieval mock-up cellar, all warping crossbeams and sinister, poorly lit alcoves where even the shadows wouldn't run from a lamp. Shelves of old books, most of which had been washed up on the beaches or plucked out of the river and dried, filled every available space. A mixture of subjects and seriousness, seemingly at random, from all points in history. Benjamin found novels in the sci-fi section with publication dates of 2800 A.D. or beyond, so many of the mysteries of Endinfinium could possibly be solved with a large-scale blitz of the library. Unfortunately, wading through shelves of tatty history books was as boring for Benjamin as it would have been for any other twelve-year-old. And the library at Endinfinium, of course, was unlike any other.

With the exception of one small section—books written in Endinfinium itself—all shared a common theme:

shabby and water-damaged, often incomplete. And they had a tendency to reanimate. Once a year, the library itself was sprayed with deanimation fluid to stop the walls from moving around, but at any one time, you could put your arm across the spines of a row of books and pick out one or two that were warm or even tingling. Some even shifted around, as if fighting to break free.

'Look, there's one of those people,' Wilhelm said as they turned the last corridor before the library's entrance, a large archway with trellised doors. 'Wow, he must be two hundred years old.'

The shuffling man carrying a basket of books looked up with a crinkled face framed by white hair, though his eyes stared right through them at the wall beyond. Stooped low, the old-timer stumbled past, clutching the handles of the wire basket in two gnarled hands as he headed for the stairs leading down to the locker room. As he got close, Benjamin and Wilhelm flattened themselves against the wall as if the vacant creature might turn full zombie and try to rip out their hearts.

'Anywhere else, they're cool,' Wilhelm gasped while the man started down the stairs. 'But here, there's just something about them that chills the blood, isn't there?'

'It's like they were designed with this job in mind,' Benjamin said.

A team of cleaners worked around the clock, picking out books close to regaining a life of their own and hauling them down to the locker room, where kids sent for punishment deanimated them with chamomile-based liquids. Then the cleaners would carry them back up and slot them into the correct shelves.

The shock of the stumbling, near-lifeless cleaners only lasted for the first few days in Endinfinium, since they were everywhere, given menial work from cleaning to

Benjamin Forrest and the Bay of Paper Dragons

maintenance to preparing school dinners. Corpses of the long-dead, controlled by the same reanimation magic that permeated everything. Generally, they appeared across the river in the Haunted Forest, periodically collected and brought to the school to keep them out of trouble. However, while most could be mistaken for regular people, the teachers had seemingly placed a cruel trick on any pupils wanting to study in the library by staffing it with the most ancient, most ghastly cleaners, who stumbled through the dimly lit corridors like the ghosts of dead librarians.

With the cleaner out of the way, Benjamin and Wilhelm ran for the entrance, clutching each others' arm for moral support. As usual, no other pupils were in the library, and the tall bookshelves led off in multiple directions, like the entrances to some vast subterranean labyrinth.

'What do we do now?' Wilhelm asked.

'Let's split up,' Benjamin said. 'You go left, and I'll go right. Call out if you find the maps section.' At Wilhelm's horrified stare, Benjamin grinned. 'Only joking. Let's stick together. Left or right?'

As a wild-haired cleaner lumbered out of the stacks to their right, Wilhelm signaled left, and they hurried away as if fleeing from a chilling breeze.

Benjamin had only been in the library a handful of times, always with the rest of his class as part of a library study period, and it didn't seem so bad when there were fifteen kids and a teacher wandering about. Now, it just seemed sinister, as if the lights might go down at any moment to leave them floundering in the darkness.

They were quickly lost among the bookshelves. The library had more than one floor, with several mezzanine levels at the top and bottom of rickety staircases, seemingly not connected to the walls. Dark spaces over the bannisters plunged into immeasurable black depths below the school.

'Reckon if I toss a book down there it'll make a splash?' Wilhelm said, leaning over the corner bannister of one especially unstable staircase.

'I don't know about that,' Benjamin said, 'but you'll get a thousand cleans if anyone spots you. You remember how these books are supposed to be priceless?'

'Of course they're priceless. They're worthless. No one would pay for any of this junk. The smell alone is doing my head in.'

Everything stank of salt underneath a layer of chamomile, though it certainly could have been worse.

None of the shelves were labeled, so they quickly lost their bearings. 'This is a waste of time,' Benjamin said, pushing back into the shelf a book on eighteenth century postal systems. 'There's no order to anything.'

'Perhaps we should just give up,' Wilhelm said, tugging at Benjamin's arm.

'Maybe you're right.'

They headed back to where they guessed the entrance should be, just as the shelf to their left creaked and a cleaner stepped out in front of them.

Together, Benjamin and Wilhelm gasped as the shaggy, grey-white mop of hair lifted and a pair of vacant eyes peered out of a partially decayed face.

'Business?' wheezed ancient lungs.

The boys exchanged a look. Cleaners, to the best of their knowledge, couldn't speak. Something about that part of their brain having never returned from the dead.

'Um ...'

'Louder. Ears ... broke.'

'Um ... the map section? I'm looking for a map of Endinfinium.'

The cleaner grunted, then nodded to the right as though to indicate they should follow him that way.

He moved slowly, dragging one leg behind him, holding on to the bookshelf stacks for support. Benjamin glanced back at Wilhelm who mouthed, 'He's not a cleaner, is he?' though he had no time to reply as the old-timer increased his pace like an old car warming up in the sun, jagging back into barely visible shelf stacks as if purposely trying to lose them.

Finally he came to a halt at a little wooden table that stood surrounded on all sides by shelf stacks.

'Map section,' the man said, stepping back against the wall to let them pass. As Benjamin nervously picked a book off of the shelf, discovering a map book of the Edinburgh sewage system circa 1920, the man added, 'Left stack. Fourth shelf.'

'Thanks.'

The wild old man showed no intention of leaving as Benjamin pulled a wooden box with the single word 'WORLD' on its spine and placed it onto the table. He lifted off the lid to reveal a folded parchment map like something out of a museum, aware of the old man's gaze on the side of his face. Wilhelm stood on Benjamin's other side, as if using him as a human shield.

'Um, thanks,' Benjamin said again, hoping the prompt would encourage the old man to move on, but when it became clear that he wouldn't, Benjamin instead asked, 'Who are you? You're not a cleaner, are you?'

'What? Ears ... louder.'

'You're not a cleaner!' Benjamin shouted, and even in a library where the three of them were likely the only living people, he still felt internally scolded for breaking the most sacred of library rules.

'No need to shout. Name's Cleat. Harold Cleat. Head

Librarian.' His lips wrinkled in the hint of a smile. 'Only librarian.'

'You're not a cleaner?'

'What?'

'A cleaner!'

Cleat shook his bushy head. 'Nope.'

'Not one for conversation is he?' Wilhelm whispered.

'Um, Mr. Cleat, can you tell him how long ago this map was made?'

'What?'

Benjamin repeated his request with another shout.

'How long have you got?'

'How many years ago was it drawn?'

Cleat shrugged. 'No need to shout. Hard to tell. Time ain't like normal time here.' He shuffled forward, gestured for Benjamin to open up the map. He did so, spreading it out onto the tabletop in a plume of dust.

At first it was difficult to understand, having been drawn up like the kind of ancient maps Benjamin had seen in dusty old museums, although with strange markings and unfamiliar symbols. Then, when Wilhelm pointed to a thicker line that appeared to be the coastline, it all began to become clear.

'We're going to the Bay of the Paper Dragons on a school trip,' he said to Cleat. 'Where's that?'

Cleat poked a stubby finger at a point near the top of the map. 'Here.'

Benjamin leaned closer. The coastline cut into a tight inlet where something was drawn swimming in the water, though it was too faded to make out clearly.

'Sea monsters!' Wilhelm said. 'Not dragons, sea monsters!'

'One and the same,' muttered Cleat.

While Wilhelm still talked excitedly about the dragons

and Cleat squeezed out a few words in response, Benjamin turned his gaze inward, picking out the dark line of the meandering river in the hills to the west of the school. He put his finger on it, then slid it up toward the top of the map, but rather than going over the edge like it did on the map Loane had given them, it stopped at an abrupt black smudge, with a little space beyond it for more rolling hills.

He put his finger on the black mark. 'What's this?' he asked Cleat.

'That?'

'Yes.'

'River source.'

Benjamin stared at him, frustrated, his old anger beginning to rise. Too many questions, not enough answers.

'But what kind of river source is it? Like a spring or something? Doesn't look like it just fades into nothing like a normal river should.'

'Culvert.'

'A what?'

'Culvert.' Cleat made a pouring gesture with his hands. 'Water comes out. Makes river.'

'What's on the other side of the culvert?'

'What go in.'

'Where from?'

Cleat looked up at him and a steady smile spread across his wizened old face. 'Head librarian,' he said, poking a bent finger at his own chest. 'No architect.'

Finally the old man thought of something else to do, and he stumped off into the shelf stacks. Benjamin stared at the map for a long time, even after Wilhelm had gotten bored and wandered off to look for comic books.

Benjamin was still staring at the map when Cleat reappeared clutching something big and dusty in his hands, which he dumped onto the table, and a plume of dust made Benjamin cough.

It was a thick book with browned, brittle pages. Cleat opened it to a place somewhere in the middle bookmarked with a ruler to a page covered in handwritten text, nearly impossible to read.

'Sixty-four years,' Cleat whispered, leaning forward, and Benjamin smelt musty carrots on his breath as if the old man chewed them straight out of the ground. 'We all come here young, like the old don't believe enough to make it. I was like you, once. Dreaming of a way out. Still am. Just too old now, even if I do find something.' Cleat grinned suddenly, mouth widening against rows of irregular-shaped teeth, as if he'd stolen them from the dead and had arranged them in the dark. 'Say Cleat's mad, some do. All these years holed up in this dusty place, picking through books no one wants, only the cleaners for company while just one step away from being one myself.' Cleat gave an exaggerated shake of his head. 'Not mad, just persistent.'

Benjamin looked down at the book Cleat held open. He squinted at it, trying to get the faded grey script to form into words.

"Spring water can come from the ground, but junk … junk has to come from somewhere." Benjamin looked up, realising Cleat was reciting the passage from memory. "The river is full of junk that has the distinctive markings of companies well known by people from Earth. It comes through the gushing culvert at the top of a sloping hillock I've named Source Mountain for simplicity's sake. The water could come from the ground, but the heaps of junk … they have to come from somewhere. I have thereby tasked myself with entering this culvert and somehow finding a way through."

Benjamin peered at the words, guessing what point Cleat was up to. He was pretty sure he'd figured out which of the scribbles meant 'junk' when Cleat abruptly slammed the book shut.

'I was, um, reading that.'

Cleat sighed. 'You won't find anything else of use. I know. I've read it six times. Essays by different travelers who went off to explore the farthest reaches of Endinfinium. The traveler who went looking for the culvert was a well-known botanist named Jeremiah Flowers. He seems to have had a bit of an obsession with his object's namesake; I've found several books that he wrote describing Endinfinium's flora. But anything after this short passage ... nothing.'

'So he made it through?'

'Or perished trying. Who knows?' Cleat shrugged, then prodded a finger at the tabletop. 'The only thing that's certain is that he never came back.'

7
DATE

'A thousand years, at least,' Miranda said as they walked to class, Benjamin on her right, Wilhelm on her left. 'The school's at least that old. Perhaps ten thousand. And in all that time, they've never admitted that there's any such thing as magic. It's all quite exciting, really.'

'Well, it's not really magic, is it?' Wilhelm replied, earning a stern glare for his disagreement. 'It's just a kind of science that we don't understand yet. What else could it be?'

Miranda scoffed. 'You're such an unbeliever. They should burn you at the stake for the heathen you are.'

'I just don't buy into all that hocus-pocus stuff. What about you, Benjamin?'

Benjamin shrugged. Not that he didn't believe it, he just had no choice. Whether he liked it or not, he could do what he could only describe as magic.

And it had nearly killed him. Now, only with careful, private practice with Grand Lord Bastien had he learned how to use it without immediate danger to himself, though should another dangerous situation arise, he doubted he would remember his training in time.

The fifteen first-year pupils crowded into a concrete science laboratory with shelves and cupboards brim-full of all manner of dusty bric-a-brac. The only difference between this room and one of Benjamin's former school's science laboratories was that some of the items in glass jars and cages were alive.

One metal cage flickered with trapped Scatlocks. Another sealed glass tank contained several soda pop cans bouncing off of each other and knocking into the glass.

'They could make a zoo out of this place,' Wilhelm said as they shuffled behind a row of benches and sat down. 'Not sure I'd want to pay to come in, though.'

The pupils were still chatting when a door on the other side of the room opened to allow in Professor Loane. The tall, boyish teacher, who wore an expression of part smug, part embarrassment, went to a podium in front of the blackboard and called for quiet.

'Hello, everyone. As you know, this is your first lesson of a new course. Animation Science. I suppose you're wondering what that means. Well, for almost the length of time this school has existed, we have lived in the shadow of … um, our circumstances. As you've probably noticed, this world isn't quite like the one you may have come from. It has certain … peculiarities….'

Wilhelm rolled his eyes so much, Benjamin wondered if they wouldn't get stuck on the wrong side of his head, and Miranda stared at the door as though she had forgotten something back in the dorm. Benjamin tried to concentrate on the professor's speech, which was sounding far too much like an apology than an explanation.

'It was believed by the Teachers' Inner Circle that studies

of reanimation and ... um, what abilities you might have to influence it, were detrimental. However, we have now decided to take a more modern view of things, on a short-term, trial basis.' At the sound of an exaggerated sigh from the back, he concluded, 'So without further ado, let me introduce you to your new Animation Science teacher, Professor Caspian.'

'Edgar!' Miranda cried out as the door opened again and a diminutive, old man dressed in a medieval tunic entered the room. Edgar Caspian, the one who had helped them in their battle against the Dark Man, had always been considered an outcast because of his refusal to hide the existence of reanimation magic. He lived in a rather unique cave down on the beach, where, among other things, he was Miranda's secret magic teacher.

'Um, Professor Caspian will do,' Professor Loane said. Then, with a flourish of his hands, added, 'Over to you, professor.'

'It's nice to be here in front of you,' Edgar said, his small, knowing eyes taking in all of the gathered faces. 'Many years ago, I used to teach in this very same room. Unfortunately, circumstances had led me to take a break for a few decades.'

Miranda glanced across at Benjamin and Wilhelm, and her face glowed with justification. After all, Edgar had been the only teacher to look out for her. Aware she had a special skill who no one else in the school would admit to, she had been wandering, lost and afraid, when Edgar had come across her down on the beach and taken her on as a pupil.

'First of all,' Edgar said, 'I'd like you to make pairs. We're going to do a little experiment so that you understand what reanimation really is.'

'You can work with Snout,' Wilhelm said to Benjamin, shuffling his stool across to Miranda.

'Oh, wait!' Edgar called. 'I almost forgot. We have a new pupil today. Cuttlefur, will you please come in?'

The boy with the deep blue hair strode in through the doorway. He looked like an avant-garde fashion model, and when he went to stand beside Edgar with a shy grin, an audible sigh came from all of the girls in the room.

'He's supposed to be in the third year, isn't he?' Wilhelm hissed into Benjamin's ear.

'I thought so.'

'Please welcome Cuttlefur to our class,' Edgar said. 'He's newly arrived in Endinfinium, and while he'll be moving into the third year in a few weeks, he's joined us in the middle of the term, so we felt it best to give him a few catch-up classes. For the next few weeks he'll be treated as an honourary first year. Please treat him like one of your own.'

A round of applause came from the girls. Wilhelm gave one sarcastic clap and glared at Cuttlefur as though trying to melt him with his eyes.

'Oh, you'll need a partner … how about Ms. Butterworth? Miranda, would you mind partnering with Cuttlefur for the next few lessons? Thank you.'

Wilhelm looked so aghast as Cuttlefur took his seat beside Miranda that Benjamin almost laughed. Instead, the smaller boy shuffled toward Benjamin.

'I suppose it's you and me, old sport.'

'And it looks like we have one odd … Simon, would you mind joining with Benjamin and Wilhelm? Thanks.'

Wilhelm sighed as Snout pulled his stool over. Benjamin couldn't help giving Wilhelm a playful nudge under the table, but instead of kicking back like he would have done if in a good mood, Wilhelm just slumped forward like a deflated balloon.

'Let's get this over with,' he grumbled.

An hour later, after a series of experiments to define what kind of state an inanimate object might reanimate into, the bell rang for the end of class. Wilhelm automatically looked around for Miranda, though they caught only a glimpse of her hair as she hurried out of the room in pursuit of Cuttlefur.

'What's gotten into her?' Wilhelm said. 'I mean, she can't be buying into all that cool, older boy stuff, can she?'

Benjamin shrugged. 'She's a girl, so who knows? But it's more than that, isn't it? He's from where she's from. It's that link they share.'

Wilhelm rolled his eyes. 'I suppose you're right.'

Benjamin grinned. 'Anyone would think that you might be a little—'

'What?'

'Jealous?'

'Of what?'

Benjamin just shrugged.

'You think I want to hang around with Miranda? I'm just concerned for her well-being, that's all. And I didn't want to work with Snout.'

'What's wrong with Snout?'

'Nothing! He's just, you know—'

'Not a girl?'

'I don't want to work with a girl. Miranda's not a girl, she's a ... friend.'

Wilhelm was getting increasingly flustered, and Benjamin gave him a nudge in the ribs. 'But doesn't she punch you all the time?'

'That's her way of showing affection.'

'Do you think she's going to punch Cuttlefur?'

Wilhelm glowered. 'She'd better not.'

'So what you're saying is that we need to protect Cuttlefur from Miranda?'

Wilhelm snapped his fingers. 'Yes! Exactly that. I feel for him, I really do, getting her attention like that.'

'You must be pretty glad she's no longer interested in hanging around with you.'

Wilhelm nodded. 'I wouldn't mind if I never saw Miranda again. She's a hothead and she has a bad attitude—'

Just then, Miranda stepped out of the girls' lavatories immediately to their left. 'Excuse me?' she said. 'What are you two talking about?'

'Wilhelm was just saying—'

'No, I wasn't!'

Miranda glared at him. 'I heard you.' Lightning fast, a bony fist shot out to cuff Wilhelm across the shoulder.

'Ow!'

'Serves you right. I have other friends, you know. Cuttlefur and I and going to watch the fourth years do a theatre presentation of West Side Story. You two can have a nice time playing together in the sandpit.'

And with that, she marched off, leaving them staring after her. After a pause, Benjamin said, 'Did you hear that? They're going on a date.'

'No, they're not. Watching a bunch of fourth years flounder about on a stage is hardly taking her up the West End, is it?'

'It's about as good as you can get in Endinfinium.'

Wilhelm fell silent, and Benjamin made to nudge him for a response, when he answered, 'This cannot be allowed to happen. He's a third year. He should hang out with other third years. And I don't trust him. There's something about him that's kind of ... odd.'

Benjamin nodded. Very little in Endinfinium wasn't odd, but something about Cuttlefur had gotten his own hackles up. Pretty much everyone he'd met here in

Endinfinium had problems of one kind or another, but Cuttlefur … he was just too perfect.

'What are we going to do?' he said.

'We have to watch her, to make sure she's all right. And we have to spy on him.'

'How? She'll kill you if she finds out, and if he's anything like her at all, he might be ten times worse. He might tie you up in the Haunted Forest and leave you to the wraith-hounds.'

Wilhelm rubbed his chin. 'I think I have an idea,' he said, a slow smile spreading across his lips.

8
THEATRE

Neither Benjamin nor Wilhelm really understood. Miranda wasn't surprised Wilhelm didn't get it—after all, he was a nitwit at the best of times—but she'd hoped Benjamin might have understood, particularly after what had happened with his brother.

Didn't matter how many friends you made, nothing was as special as a link to home.

Even with a home like hers, growing up in a people-making factory, it was still all you knew. And while Miranda had adjusted to life in Endinfinium better than most—enjoying it for the most part, despite its peculiarities—it was still an alien place that had claimed her without warning or reason.

A thousand theories abounded as to why each of them had woken up in Endinfinium one day, with no recollection of what might have caused it. Some of them were fanciful, such as that aliens had finally shown up and Endinfinium was a giant zoo for humans caught across dozens of time periods, while others were more realistic, including that everyone on Endinfinium shared a biological quirk allowing them to step through some spacetime continuum wormhole that had then conveniently closed behind him.

Miranda rather liked the latter theory, though the only problem with verifying it was that no one here had any idea what that quirk might be, and no scientists were around capable of looking for it.

Cuttlefur waited in the school entrance lobby, a wide internal courtyard lined with offices on one side and great glass walls on the other. Outside, a wide terrace sat on the very edge of the clifftop, from where panoramic views of the yellow sun's setting could be seen every night, and where you were perfectly safe, provided you got back inside before the black-winged haulocks took flight just after sundown.

'Hey,' he said, standing up from one of the hard, metal seats outside of the school office. 'Did you change your clothes? You look really nice.'

Miranda shook her head. Had Wilhelm or Benjamin said such a thing, she would have immediately gone on the attack against a comment surely dripping with sarcasm. But Cuttlefur's smooth voice left no doubt that he was sincere.

'No, I didn't,' she said. 'This is my regular school uniform. Thanks for asking, though.'

Cuttlefur led her through the corridors, toward the fourth years' area. Each school year had a section of rooms used for their basic studies—languages, math, Earth history—and there were far more rooms than pupils, suggesting a far more widespread population in years' past. Several rooms had been left empty, but in the fourth years' area, one had been turned into a makeshift theatre.

They took a seat at the back, and Miranda felt a little conspicuous since she was one of the youngest pupils present. Plus, it seemed every girl they passed wanted a second look at Cuttlefur.

'Don't they look at you like they look at me?' he asked in the end after two third-year girls had giggled past them.

Miranda shrugged. 'I suppose they got bored.'

'I mean, we were made physically perfect. That was the whole point.'

'Except they missed a bit.'

'Where?'

Miranda tapped the side of her head. 'In here. Keeping us in a dorm with forty-nine others who looked exactly the same wasn't really the best way to give us an emotional background.'

'I suppose not.'

The play started, and within the first few minutes, Miranda realised she really didn't like the theatre all that much. But Cuttlefur stared at the stage, eyes glazed as if viewing a reenacted epiphany. The production was a grown-up love story, though it seemed like the script was incomplete; every so often scenes jumped forward without any kind of reason. Miranda remembered something Benjamin had said about the library being full of water-damaged books. Perhaps that was where the fourth years had found the script.

Miranda was glad when it was over. Cuttlefur stirred as if he'd been sleeping for the last hour. He turned to her and smiled.

'You know what?' he said. 'All those years growing up in the institution, I never realised how much I missed seeing the sunset. I've watched it every night since I came here. Shall we go and look after dinner?'

Miranda returned his smile. Again, had anyone else said such a thing, she would have punched them. Cuttlefur, though, seemed genuine. Was it normal for fourteen-year-old boys to be so romantic? She glanced down at his hands resting in his lap. If he reached out to hold hers, she would certainly let him. It was a weird feeling.

Cuttlefur stared at her and Miranda realised she hadn't answered. 'Yes!' she blurted, and a couple of the fourth years in the seats in front glanced back with frowns.

'Great. Well, I'd better go and get ready. I have to get some stuff from my room.'

'Who are you sharing a room with?'

He grinned. 'Simon ... what do you call him? Snout?'

Miranda laughed. 'Yeah, some people call him that.'

'He's an odd character. I gather his old roommate disappeared?'

'Godfrey? Yes, a few weeks ago. He was a complete horror. He tried to kill Wilhelm, Benjamin, and myself. We don't know where he went. Maybe the Dark Man took him.'

Cuttlefur's eyes had glazed over again. How much had he actually heard? 'Benjamin,' he said. 'Benjamin Forrest? He's your friend.' It wasn't a question.

'Um, yes.'

'He's quite a famous boy in the school, isn't he?'

'I suppose. Why?'

'Just that lots of the others talk about him. You know, when he's not around.'

Miranda frowned. 'What do they say?'

Cuttlefur shrugged. 'Oh, this and that.' Then he gave an exaggerated shiver, as if to shake off the conversation. 'Anyway, I'll meet you in the lobby after?'

'Sure.'

Cuttlefur smiled, holding her gaze. Miranda tried to smile back, though half of her mouth was too nervous, so she just gave an awkward grimace, and when Cuttlefur left, it was almost a relief. Miranda stood around awkwardly for a moment, half wanting to follow him to see where he was going, half wanting to run in the other direction. In the end, she headed for the dining hall instead.

She had to admit she was feeling a little guilty about not spending much time with Benjamin and Wilhelm. After all, they had been inseparable ever since the Dark Man had attacked the school.

Well, not very guilty, but definitely a little.

9
SPY CAMERA

'Look, if you wanted to get into the locker room, you should have just stolen Ms. Ito's shoes or something.'

Wilhelm shook his head. 'I don't have time for a thousand cleans; this is a covert operation.'

'What kind of covert operation?'

'I have some concerns I need to put to rest, and I think I've found a way to do it.'

On the level below the library, the walls in the basements this far below sucked up any attempt at light, despite the fluttering of the reanimated candles affixed into the wall's metal clasps. From everywhere around came a hum, as if from machinery, and while some of it was just that, a lot of the noise came from the creaks and groans of the old school itself. Built in stages over several centuries, the school was a collision of ancient and modern. Down this far, the corridors had been hewn out of solid rock, but on the higher levels, the school had sections of wood, stonework, and even prefabricated plastic and glass.

Up ahead and beside a closed door, a figure stepped out, pulling a sword from its belt.

'Hail, Sin Keeper.' Wilhelm lifted a hand toward the reanimated suit of Samurai armour that guarded the locker room. 'May we go inside? We have a special request from Professor Loane himself to collect something that was wrongly sent for cleaning.'

The sin keeper said nothing, though he swung his sword across in front of him, then slid it smoothly back into the scabbard fitted to his belt. With a flourish of a chainmail glove that lacked a hand or fingers, the sin keeper stepped aside to bid them entry.

'Lucky for you he's so trusting,' Benjamin said.

Wilhelm smirked. 'I've been sent down here so many times, we're practically brothers,' he said. 'If I ever get married, he can be my best man.' He shrugged. 'Or perhaps security.'

The locker room was a row of cubicles that opened onto a conveyor belt. Punished pupils had to sit in one of the cubicles to pick items off of the conveyor, then give them a polish with the deanimation fluid, then drop them into a basket. Every few minutes, cleaners lumbered through to collect the baskets and carry them into a back room for sorting. Anything cleaned properly was returned to its place; anything still reanimated was put back on the conveyor. In each cubicle was a counter, and when the number reached zero, the pupil was free to go back upstairs. The most cleans Benjamin had had so far was five hundred, after falling asleep in a math class. On a couple of occasions, Wilhelm had broken two thousand, which meant he'd had to stay overnight.

Wilhelm headed straight for the cleaners' office. Three or four cubicles were currently occupied with pupils scrubbing away at a variety of items in the hope of getting back upstairs before breakfast. The grumbling of Derek Bates, one of Godfrey's cronies, came from the middle cubicle. Benjamin had learned early on that if you got your choice of cubicle, you should take one near to the conveyor entrance, so you could select the easiest items to clean before anyone else got to them.

'Surely we can't just march in there?' Benjamin protested as Wilhelm pushed through the swinging doors and into a room that resembled an Aladdin's Cave of junk. At one end, assorted objects backlogged a chute from some higher floor while at the other end, a conveyor swung in and out of the wall like an airport luggage system. Between the two were heaps of things all roughly sorted into types —books in one pile, electrical items in another, kitchen utensils in a third—monitored and arranged by the zombie-like cleaners who moved from one pile to another in a languid, syncronised dance.

'Wow, it's ... alive.'

Wilhelm grinned. 'Never been back here before? Quite a sight, eh?'

Everything appeared to be moving, as if the room was a giant termite mound, and a little queasiness rose up in Benjamin's stomach at the sight of it.

'I never realised so much stuff reanimated so quickly,' he said.

'This is a big school,' Wilhelm answered. 'There are rooms and rooms of just junk. Whoever built this place was clearly a massive hoarder.'

'What are you looking for?'

Wilhelm dodged among a group of cleaners headed toward a large, shiny, silver pile of electronic items— mobile phones, fax machines, and all manner of other gadgets that had been invented far into the future from what Benjamin knew. Amazing how Endinfinium seemed to have no concept of time. While he had met several people from the future, he hadn't yet met anyone from the distant past. Certainly there had to be someone around here, somewhere, whose idea of technology was the printing press.

'Okay!' Wilhelm shouted, poking his hand into the pile and withdrawing a small, silver object that looked like a miniature camera. It was so small, though, he could balance it between his thumb and forefinger.

'What is it?'

'A spy cam,' he said, 'for getting juicy goss on celebrities, I imagine.'

'What are you going to use it for?'

'That very same thing. Only difference is that my celebrity is Miranda.'

Benjamin lifted an eyebrow. 'She will literally kill you if she finds out,' he said. 'She thinks its amusing the way you spy on Dusty Eaves, but if you try the same thing on her, she'll probably pull out your limbs, one by one.'

Wilhelm gave Benjamin a forlorn look. 'You think?' Then a massive grin beamed across his face. 'A good job she has no chance of finding out, then, isn't it? My plan is failproof.'

'How on earth are you going to spy on her, anyway?'

Wilhelm lifted a finger. 'That, my friend, is part two of my plan.'

∽

'Look, what I'm about to show you is top secret,' Wilhelm said. 'And I mean, top secret. As in, no pretending not to talk about it and then tell someone else behind my back. Like Snout, for example.'

'Why would I tell Snout?'

'Don't pretend you haven't started thinking about him as a mate now that Godfrey's not around to lead him astray. I know you enjoyed working with him in science class until that punk new kid showed up.'

'He's all right, but I wouldn't tell him anything important.'

'Good. If Old Gubbledon finds out, I'll not only get sent to the locker room, probably forever, but I'll also lose my only chance to keep an eye on Miranda.'

Benjamin rolled his eyes. 'Let's talk about the secret and not what your plans are for it. I really don't want to think about you spying on Miranda.'

'It's for her own good. That new kid is up to something, I'm sure of it, and I'm going to find out what.'

Wilhelm knelt and reached underneath his bed to pull out a cardboard box whose top was sealed shut with tape. From the way it hung loose over the edges, though, Benjamin could see Wilhelm had opened it and closed it many times.

'Remember,' Wilhelm said, 'top secret.'

He opened the box.

'What the—'

A near-transparent plastic bag crinkled and crunched into a shape resembling a butterfly and fluttered up out of the box. It did a circuit of the room then came to rest on top of Wilhelm's head, where it sat with an air of contentedness, its wings slowly opening and closing.

Benjamin shook his own head. 'Oh, my. When Gubbledon finds out about this, you're a dead man.'

Wilhelm grinned and said, 'His name's Rick.'

10

SHIFTING INTENTIONS

Somehow, not being in chains or confined to some dark cell with bars over the window was more terrifying. Left to roam the corridors of the vast mountaintop castle with its shifting rooms and corridors that left no route the same for more than a couple of minutes, Godfrey lived in constant terror that the floor beneath him would shift to send him plummeting to the ground far below. He knew from the way the Dark Man's hideous minions were able to find him at will that there had to be a sense to it all. But even without any bonds, Godfrey was left as immobile as any shackled prisoner.

As always, when he woke in some deserted bedroom he had chosen to sleep in, during the night he had invariably descended several levels, the blocks of rock, wood, plastic, and even glass, seemingly unlocking and lowering like a monstrous game of connect. And as he always did, after eating his plate of whatever gruel was considered food here, he began the long and arduous journey up through the twisting, rising, and falling corridors, up staircases that dipped in mid-climb, sending him back down as he endlessly tried to get to the top part of the castle where a handful of galleries and balconies remained stationary for the most part, at least in comparison to the rest of this place he had overheard the teachers at Endinfinium High referring to as the Shifting Castle.

On a bad day, he would get one of the castle's rear balconies, one that faced inland toward one of the few snowy ridgelines poking up out of the grey clouds, and then just grey cloud itself beyond. He wondered how many people had tried to find a way out by hiking off into those grim peaks. But the view was so uninspiring that, after a half-hour of wishing for something to change, he would curl up in the corner and do his best to fall asleep.

On a good day, however, he would randomly find himself on one of the balconies that faced back the way he had come, the sea and Endinfinium High School.

The Dark Man had chosen to make his base a safe distance back into the mountains, so in the immediate foreground stood a series of jagged peaks that looked nearly impossible to cross—all snowy gullies and grey rock crags. Beyond those, though, the world opened out into a patchwork blanket of green: rolling hills and forests, open meadows and high moorland.

Rivers and lakes were in there, some of them glacial or comprised of snowmelt, plus the Great Junk River that the Dark Man claimed was the beginning of all things.

And beyond that lay the accursed place that had tried to force an education into him: Endinfinium High.

Godfrey couldn't help scowling through the battered telescopes that topped some of the largest galleries, as if the castle had once been open to tourists before being teleported into a strange new world. The resolution wasn't strong enough to make out people, but the ugly cluster of towers and battlements that was the tamest of versions of the Dark Man's mighty abode, were easy to pick out of the sea beyond. From here, it looked like a black speck of dirt, easy to condemn to the water forever with one flick of a giant's finger.

When he wasn't overcome with hatred—which happened far more often than he would like people to believe, though when you had nothing to do but hate your enemies, you tended to get bored after a while—he mused on how he could see so far, despite the distance being so vast.

After a few weeks of consideration, he had understood why.

Unlike the England he had come from—a wealthy country estate just outside of Shrewsbury in 2113, to be exact—Endinfinium, what there was of it, was entirely flat.

And it was still building itself.

He couldn't be sure, of course—the Shifting Castle's telescopes weren't that good—but he suspected that the sea horizon was a fraction further away than when he had begun his de facto imprisonment. The Great Junk River and its load were slowly filling up the sea.

Today, he had gotten lucky and found a nice, relaxing balcony near the very top of the castle, one with panoramic views to the south and east. Clouds had rolled in across the south, but he could still see as far as the dark green strip of the Haunted Forest before the haze had begun to obscure the landscape. At a rough estimate, it was a couple of hundred miles from here in the Shifting Castle back to Endinfinium High School, and the mixture of different landscapes was elaborate. Who- or whatever had created this place had tried to fit in as much variety as possible.

A creak behind him nearly made him jump up and over the balcony's edge. A door opened, and a squat, box-shaped creature stumbled in, all flaps of cardboard and loose, flickering tape, its marble-like eyes searching for him from the top of antennae made out of wire cord.

'The Master will see you,' it said in a strange, hollow voice that came from everywhere in the room at once. 'He's waiting.'

'Where?'

'Follow.'

Godfrey stood up, brushed down his clothes as though going to a job interview, and walked stiffly after the box-creature.

'Do you have a name?'

The box swung from side to side. 'No.'

'Can I call you Boxy? You know, since you're a box.'

'You can call me what you like.'

Godfrey shrugged. As the creature waddled in front of him, its feet made by two lower flaps of cardboard folded and bent into pyramids, he had an urge to kick it, just to see if it was hollow or whether something was contained inside.

The corridors stayed quiet for Boxy as he led Godfrey to his waiting audience. Godfrey hadn't seen the Dark Man since the army had returned in disarray to the valley below the Shifting Castle, having been routed by the little upstart Benjamin Forrest and his friends. In Godfrey's own opinion, the Dark Man had been a little too obvious with his attack. But what did he know? He was only thirteen, and the only wars he knew about had been acted out in his vast back garden with one or two of the servants acting as mobile targets for his slingshot.

Boxy finally paused at a couple of wide, ornately decorated doors. 'Enter, please,' he said.

Godfrey took a deep breath. He didn't really feel afraid. After all, if the Dark Man had wanted him dead, he would have been thrown over a balcony weeks ago. This felt like the start of something. Ideally, the revenge Godfrey so wanted on Benjamin Forrest and his idiot friends.

'Thanks, Boxy,' he said, patting the top of the box-creature's head and shoving through the doors like he had done daily back on his parents' estate. He was Godfrey Pendleton, after all; he had half a mind to request the Dark Man kneel for him.

He had expected a bigger room, like an audience chamber off a television show, but the Dark Man stood with his back to Godfrey in a room so small, Godfrey had stepped on the edge of a billowing robe before he had a chance to stagger backward and correct himself.

'Welcome, boy,' said a low, growling voice. 'At last I have a task for you and all of that anger you enjoy so greatly.'

Godfrey inched backward. The door had swung shut, but as his desperate fingers found the cold metal of the handle, he realised that either Boxy had locked it or the Dark Man had some other way of keeping him inside.

'You are a powerful Summoner, Godfrey,' the Dark Man whispered, still not turning around. He moved forward a few paces, seeming to grow in height. Only when steps appeared beneath his feet did Godfrey realise he was ascending a stone staircase toward an archway set high up into the wall.

Without another word, Godfrey followed as the Dark Man swept through the arch and out onto a freezing tower balcony at the very top of the Shifting Castle. Godfrey balked at the sight of the castle's slowly shifting walls and buttresses; if you glanced away you would never look at the same exact design twice. He wondered how he had climbed so high along the flat corridors that Boxy had led him through until he realised they were rising up into the air like a giant periscope on top of a submarine.

'Tell me what you remember of your life before you came to Endinfinium,' the Dark Man said, cloak billowing out behind him.

Godfrey opened his mouth to a flood of freezing air. He gasped for breath, then leaned back against the stonework to collect what little warmth he could find.

'I lived mostly alone on a big, rambling estate,' he said. 'My parents were usually away. My father was a banker, my mother an actress. I had twenty servants to do my bidding.'

'And you were cruel to them, were you not?'

Godfrey scowled. 'I only punished them when they deserved it.'

'Which was frequently?'

'What use are servants when you can't tell them what to do?'

The Dark Man nodded. 'Quite. Remind me of a particular form of punishment.'

'I could make the walls hold them.' Godfrey grinned, remembering the poor cook he had suspended from a second-floor balcony and had left for two days, until the sun had practically baked her.

'Explain to me how you could command the walls to move.'

Godfrey shrugged. 'I don't know. I could tell them what to do. I remember once being angry, and I demanded that the walls swallow up one of the butlers. And they did. It took two stonemasons three days to set him free.'

'And you went unpunished for this?'

'No one knew it was me. With my mind, I could tell the walls what to do.'

The Dark Man nodded. 'And your house? Did no one raise a suspicion?'

Again Godfrey shrugged. 'Some staff quit, but my parents just hired more. People said the place was haunted, but my parents didn't care.' He grinned again. 'It was haunted—by me. I suppose some people will put up with anything if you offer them enough money. I learned how to scare them just enough to make them afraid, but not enough to make them leave. Oh, the games I used to play.'

'I can imagine. And what happened when you used this power of yours?'

'At first I thought nothing happened. Then I realised trees and flowers were beginning to die. The connection wasn't obvious, but over time it seemed the only likely thing.'

'And did this cause you to stop?'

'Why would it? It was only a bunch of stupid trees and flowers. Who cares?'

The Dark Man spun around, and Godfrey gasped, shrank back. But beneath the hood came only the glimmering white of the Dark Man's eyes and the vague outline of his face.

'Most die,' he mused. 'Most Summoners die before they ever make it to Endinfinium. You were a lucky one. You had natural control of the power. You could be dangerous, Godfrey. A great asset.'

'I want to punish Benjamin Forrest.'

The Dark Man laughed. 'Do you, now? Well, I have news for you. I very much want to meet Master Forrest, but he is proving elusive. I have, however, found a way to bring him to me by his own accord. And in order to achieve that, I require your help.'

'What? I'll do anything.'

'Good, good. Now come. We must make haste. Our window of opportunity swiftly swings closed.'

The Dark Man swept past him, pushing Godfrey back against the wall. The billowing cape snapped in the air, and then he was gone, headed back into the tower. Godfrey took a deep breath and, with one last glance at the distant sea, hurried after his new master.

While they had talked on the balcony, the staircase had altered, and now it stretched down into darkness. Godfrey had to hurry to keep up, running one hand along the wall in case he were to trip and stumble forward, with only the Dark Man's back a cushion for his fall.

They descended deep into the castle, deeper than Godfrey had ever gone. The walls closed in, and the hum of machinery surrounded him, as though they were entering a giant, subterranean engine.

Godfrey caught sight of scurrying and slithering creatures down side corridors. Like Boxy, many of them were reanimated objects: snakes made from electrical cable, heaps of rags that walked upright like men, chairs and stools and tables that shuffled along like crippled soldiers returned from war. He tried not to entertain the thought that disobeying the Dark Man might leave him like this—a remnant of a man, discarded and forgotten into the darkness at the very bottom of the Shifting Castle.

Finally the Dark Man paused in front of two wide doors.

'Behold!' he shouted, raising his arms above his head in the most animated way Godfrey had ever seen him. 'The Paper Room!'

The doors burst open and a sound like a thousand fluttering newspapers filled Godfrey's senses. The room glowed with a kind of half-light, and in its illumination, a cyclone of paper raged against the walls and the ceiling far above.

'Come, boy, let me pack you into something that can help me.'

Godfrey shook his head, never having felt such an urge to run, and he turned on his heels to make his escape, only to find braids of paper encircling his ankles, pulling him back. He screamed as they dragged him into the maelstrom until there was nothing but a howling storm of scrap paper as it wrapped and formed around him.

As his body grew heavy and tired, he understood why the cyclone of paper had appeared to glow—it was damp with glue, and it now knitted around him, sticking close to his skin, reforming him into a papier-mâché monstrosity at the Dark Man's command.

When finally he was put down onto ground and the maelstrom had died down, he peered at the Dark Man standing before him through a face that no longer felt like his own.

The Dark Man's laughter was the only sound that remained. Godfrey turned his now-cumbersome body around and saw the paper piled in a heap that towered over his head.

'Wonderful!' the Dark Man cried. 'Perfection itself! Would you like to see how you now look, boy? Behold.'

A great curtain slid down from the wall to reveal a huge mirror towering over him, and Godfrey screamed at the sight of the man staring back at him. Nothing remained of the boy—a rather a good-looking one at that, he thought, despite some whispers that he was quite sour-faced—he had been when he had entered the room.

'It becomes easier with time,' said the Dark Man, a towering shadow at his shoulder. 'You must now be tasked with the intricacies and requirements of your new role. But first, it might serve you well to understand why I need to meet with Master Forrest as a matter of some urgency. Turn around. Look on my face.'

Godfrey wanted to do nothing less. He squeezed his eyes shut, only to be forced by invisible hands pushing his eyelids open and turning his body around. His head lifted without his intent, and he stared into the face of the Dark Man, just as the room was bathed in white light.

The Dark Man smiled, and finally Godfrey understood.

11

BASIL

Benjamin leaned close to the floor and gave the wooden boards a heavy tap. Shiny with lacquer and toughened with age, they felt solid and immovable. He tapped again, then closed his eyes as the Grand Lord had taught him, concentrating, searching for a wisp of air and channeling his power through it. His mind felt for the boards beneath his fingers, and then they were loose, humming with reanimation as they easily slid to reveal a space large enough to crawl through. Benjamin glanced up the corridor to make sure he wasn't being watched, then ducked down into the space and slid the boards back above his head. A little surge of his magic, and they were as firm again as if they had never been moved.

He was in a space barely high enough to sit up in, but a little further along the dusty stone under the floor became a stairway and he was able to stand up straight. At the bottom of this short flight of steps stood a door upon which he gave a solid knock, using a code he had been taught some weeks ago.

The door swung open. 'Welcome back to Underfloor,

Benjamin,' came the muffled voice of what looked like a cross between a bookshelf and a man—all protruding corners of wood and metal braces, yet with a vaguely human face carved into one end.

'Steven,' Benjamin greeted the shelf-man, a name he had chosen for the creature himself. The Underfloor reanimates had no use for names amongst themselves, taking on human shapes and forms only when they had to speak to a human from the school, communicating with each other in ways that even the teachers who knew of them didn't understand. While 'Steven Shelf' was the name a lonely boy might have given to part of his surroundings, the shelf-man had rather liked it.

'Sorry it's been so long,' Benjamin said, 'but you know, schoolwork and all that.'

'Even in a place like this, they dump algebra on you like a big, fat cat,' Steven said, making Benjamin smile. Sometimes he felt the shelf-man had swallowed a few of the books he might have once held and liked to regurgitate lines in an apparently random order.

'We have a test next week,' Benjamin said. 'I'll probably score higher than Wilhelm, but that's about it.'

'The bottom five go to the lockers?'

Benjamin grinned. 'We get to keep each other company.'

'Why can't you be more like that Miranda? She's such a good girl. Studies like a squirrel collecting acorns for the winter, at least that's what Wilhelm said.'

Benjamin wasn't quite sure Wilhelm would have put it that way, but Steven was Steven. 'Is Moto around?' he asked. 'I want to ask him something.'

'Sure. Head on in.'

Moto, a reanimated motorcycle who stood on one wheel and revolved the other to show a variety of facial expressions, was the unofficial leader of Underfloor. He had helped out Benjamin before, and they had become friends. While some of the teachers were aware of Underfloor, few had any contact with its inhabitants, many of whom had been roaming the hidden rooms and corridors for almost as long as the school had been in existence.

Feeling strangely comforted by the unfolding world within a world as he made his way through Underfloor's warmly lit rooms, Benjamin tried to take a step back and appreciate the strangeness he saw wherever he looked. In one room, a group of shop mannequins sat around a bar, served by a table passing around glasses and ashtrays, its legs flexing and bending with the elasticity of human arms. That the glasses were empty and the ashtrays filled with sawdust from the sticks of wood the mannequins chewed on was one of the least unusual aspects of the scene. Far more bizarre was that they moved and gestured like real humans, without making any sound.

In another room, a variety of reanimates sat around a poker table, playing with water-damaged trump cards and betting with handfuls of ancient coins that rattled and scattered to the floor every time one moved an awkward limb to pull in a sizeable win.

In a third room, larger than the others, a band played on the stage, performing a discordant drone that did nothing for Benjamin but delighted the couple of dozen reanimates moving around to the rhythm. Their dancing was so fascinating, Benjamin wanted to stay and watch, but his housemaster, Gubbledon Longface, was up on the stage, playing a battered piano, and getting caught in Underfloor when he should have been in the dorms would be worth a punishment Benjamin didn't want to think about.

He found Moto sitting in a library room, a kick-start lever Steven would probably say resembled a T-Rex's puny forepaw in comparison to Moto's size, flicking through pages of a tatty motorbike magazine.

'Family album?' Benjamin quipped, before suddenly wondering if the bike might be offended. 'Sorry—'

Moto's front wheel spun in a gesture that Benjamin knew meant amusement. 'You've been hanging around Wilhelm too much,' Moto said. 'That joke was straight out of his stand-up routine.'

'He tells them better than me,' Benjamin said.

'What brings you down here to Underfloor?' Moto closed his magazine. 'We haven't seen you in a while.'

Benjamin shrugged. 'Just schoolwork. And trying to stay out of trouble.'

'Not easy with Wilhelm around?'

'Impossible.' Benjamin grinned. He considered telling Moto about Wilhelm's plan to spy on Cuttlefur, but he didn't feel as happy as he had tried to make out. 'Moto ... I was wondering if I could ask you a question. More of an opinion, really.'

'Sure, anything.' The bike's front wheel cocked to the side. 'Are you still thinking about how to get home?'

Benjamin sighed. 'It's all I think about. I try not to, but ... it's just ... I don't feel like I belong here. I can play the game for a while, but when I'm lying awake at night, I can't stop thinking about home.'

'It was different for you,' Moto said. 'Your brother was here for a time, too. That tie with home is not something most people have.'

Benjamin shrugged. 'And that I feel my being here is putting the rest of Endinfinium in danger.'

'I don't think the Dark Man will be back for a while

yet. He was soundly beaten, and his resources must be almost depleted.'

'I still think it would be safer for everyone if I left.'

'But it's impossible.'

'Is it? We got here, didn't we? If you can walk in one direction, you can walk back again.'

'Not if you go through a door that locks from the other side once you've passed through.'

Benjamin rubbed his chin. 'I'm not so sure it's locked.'

'What do you mean? Do you think you know a way to leave?'

'The river. We're going on a school trip next week and we'll be near the source. I want to see where that water comes from. I mean, water can come from the ground, but the rubbish it carries can't. It has to come from somewhere.' He pounded one fist into his other palm. 'It has to.'

'And how do you think I can help? I can't go with you.'

'I want to know if you have any memories of your time before. If you remember coming through whatever valve brings us into Endinfinium.'

'I can't have, I didn't become … well, me, until I came through.'

'Professor Eaves says that everything already had a soul before. It just took a little magic to wake it up.'

'I'm not sure I could believe that.'

'Can you tell me if there's anything you remember? Anything at all.'

Moto's head rolled. 'I became aware of myself part of the way down the great junk river. My earliest memories are of swirling in dark water among thousands of other objects, some reanimated, some not. I was in the waters of the sea before I could move, but I was caught in a drift current and found myself on a shore.' The bike's handlebar-shoulders lifted in a shrug. 'And eventually I found myself here, in Underfloor.'

Benjamin nodded. Moto had told him similar before, but none of it helped to unravel the mystery. 'How long have you been here? Were things different then?'

Moto's head-wheel spun. 'The world was smaller. The edge of the sea was no more than a mile offshore. I remember stories of people going out in boats to see it, only to never come back.'

'They fell off the edge?'

'Who knows? Maybe they found a way home. I wouldn't chance it, though.'

'And the river? The water has to come from somewhere.'

'There are stories, of course. We've all heard about the kind of stories you had back in England. Folklore. We have some of that here, too.'

'About the river?'

Moto's wheel revolved to a smiling face. 'The Great Junk River is the bringer of all life. That is what we believe.'

Benjamin wanted to jump up and down in frustration. 'But where does it bring it from?'

Moto's wheel revolved back to a sterner expression. 'We here in Underfloor don't like to think about it too much. We leave speculation up to humans. We have been granted this chance at life that only humans were once privy to. We are afraid that to question it too much will see it taken away.'

Benjamin opened his mouth, but Moto's kick-start pedal lifted in a gesture that he hadn't finished.

'However,' he added, 'we have no control over what humans do. There's a story of a man who tried to find out where the river came from. Have you heard it?'

'Jeremiah Flowers.'

'Yes! So you know of him?'

'A librarian called Cleat told me a little about it. He escaped, didn't he?'

Not exactly what Cleat had told him, and Benjamin wondered whether Moto might be holding something back. If it was dangerous to climb Source Mountain to see the culvert through which the water flowed, then his friend would obviously not want him to go. Yet Benjamin had been obsessing over it for days, and it was less a case of 'if' rather than 'when.'

Moto rose up onto his back wheel, his full height a head taller than Benjamin. 'Many residents of Endinfinium think that that story of Jeremiah Flowers is a myth. A folktale, a legend. It would make a good one, no?'

'What do you think?'

Moto's head-wheel spun. 'It isn't what I think, young Master Forrest, but what I know. Here in Underfloor, most of us might not care much for what you humans do upstairs, but that wasn't always the case. In fact, at one point or another, most of us served some use.' His kick-start lever waved. 'Follow me.'

He led Benjamin down a series of stairwells and along several corridors, until the air was cold and damp and Benjamin felt like they were far under the earth now, perhaps lower than he had ever been. Eventually Moto stopped at a featureless wall, only for it to slide back at his touch of a hidden switch. They stepped out into a cold, stone corridor with boxes piled high on either side. Some were sealed shut, others had broken open and spilled out all manner of assorted, inanimate objects.

Down here, though, nothing moved. The school was as quiet as he had ever known it.

'We've just left the main region of Underfloor,' Moto

said. 'We're near the very bottom of the school, but we're not quite there yet. Like everything else, Underfloor has evolved, too, and over the years several sections have become separated from the rest. I'm taking you to one of them now.'

'It's so cold down here,' Benjamin said. 'And why isn't anything reanimating?'

'Even magic has a lifespan,' Moto said with something like regret. 'Just like when a tree dies, reanimates who have lost their magic tend to sink, just in different ways. More often than not, they get brought down here. Not everything is dead, though.'

'Who'd want to live down here? It's so creepy.'

'People looking for peace and quiet,' Moto replied. 'Stay quiet now, Benjamin. He gets upset easily, and then he doesn't want to speak.'

'Who?'

Moto's face revolved around to a smile. 'You'll see.'

Benjamin followed Moto up the corridor a short way, before Moto poked his kick-start into a tiny crack in the wall. With a plume of dust, a stone door slid open and inside were none of the dim candles hanging from the walls of the corridors, so Moto leaned one of his headlamps forward, switching it on.

The room had been piled high with dusty junk like someone had packed up their goods to move house, then never got around to unpacking them. Boxes were stacked high, although many of the stacks had collapsed, and in one corner, several collapsed stacks had formed a natural bowl.

'Would you mind dipping your headlight? It's quite a strain on eyes as old as mine, you know.'

Benjamin did a double take. Among the boxes, something shifted, and a strange spindly creature appeared, sitting in the middle of the collapsed stack as if he were an old man enjoying his favorite recliner.

At first, Benjamin thought it was a giant butterfly, but as Moto's light caught over lengths of flexing wood and a hard, fiberglass body, he realised that, while he was in the right vicinity, this creature was something else entirely.

It was an old, propeller-powered biplane.

'Hey, Basil,' Moto said. 'Sorry to intrude like this, but I have someone here who would like to meet you.'

Yet to understand why Moto wanted him to meet something a museum could have thrown out, Benjamin forced an enthusiastic nod. 'Hello,' he said. 'My name is Benjamin Forrest.'

'Basil,' the plane said. 'Not charmed. I was sleeping.'

'You're always sleeping,' Moto said. 'You should brush yourself off and go for a fly once in a while.'

The biplane shifted, and in Moto's light, Benjamin saw how his wings dropped uselessly against his sides as if waterlogged. His propeller, too, had slumped into a drooping, tarnished chrome moustache in the centre of a painted-on face.

'Not much use in these old wings,' Basil said. 'What do you want, boy? Quickly, now. I have little enough time left as it is. I don't wish to waste any more precious seconds looking at your gaping mug.'

'He wants to ask about Jeremiah,' Moto said.

With a rustle of musty cardboard, Basil drew back into his box bed. 'Does he, indeed?'

'You knew Jeremiah?'

Basil coughed, and a dust plume tickled the air in Moto's headlight. 'We were friends, of a sort, me and him. Why do you want to know?'

'I heard he went to a place called Source Mountain

and disappeared. I want to know where he went, because … because I want to go there, too.'

Basil shook his head with a rustle. 'He was a fool, that Jeremiah. He failed to appreciate what he had here in Endinfinium. He just wouldn't give it up, and it was the death of him.'

'So he died?'

'He had to have done.'

'How do you know?'

'Because I took him there. He thought that an ability to fly might give him an advantage, that we could just fly out over the edge of the world and find out what was there … but Endinfinium doesn't work like that.'

'You went over the edge of the world?' Even Moto looked surprised as he and Benjamin exchanged a glance.

'We tried, but it's impossible. When you get within a short distance of the ocean's edge, you meet a vortex of winds that push you back. We tried several times. Impossible.'

'So Jeremiah looked for another way out.'

Basil gave a hollow cough like someone was beating a hammer against the inside of his fiberglass body. 'Fool wouldn't give it up.'

'What happened when you went to Source Mountain?'

Basil grunted. 'Think I can remember details? It was hundreds of years ago, as you people count them. I can barely remember yesterday.' He sighed and settled back into his box throne. 'In fact, I'm tiring of this conversation. Good night to you both. Thank you for the visit and all that—'

'Wait!' Benjamin put a hand on the biplane's bent wing, receiving a glare from Basil. 'Just one last question.'

'Get on with it.'

'Do you know for sure that Jeremiah died?'

Basil sighed. 'I lowered him down on a rope. He was weighted down, wrapped up in breathing gear he'd found from somewhere. He went into the water where it rises up out of a spring at the top of that ugly old hill.' Basil sighed again. 'And then the rope broke. I never saw him again, even though I circled that hilltop for days afterward.'

'Are you certain he died, that he didn't make it through the other side?'

'That's two questions! Very well, if you really want to know what I think, I'll tell you.' The biplane shuddered, boxes rattling around him.

'All I know is that he didn't come back out. And that water pressure was powerful, believe me. He didn't come back out, so he must have gone somewhere. Whether that was where he wanted to go to, or some other place entirely … I don't know.'

12

SPYING

'Okay, Rick, test flight.'

Wilhelm tossed the Scatlock up into the air, and Rick did a couple of confident circuits of the room while Wilhelm looked at the computer tablet in his hand, trying to make sense of the mess of colour beamed back by the remote camera attached around the Scatlock's neck.

'Sorry, come back. One more time.'

Rick obediently swooped down and landed on Wilhelm's wrist. Wilhelm made a few adjustments to the remote camera, then tossed Rick back up into the air, and this time, the picture that transmitted to his computer screen was much clearer and smoother.

'Nice.'

Again on command, Rick alighted on Wilhelm's wrist. 'Now, you're sure you know who Miranda is?' Wilhelm asked, and Rick gave an enthusiastic nod. 'That's right, the girl with the bright red hair. The annoying one.' He grinned. 'I want you to trail her and figure out what that Cuttlefur is up to. You got that?'

Rick made a crinkling sound that could have meant

anything. Wilhelm shrugged. 'Right. I suppose that'll have to do. Now, I'm not worried about her so much, but when he's alone, I want you to follow him. Keep a safe distance, though. He's obviously dangerous, otherwise he wouldn't be so creepy. Good luck, Rick. I never had a brother that I know of, but if I did, I wish he could have been just as loyal as you.'

The Scatlock with the taped wing and the tiny camera affixed to its body made the same crinkling sound. Wilhelm figured he'd have to just trust it.

He went to the window. Benjamin had earlier wandered off somewhere and still wasn't back, and most of the other pupils had gone to a team sports event in the Great Hall. As far as he knew, only Gubbledon, and a couple of nerds studying for this week's tests, were downstairs.

He pulled open the window—a cardinal sin after dark, lest any Scatlocks got in—and held Rick up to the fresh air. 'Good luck, mate,' he said. 'Do your best.'

Rick rustled and flew off. Wilhelm closed the window and went back to his bed. He had cried off sick to Gubbledon over the sporting event, and now he climbed under his blankets, taking the little computer tablet with him. It was about the size of his palm. He had traded five thousand cleans for it with a fifth grader called Martin Crown, and with a little help from Ms. Xemian, the math teacher, under the pretense of doing a school project, he had connected the camera's frequency to a program on the computer tablet. Rick's progress now came through on a grainy live stream.

'Don't let me down,' he whispered, crossing his fingers.

At first Rick dipped straight down toward the grey stretch of beach far below them, and with his heart in his mouth, Wilhelm waited as the Scatlock swooped among the roosts of his brethren clinging to the jagged points of the cliff-face. He wondered if Rick would either betray him, or be ripped apart as an impostor by the other Scatlocks, perhaps aware that he had been tainted by a human's touch. Instead, though, Rick just ducked and wheeled a couple of times as if greeting his old family, then soared back up over the cliff, rising high above the school.

As soon as he was over the top of the nearest wing of the building, however, Rick's speed dropped to a crawl, and Wilhelm realised he had been surfing the gusts of wind that blew up and down the cliff-face. At least now the camera feed had steadied, giving Wilhelm a fine twilit view of the vast school and its towers, buttresses, battlements, and annexes—a monstrosity of architectural styles crossing hundreds of years. And while it had a certain charm from the inside, on the outside, it looked as though someone had grabbed a bucket of Lego and thrown it into a washing machine with a tub of glue. While in one corner rose an elegant tower, its foundation was a lump of ugly prefabricated concrete and plastic walls. In many ways, Wilhelm thought, Endinfinium High was a perfect work of post-modernist art—the kind of junk people paid good money to look at without really knowing why.

The yellow sun had set and the red sun lay low on the horizon, half beneath the edge of the world, as low as it ever got. Rick topped the highest part of the castle, then began a gradual descent toward the courtyard outside the main entrance, where dozens of terraces had been cut into the cliff-face. With their chairs and tables, they were a popular hangout place during summer evenings when the low winds kept the Scatlocks confined to their roosts.

Now, as Rick began to descend, Wilhelm saw the terraces were almost empty, except for a small one nearest to the cliff edge and farthest from the school, out of sight of the main entrance.

Two people sat on a bench looking out at the sea, and Wilhelm could tell immediately who they were.

One had blue hair, and the other a dark, crimson red.

13

FAMILY

'This is my favorite place of everywhere,' Miranda said. 'I mean, it's so depressing at the same time, but it's still beautiful.'

'Why depressing?'

She pointed out at the edge of the sea, a couple of miles offshore. While it looked like a natural horizon at this time of the evening, during the day, it felt uncomfortably close and unnatural, and she knew it was where the water fell over the edge of the world.

'You can see where it all ends,' she said. 'I mean, in England, back in the Facility, they didn't let us see outside much, but when they did, you could look out and know that you could keep walking and you'd find somewhere else that might be better than where you were. Here, you can't. If you swam out there, you'd fall off.'

'Are you sure about that?'

'Everyone knows it.'

'And what would happen then?'

'You'd die.'

'How?'

'You'd fall until you hit something, or if you didn't, you'd just fall forever until you got so hungry you just died.'

'What if there's something else down there?'

'There can't be.'

'Why not?'

'Because if there was, someone would have found it and come back to tell us about it.'

Cuttlefur grinned. 'Have you always been so cynical, or is that just the way your strain was brought up?'

Miranda sighed. 'I don't know. I mean, I love it here. Back in the Facility, I was no one. Just a colour and a number. I don't even know what they were growing us for. Maybe just because they could, I suppose. When I woke up here, it was like my whole life had changed. I was no longer Red-37. I was whoever I wanted to be. And I chose Miranda Butterworth.' She shrugged. 'It doesn't stop you wondering, though, does it?'

'Not at all. I suppose I feel the same as you, but I'm not quite as negative about it.'

Miranda felt the same sudden anger she often felt with Benjamin and Wilhelm, and she considered it a good thing —strong emotions for someone meant they had meaning for you. At least that's what the books she borrowed from Gubbledon's bookcase in the common room of the dormitory said. Although most of them were fairy tales and fantasies, she was still only a girl. She was allowed to dream.

'I was thinking to punch you,' she said quietly, not looking up at him, only staring at the hand resting on the bench beside her. If he made a move at holding hers, it would only be right to push it away … she just wasn't sure she would have the willpower.

'Is that a good thing, or a bad?' he said.

'I always punch people I like.'

'Really? Like Wilhelm?'

Miranda's cheeks burned with the same shade of red as her hair. Did he think Wilhelm was her boyfriend? He was more like a little brother, but if Cuttlefur thought—

'I'm envious of your friends,' he said. 'I hope I can be one of them.'

Her heart pounded. Was she in love? Was this what it felt like—a strange, fluttery feeling like her heart might burst out of her chest and float off into the sky?

'Well, um, sure….'

'I have something for you,' he said, and she almost gasped when he lifted his hand. But it wasn't to touch hers, only to put it back into his pocket. 'I know it's not much, but while I was down on the beach, before you found me … I saw this lying in the sand and couldn't stop myself from picking it up. Later, after I met you, I understood why I had. After science class yesterday, I got Professor Caspian to attach it to a chain for me.'

He lifted a necklace out of his pocket. On the end of a pretty silver chain hung a dark red stone that shone in the light of the red sun.

Miranda stared at it. It twinkled like a star fallen to earth. Her heart was still pounding like a running horse, and her fingers shook as she reached out and took it from him.

'What is it?' she said. 'I've never seen one before.'

'It's a ruby. Here, let me put it on.'

He leaned over, took it from her, unclasped it, and slipped it around her neck. She couldn't bring herself to look at him this close. Like herself, he had been created flawlessly. Plus, he was a couple of years older, which automatically made him boyfriend material.

What if he tries to … what if he tries to….?

Cuttlefur pulled back. He smiled. 'There. You look perfect.'

'Thank you.'

His smile dropped. 'That's not all, though. There's something else.'

Miranda frowned. She didn't dare hope for another present. She was humming with happiness as it was. 'What?'

'I didn't tell the whole truth about coming here.'

Miranda drew back, her hackles rising. She'd learned quickly to be alert for danger in Endinfinium. When literally anything could come alive in moments, potential hazards lay at every turn.

'I'm a Channeller,' she said. 'I can blast you right over onto that beach—'

Cuttlefur smiled and lifted a hand. 'It's not bad,' he said. 'It's good. It's about you, Miranda.'

'What?'

'I came here to get you. I came to take you back.'

Back? His proclamation was so ludicrous, Miranda coughed, then immediately felt embarrassed and slapped a hand over her mouth so hard it made a sharp snap.

'Don't be ridiculous. You can't leave again. Everyone knows that.'

Cuttlefur shook his head. 'Most people can't. But most people aren't you and me. I was sent here to find you. When I first arrived, I was a bit disorientated and wasn't sure what was going on.' He shrugged and flashed that disarming smile she was learning to love love *love* ... 'Then it slowly came back to me after the last few days. I was sent here to find you, and to bring you back.'

'Why? How? W—'

'When? Where? What time?' Cuttlefur smiled again, and this time, he put a hand over hers. Miranda felt like her heart had just exploded. She wanted to rip her hand away, push him off of the bench, and then run all the way back to her room, where she would no doubt spin around in circles, screaming about how stupid she had been.

'You'll have to trust me,' he said. 'I can't tell you everything, because I only got told certain details. What no one's telling you about Endinfinium is that being here is optional. It's just that no one knows how to get back.'

'That's crazy.'

'Sounds it, huh? Listen, in a couple of days, we're going off on a school trip. There's a place near where we're staying where we're going to meet someone from the other side who will show us how to get back.'

'What do you mean, "from the other side"?'

'From England.'

Miranda started to stand up. 'Look, if you're just messing with me, this isn't funny.'

'Sit down.'

Something in his eyes made her obey. Both Benjamin and Wilhelm would have gotten a punch just for telling her to open her book in class, but Cuttlefur had a hold over her that she couldn't quite—or didn't want, if she was honest about it—to understand.

'I got told to take you to a certain place,' Cuttlefur said. 'I didn't know where it was until I came here and I looked at a map. "Where dragons swim in the sea," was what I was told. So the Bay of Paper Dragons makes sense. However, this is just for you and me. We can't take anyone else back with us, and once we're gone, we can't return.'

Miranda looked down at her hands. But she was happy here ... wasn't she? She'd never had a life back in the Facility, so why would she even consider going back with Cuttlefur? Slowly she looked up, shaking her head. 'I can't go back,' she said. 'There's nothing for me there.'

Cuttlefur shook his head. 'Oh, but there is. They're closing the Facility. They're sending you home.'

'What home? The Facility is my home.'

'No.' Again Cuttlefur shook his head. 'Your real home. Your family.'

'I don't get what you mean.'

This time, Cuttlefur took both of her hands in his. 'There were some things the Facility didn't tell us about where we came from. We just assumed certain things ... but they weren't true.' He grinned. 'You're going home, Miranda. You're going to see your family again.'

14

MISTAKES

'No! You complete liar! That's not true and you know it!'

Wilhelm jumped up, hitting his head on the wooden slats of Benjamin's bunk. As he rubbed his head, he wished Benjamin were here to see this, but Benjamin still hadn't come back from whatever he'd gone off to do. So instead, Wilhelm was stuck on his own, watching Cuttlefur's lies.

Rick, perched on a little crag right behind Miranda and Cuttlefur, had caught their whole conversation, both pictures and sound. Miranda had gone now, headed back to the dormitories, but Cuttlefur still sat there with a smug grin as he watched the sunset.

'Everything all right in here?'

A long, zombified horse's face peered around the door. Gubbledon Longface, their housemaster, glared at Wilhelm.

'Sorry,' Wilhelm said, quickly throwing a pillow over the little computer screen. 'I was doing my math homework. I didn't, um, agree with the answer to one of the equations.'

'I'm sure Ms. Xemian will be happy to know about

your enthusiasm. But remember, some pupils are already sleeping.'

'Sorry.'

Wilhelm waved him away, and the housemaster finally closed the door. For a few seconds, Wilhelm listened to the hooves clomping on the stairs, before going back to his video feed.

Cuttlefur was now inside the school. Rick fluttered in the air above him, so must have sneaked in when Cuttlefur opened the door. The boy wasn't headed for the dorms like he was supposed to, however, but back toward the science wing.

'Where's he going?' Wilhelm muttered. 'What are you up to, you scoundrel?'

Rarely did anyone other than he risk a spell in the locker room by wandering around the main school buildings after hours. It was worth a thousand cleans, minimum, but he watched with interest as Cuttlefur walked silently along the corridors to the science block, hands straight at his sides like a robot. His head didn't move, and he didn't pause at any doors, as if to meet someone and was already late.

At the end of the corridor, a set of double doors opened onto the science block. Cuttlefur stopped, standing stock still in front of them for a moment, when he suddenly turned and looked directly up at the camera. A smile creased his face, and he lifted a hand to wave.

Wilhelm gasped, a shiver of fear running through him. Then, in a movement too swift to follow and too quick for Rick to slip through, Cuttlefur pushed through the doors and closed them again.

Wilhelm jumped to his feet. Whatever Cuttlefur was up to, he couldn't sit by and do nothing.

He turned down the volume on the live stream and

stuffed the computer into his pocket. Then he ran for the door.

At the top of the stairs, he heard someone coming up, and he shrank back into the alcove of the toilet entrance, standing breathless as Miranda passed by right in front of him. He wanted to grab her and tell her that her supposed new friend was trouble, but she would never believe him. He needed evidence.

Downstairs, Gubbledon was reading books in his office, but the common room was empty. Wilhelm slipped out, quickly throwing on a Scatlock cape and dashing across the narrow cliff path to the school's main building.

He was just pushing through the doors, when he bumped into someone.

Both of them let out a scream. Expecting to see the Dark Man's face itself, Wilhelm looked up to see it was only Benjamin.

'Quick!' he hissed, pulling off his cape. 'We have to find Cuttlefur. He's up to no good.'

'What are you talking about?'

'He spouted a bunch of rubbish to Miranda about how she could leave and find her family, and then he went running off to the science block. He looked up and saw Rick, and he didn't do anything. He just smiled and waved. He knew I was watching him. Whatever he's gone to do, we have to stop him.'

'Calm down,' Benjamin said. 'Look, it might be nothing.'

'It isn't!' Wilhelm shouted. 'I'm sure of it!'

Without waiting for Benjamin to follow, he raced off, but a few seconds later he heard his friend's footsteps behind him and glanced back to see Benjamin following.

'Look, I don't have time to explain properly,' Wilhelm said, as he peered around the wall into the adjoining corridor. 'You'll have to trust me. Who goes into the science block at this time of night unless they're causing trouble or stealing something?'

'We do,' Benjamin said.

'We're a special case,' Wilhelm said. 'He's not. Man, you should have heard what he was saying to Miranda. It was just lie after lie.'

'Like what?'

'Like he had come here to bring her back home. Like they were going to find a way back to England when we go to the Bay of Paper Dragons.'

Benjamin didn't answer right away. Wilhelm turned to look at him. 'Don't you believe me?'

'Of course I do.'

'Well, come on, then.'

The doors to the science block lay up ahead, and Wilhelm broke into a run, slamming through them.

Instead of swinging open smoothly, though, they collided with something coming the other way.

'Ow!'

Cuttlefur sat on the ground, rubbing his forehead. As he started to get up, Wilhelm pushed him backward and snatched out of his hands the bag Cuttlefur was carrying.

'What have you been stealing, you villain?'

Further up the corridor, a light clicked on, while behind, Benjamin ran through the doors, right into the back of him. Wilhelm backed away as Professor Loane stepped into the corridor.

'Um, what's going on here, then?'

'I caught him stealing stuff from the science labs!' Wilhelm shouted, pointing at Cuttlefur. 'Didn't he, Benjamin?'

Benjamin shook his head. 'I don't know....'

Professor Loane's face was as dark as a thundercloud.

'Cuttlefur came to collect some catch-up homework I had him do,' the professor said. 'And it looks to me that you two are not only out of your dorms, but that you also just assaulted him.'

'We did no such thing!'

'It was an accident, sir,' Cuttlefur said, glancing up at Wilhelm to give him the tiniest of private smiles. 'I don't think they knew what they were doing. They were just kids playing games. It's a bit late at night to be playing kiss-chase, but thats what it looks like.'

'That's very nice of you to say, Cuttlefur,' Professor Loane said, 'but discipline is important, and I think these boys need to learn some.'

Wilhelm glanced back at Benjamin, who rolled his eyes and gave a little shake of the head. *Nice one*, he mouthed.

15

DISCOVERY

'He got a thousand and I got five hundred,' Benjamin said. 'And we have to apologise to Cuttlefur in front of the school at tomorrow's Monday morning assembly.'

Miranda's eyes were like smoking coals. 'He'll wish he could have stayed in the locker room forever after I'm done with him,' she said. 'Where is he?'

'He's still down there. He's not talking to me, either, because I didn't back him up. What was there to back up, though?'

'How did he know Cuttlefur was going to the science block?'

Benjamin said nothing. If Miranda found out about Rick and the spy camera, she would never speak to Wilhelm again. The situation was bad enough without him making it worse, and he did feel bad for not sticking up for his friend. While he didn't particularly like Cuttlefur much, he couldn't just spread lies about him. And Cuttlefur hadn't actually done anything wrong that Benjamin could see. If he liked Miranda, it was understandable. She was kind of fiery ... but also kind of nice.

Not that he'd ever let her know that.

'I told him I saw Cuttlefur heading that way, and I think he got the wrong idea,' Benjamin said. 'It was probably all my fault.'

Miranda shook her head. 'He always wants to believe in conspiracies. I mean, haven't we got enough to worry about without getting after each other? Cuttlefur's stuck here, just like the rest of us.'

Benjamin didn't know what to say. He wanted to ask Miranda what Cuttlefur had said about leaving Endinfinium, but that would betray Wilhelm.

Instead, he decided to go and see if Wilhelm had finished in the locker room yet.

Fifteen minutes later, he squeezed into the little cubicle where Wilhelm sat, having managed to blag his way past the fearsome sin keeper by pretending to have forgotten something.

'Well, if it isn't the traitor himself,' Wilhelm said. 'Did I thank you for sticking up for me? If I didn't, it must have slipped my mind.'

'I'm sorry, but you have to admit, you went a bit crazy, there.'

Wilhelm tossed the object he was cleaning back onto the conveyor belt. 'You weren't there. You didn't see the way he looked at Rick. He's up to something, I know it.'

'Did you record the video? Perhaps you could show it to the teachers.'

Wilhelm shook his head. 'The computer tablet I've got it hooked up to doesn't work properly. It's only got a live-stream mode. I don't know how to get it to record.' He turned back to the conveyor belt, then stopped. 'I don't suppose you could ask someone for me? I got Ms. Xemian to help me with it, so you can't ask her, but one of the science teachers might help if you pretend it's for a school project.'

Benjamin tried to look enthusiastic, having now regretted coming down here. 'Look, just tell me where it is and I'll see what I can do.'

'In the box under my bed. Can you have a look at the video and find out where Rick went? I didn't have time to call him back before I was sent off to enjoy myself down here.'

'Sure, I'll see if I can figure it out.'

'Thanks. And about all that mess with Cuttlefur ... I don't know, maybe I was overreacting. Probably not, but maybe. Thanks for showing up, though. Anyway, I'd better get back to this, otherwise I won't finish in time to join the school trip, and Professor Loane said I'd get left behind.'

Benjamin returned to the dormitories, where the clock on the wall above Gubbledon's office told him he was late for lunch. Ordinarily that would have bothered him, but with everyone out, he had a chance to check out this camera of Wilhelm's.

The box was under the bed as Wilhelm had told him. He pulled it out to find a little cardboard nest where he supposed Rick would sleep—assuming reanimated plastic bags needed sleep—and a square computer tablet which he switched on.

A grainy, live video feed appeared. At first, Benjamin wasn't sure what he was seeing, until he realised it was a shot of Cuttlefur walking through a tunnel, illuminated by occasional candles flickering in braces on the walls.

So, Rick had picked up his trail again in one of the basement levels, though Benjamin couldn't be sure. Intrigued to see where Cuttlefur was going, he squatted down and pulled the computer up onto his knees.

'What have you got there?'

At the sound of Miranda's voice, Benjamin spun. She was standing in the doorway, hands on her hips, one fiery red eyebrow raised.

'You're supposed to be at lunch,' Benjamin stammered.

'So are you. What's that? I saw you pull it out from under Wilhelm's bed.'

'Nothing.'

He tried to hide the computer tablet under his arm, but it was too late. Miranda had marched across the room and man-piled him, shoving him to the floor and jerking it out of his hands.

'What is it?'

She turned it over just as Rick dove at Cuttlefur, and the blue-haired boy's face was caught in the centre of the screen.

'Oh!' Miranda cried, dropping the computer with the suddenness of surprise rather than anger. The tablet spun and landed facedown on a little nodule of wood sticking up from the floor. Its plastic screen broke with a soft crack.

'You're spying on him!'

'Not me—'

'Wilhelm, then. That scoundrel. How?'

Miranda grabbed the box and pulled it forward. One corner of a piece of plastic packing tape lay among the box nest of shredded cardboard, and Wilhelm had written *Rick* on the side of the box in ornate felt tip pen.

'What's "Rick"?'

Benjamin didn't dare lie. 'His Scatlock. He found it while helping Professor Eaves. It had a broken wing and he … tamed it.'

'Showing his sensitive side, eh? That little runt. I'll kick his butt for this.'

And before Benjamin could say anything else, Miranda had marched off to start a war.

16

CAPTIVE

Miranda felt like crying, but that wouldn't solve anything. Instead, she found a net in the biology department. From the glance she had gotten of Cuttlefur before the screen had broken, it looked like he was headed for the library. No matter, because he had arranged to meet her on the clifftop an hour before lunch for a quiet nature walk.

Wilhelm and Benjamin were her two closest friends, the only two people she considered true friends here in Endinfinium, and they had both betrayed her. And while she might eventually forgive Benjamin for being an accomplice, Wilhelm would forevermore be an enemy. Some things you just didn't do to your friends, and one of those was spy on them.

While technically forbidden to go outside the school buildings after dark, during the daytime on weekends, most of the cliffs and a couple of miles inland were considered safe enough for pupils to wander as they pleased, provided they appeared at mealtimes. Benjamin had been Miranda's regular walking companion until the day they had found Cuttlefur, though now it was clear his loyalties lay with Wilhelm. Even if she hadn't been desperate to punish her former friend for spying on her, she was growing tired of their childishness. Cuttlefur was so much more mature.

He waited by a scraggly tree in a hollow near the cliff edge. A few exposed rocks made crude seats, where he sat on one, staring at the ground, twisting a lock of his blue hair around in his fingers.

'I'm sorry I'm late,' she gasped. 'I had a few, um, issues to take care of.'

Cuttlefur smiled, and as always, she wanted to melt. 'I was just enjoying the day,' he said. 'It's a lot nicer than living in an institution, isn't it? You know that, when you go back, you'll never return there, don't you? We'll be going to proper homes with proper families. You'll have a real mum and dad.'

She hadn't even sat down yet, but her stored up anger was immediately replaced by the dreams he was telling her. What would it be like to have a real family? Benjamin had told her about his. Someone to comfort you when you were sad, to cheer you on when something good happened ... she couldn't wait.

'You'll get your own bedroom,' Cuttlefur said. 'And I don't mean like one of the dorms here, where you have to share with someone. One of your very own. You'll be able to decorate it how you want, put up posters on the wall—all sorts of things.'

His hand had already taken hers, and she shifted just a little closer, envisioning the warmth if they touched each other. With their clothes on, of course—but maybe if it was a little chilly, he might put his arm around her to protect her from the cold—

'If we go back, will we still see each other?'

Cuttlefur smiled again. 'Of course. We'll be living in

the same part of town. We can walk to school together, if you like.'

'We'll still be going to school?'

'Sure. But, you know, a regular school. There won't be any lessons about objects coming back to life or anything like that.'

Miranda shrugged. 'I wouldn't miss it.'

And as she said it, she wasn't sure she would. Even here in Endinfinium, being a Channeller had made her feel like a freak. Until the Dark Man's attack on the school, the teachers had denied all knowledge of the reanimation magic that permeated the very fabric of this world, and Miranda had been forced to seek guidance from Edgar Caspian, a once-exiled professor. Even now that reanimation magic had been accepted—grudgingly, she was sure—and Edgar had been restored to a teaching position, she remembered how much of an outcast she had felt.

With her glowing red hair marking her out as not just diverse but also completely different, she knew she hadn't quite shaken off her outcast label.

Benjamin and Wilhelm had accepted her. Benjamin and Wilhelm—

A glittering thing in the sky just beyond Cuttlefur's shoulder brought her old anger gatecrashing back. Didn't matter that Cuttlefur hadn't even asked why she had a net with her; she just leapt to her feet and pushed past him, swinging the net with all her might to snare the fluttering thing hovering just over their heads.

Scowling, Miranda hauled in the net and examined the little creature caught up inside.

'What is it?' Cuttlefur said.

'A Scatlock. They're made out of reanimated plastic carrier bags. They roost in crags on the cliff-face, and they're most active at night. You really don't want one getting into the dorms, or they might leave a crack big enough for others to follow.'

'That's why we wear those capes to cross over, isn't it?'

Miranda nodded. 'They're horrible little things. And this one is the most horrible of all.'

She reached through the netting to take hold of the tiny camera tied around the part of the Scatlock she guessed was the neck.

'It's disgusting,' Cuttlefur said. 'Kill it.'

His tone had hardened, and Miranda's fingers tensed, ready to rip the thing in two. After all, it was only a plastic bag. Endinfinium's reanimation magic might make it act like it was alive, but it was on borrowed time.

The Scatlock gave a little squeak. Miranda paused.

'I … can't.'

'Why not? Give it here. I'll do it.'

Cuttlefur reached for it, but Miranda pulled it away. She felt a sudden urge to use her magic, but reined it in before the feeling overwhelmed her.

'Don't.'

'What's the matter? It's a silly little plastic bag.'

'It's no sillier than we are. We were made in a lab, too, remember?'

Cuttlefur smiled. 'Oh, I see. You're feeling that sense of being, aren't you? Everything deserves life, especially when none of us deserve it?'

She shrugged. 'I can't just kill it.'

'What's it doing here? Why isn't it roosting with its plastic bag friends?'

Miranda cradled the little Scatlock in her hands. 'Rick,' she said, and the Scatlock rustled. Miranda looked up at Cuttlefur. 'Wilhelm sent it to spy on us.' She opened her hand to reveal the little camera tied around Rick's neck.

Cuttlefur looked about to say something harsh, but then, as if catching himself, he smiled again. 'Perhaps you shouldn't spend so much time with me,' he said. 'Your little friend is jealous. Why else would he attack me in the science block and then send this creature to spy on me? Perhaps we shouldn't hang around for a while.'

'No!'

Her surge of guilt and sadness faded, replaced by the old anger. 'He can't just spy on you. I need to teach him a lesson.'

'How?'

'This is his pet, right? He called it Rick. Well, now it's my pet. And he can't have it back until he's proven to me —and to you—that he's grown up and changed his attitude.'

Cuttlefur grinned, resting his hand over hers, and their connection—briefly tenuous—was restored.

'Sounds like a great idea,' he said.

17

PUNISHMENT

Benjamin felt like an idiot. Assembled on the floor of the Great Hall below, everyone in the school—teachers, pupils, and even some of the cleaners with their vacant eyes and dopey grins—stood watching his and Wilhelm's ritualistic humiliation.

'Shh!' Captain Roche hissed, stilling a group of third-year boys who couldn't stop sniggering behind their hands. Standing at the back, Gubbledon Longface gave a comical snort that only set them off again, while beside him, the sin keeper—having made a rare appearance outside of the locker room—gave a rustle of armour that could have meant anything.

The biggest disappointment for Benjamin was that Grand Lord Bastien—perhaps the only teacher on his side—hadn't shown up. Since Benjamin and his friends had freed him from the Dark Man's clutches, he had been noticeable by his absence from public view. Apart from a brief appearance at a ceremony marking the beginning of the second term, no one had seen him. Benjamin had grilled Edgar, but his friend's only response was that the

Grand Lord liked his contemplation time, and that he didn't consider the days' passing with the same urgency as they did.

Now, with the exception of Edgar, who wore an amused smirk, the rest of the senior teachers—Professor Loane, Captain Roche, Ms. Ito, and Professor Eaves—glowered at them from the side of the stage.

Professor Loane stepped forward and lifted a microphone. He tapped the end, and a crackle burst out of a speaker at the foot of the stage.

'I'm sure many of you would rather be learning math or science right now—'—boos and muffled cries of 'no' greeted him—'—but I'm afraid you have been gathered this morning in order for us to uphold one of the great virtues on which this school has been built.' He paused, but the sniggers and muffled chatting refused to obey his desire for a dramatic silence.

'I'm talking about unity,' he said. 'No one knows for sure why we all came here, but it is a situation that we have so far faced with dignity and gumption and, most of all, togetherness. As you are aware, there aren't many safe places in Endinfinium. This school was built to protect us all, but it is imperative that within its walls, we show each other the utmost respect. We have few rules—'—here, there were guffaws, and even Captain Roche cracked a smile—'—but those we do have, we expect you to protect.' He paused again, face reddening at the pupils' stubborn refusal to stay silent. 'A great many dangers lie outside our walls, but the great one from within starts with a capital B. Bullying.'

Benjamin's face reddened, though not with shame but with frustration. Godfrey never got pulled up in front of the school for calling him 'bird's nest' and 'runt' and assaulting him, but then, Godfrey was probably dead right now, and the dead always got respect, even if they were idiots while alive.

'Hurry up,' Wilhelm, standing beside him, hissed through gritted teeth.

'Wilhelm Jacobs, Benjamin Forrest … please step forward.'

Benjamin waited for Wilhelm to move, but his smaller friend was in stubborn mode again, edging forward in tiny steps that made Professor Loane grimace. When they had shuffled onto the middle of the stage like a couple of prisoners with invisible bonds, the professor lifted the microphone again.

'We don't condone bullying in our school,' Professor Loane said, 'but since there is nowhere to which you can be expelled, we must be lenient. Two days ago, Master Jacobs, accompanied by Master Forrest, assaulted the newest member of our school, Master, um, Cuttlefur, and made some strong allegations against him that were, of course, one hundred percent false. Step forward please, Cuttlefur.'

The blue-haired boy emerged from the middle of the group, wearing a forlorn, woe-is-me look as he glanced from one to the other. Benjamin looked for Miranda, who stood with the other girls off to the left, but her gaze was on the ground as if this was equally as embarrassing for her.

'Master Jacobs and Master Forrest will now make a public apology to you for their behavior. Master Forrest, you may go first.'

Benjamin took two steps forward, then took a deep breath. 'I'm sorry for bullying you,' he said, ignoring the sniggers. 'I won't do it again.' He glanced up at Cuttlefur, scanning his face for any sign of amusement, but there was none. If he was some kind of impostor like Wilhelm thought, he hid it really well.

'Apology accepted,' he said.

With a dismissive wave from Professor Loane, Benjamin stepped back. He took another deep breath, trying to calm his beating heart and chill his smarting cheeks.

'Master Jacobs, it's your turn. Since you were the ringleader in all of this, I would like a longer explanation for your actions, if you please. Step forward.'

Wilhelm sighed and shuffled forward. Benjamin saw Miranda look up, face filled with anger. She hadn't told the teachers about Rick and the spy camera, and Benjamin wondered if she was saving that up for her own personal ear-bashing. He was glad he wasn't Wilhelm.

'We're waiting, Jacobs,' Professor Loane said. 'Let's not keep everyone from class, shall we?'

'Keep us from class!' called a couple of the fifth-years, receiving a strong *shh* from Captain Roche for their troubles. The wide gym teacher rubbed his hands together and raised an eyebrow as long as a slug, the teachers' universal sign for a threat of a locker room spell.

Wilhelm took a deep breath, and then muttered, 'Sorry,' looking at his feet.

'Is that it?'

'Sorry.'

Professor Loane cleared his throat. 'Um, Master Jacobs ... this is a very serious matter. Bullying is the worst of all crimes between pupils and will not be tolerated. I will ask you one last time.'

Miranda's face was so crimson, it was almost on fire, and she was grinding her teeth as if ready to eat Wilhelm whole.

'Sorry,' Wilhelm muttered again.

Professor Loane sighed. 'Very well. Leave the stage, please.'

Wilhelm shuffled off, and Benjamin glanced up again, this time catching the faintest of smiles on Cuttlefur's lips. Too little to confirm Wilhelm's suspicions, but it was there. Miranda, however, looked like a deflated balloon. With shoulders slumped, she stared at the floor as if distraught Wilhelm had forgone his last chance at redemption.

'And you, Forrest,' Captain Roche grunted, pointing at the door at the back of the stage. 'Professor Loane isn't done with you, either.'

He followed Wilhelm into an office room behind the stage. Captain Roche came in and closed the door behind him.

Professor Loane glanced from one to the other, although Wilhelm wouldn't meet his eyes. 'Do you boys understand the seriousness of what you did?' he said. 'We can't have bullying here in Endinfinium High. We have to be united.'

'Yes, sir,' Benjamin said, looking at Wilhelm, who said nothing.

'Master Forrest, you can go back to class. Don't forget to get your things ready for the school trip tomorrow. We leave at eight a.m., sharp. Anything you forget, you will have to do without.' He turned to Wilhelm. 'You, however, Master Jacobs, in the unlikely event that you have actually begun to pack, can go right back to your dorm and unpack. You will not be going on the school trip. Instead, you'll be staying behind to assist Gubbledon and the cleaners deanimate the Great Hall and—' Here, he paused, this time in a silence so dramatic, Benjamin felt like he was watching an old black-and-white movie. '—the toilet block outside the gym.'

'No!'

Wilhelm sank to his knees in utter despair. Deanimating the Great Hall was one thing—it was a hard couple of days of spraying chamomile—but the gym toilet block was another matter, considered so foul even the teachers wouldn't enter them. The joint toilets and showers had been off-limits for more than five years, with pupils hurrying back to the dormitories instead after gym class.

Nothing came out, and nothing went in, but school legend said that the toilets—and whatever they had contained—had reanimated to a dangerous level. The school rugby club once had an initiation game for new members to go into those toilets at night, but even the notoriously tough rugby kids now considered it too terrifying and used the toilets in the history block on the second floor instead. These were cleaned every day, so it was a ceremonial initiation rite, though little else.

'We have decided it is no longer convenient for pupils to be running back to the dorms for a shower after every gym class,' Professor Loane said. 'The cleaners will manage most of it, but one very naughty little boy will help out.'

Wilhelm looked up, the usual defiance in his expression gone, replaced by a look of defeat—the face of a general watching his army being routed on a battlefield.

'I'm sorry for bullying Cuttlefur,' he said, but Professor Loane shook his head.

'Too late, boy. Too late.'

18

FINAL WORDS

'Can you pack quietly?'

Benjamin, carefully folding items of school uniform, looked up. 'Why don't you go bully someone else?' he said, and when Wilhelm scowled, he added, 'Only joking.'

'Come on, Benjamin. You know I'm right. Cuttlefur's a creep.'

'You're lucky you didn't get caught spying on him or they might have just locked you up in the old gym toilets and been done with it.'

'I didn't want to go on the stupid school trip, anyway. "The Bay of Paper Dragons." What is that, anyway? I imagine it's just as rubbish as the rest of Endinfinium.'

'I suppose you'll never find out. I'll send you a postcard.'

'Thanks.'

Benjamin felt a sudden sense of regret. He planned to head for Source Mountain as soon as he could get away from the rest of the group, and if he did find a way back to England, he would never come back. This could be goodbye.

'Look, I'm sorry. I didn't mean to not trust you. It's just that it seems you're chasing after something that isn't true. I mean, Cuttlefur, sure, he has a stupid name and he's, you know, quite good-looking, but are you sure you're not just jealous of him? I mean, Miranda clearly likes him.'

'No!' Wilhelm threw a sock at Benjamin's head, though Benjamin managed to duck just in time, catching a whiff as it passed in front of his face. 'I'm thinking about the good of the school,' Wilhelm said. 'This kid, Cuttlefur … something's odd about him.'

'Something's odd about all of us. That's why we're here.'

Wilhelm shook his head. 'After everything we've been through, Benjamin, and you still don't trust me—'

The door flew open. Miranda stood there, hair billowing out around her face as though dragging a storm along behind her on a leash.

'You.' One finger lifted to single out Wilhelm. Was she mad enough to use her magic on him? Something so prohibited it would see her thrown off the school trip, too? But when Benjamin closed his eyes and felt for it, there was thankfully nothing.

'What? Are you happy your new boyfriend got me thrown off the school trip?'

Miranda flew at him, and Benjamin jumped between them, managing to save Wilhelm but taking a bony fist in his stomach for his trouble. Before Miranda could swing again, he managed to wrap his arms around her, interlocking his fingers as she struggled against him.

'You're not my friend,' she hissed like a fiery dragon, glaring over Benjamin's shoulder at Wilhelm. 'Friends don't spy on each other. Enjoy cleaning the toilets.' She pulled away from Benjamin and marched back to the door. 'Oh, and by the way, I've got your pet.'

Wilhelm jumped up. 'Rick? No! I'm sorry, please give him back!'

'No. Not until you've proven yourself. He's coming to the Bay of Paper Dragons with me, and when I get back, I want to see that you've changed your ways. No more spying, no more lying to people, no more attacking other pupils—got that? And if you don't, I'll … I'll … I'll eat him!'

Benjamin lifted an eyebrow, hoping she realised how bad a reanimated piece of plastic was likely to taste.

Wilhelm, though, looked somber. He sighed. 'The old gym toilet block will be spotless,' he said, eyes on the ground.

'Good!'

Miranda turned on her heels, marching out so briskly, her footfalls were almost as loud as the slam of their bedroom door.

Benjamin turned to Wilhelm. 'What are you going to do?' he asked.

Wilhelm shrugged. 'Clean like I've never cleaned before.' He looked up at Benjamin. 'Do you really think she'll eat Rick?'

'To be quite honest, I can't see it, but there are plenty of other horrible things she might do.'

'She could give him to Cuttlefur. I bet that clown would use him as a hair net.' Wilhelm stood up. 'Anyway, I'd better go.'

'Where?'

'I got given an extra thousand cleans into the bargain, just to keep me out of trouble while you leave for the school trip tomorrow morning. I think they're worried I'll stowaway or something.'

'Oh.'

As Wilhelm went to the door, Benjamin stood up,

unsure if he would really need to say goodbye or not. If he did succeed in finding a way out of Endinfinium through the culvert at Source Mountain, though, this might be the only chance he would get.

'Wait.' He ran over to Wilhelm and gave him a big hug.

'What was that for?'

'Just … you know, I know you're an idiot and everything, and that practically all of the teachers hate you, and Miranda thinks you're a bully, and you've got more punishment coming out of your ears than Dusty Eaves has tweed jackets, but … you're still my friend.'

'Well, that's nice of you to say. You do believe me, don't you?'

Benjamin paused.

Wilhelm pushed out of his grip. 'Didn't think so. Enjoy the school trip, Benjamin.'

Then, before Benjamin could think of something worthwhile in reply, something that might have been better as a final word between them, Wilhelm was gone.

19

DEPARTURE

By the following morning, the weather had turned chilly. Benjamin dragged his suitcase through the main door and stood awkwardly among the cluster of pupils waiting for the arrival of whatever transport would take them up to the Bay of Paper Dragons. With Wilhelm left behind, there were fifteen first-years including Cuttlefur, as well as twelve second-years, along with Ms. Ito and Professor Eaves, who were both in charge of supervision.

Miranda stood on the far side of the courtyard, talking to Cuttlefur, trying not to glare at two second-year girls who were also trying to talk to him. Miranda and Cuttlefur stood out strikingly as a pair, Benjamin thought, with her crimson red hair and his aquamarine blue. Now that Wilhelm wasn't here and Miranda had a new friend, Benjamin realised how few friends he had made since arriving in Endinfinium. It was likely to be a lonely trip.

The sooner he found a way to get to the source of the Great Junk River, the better.

They were due back on Friday night. Judging by the maps, twenty miles lay between the Bay of Paper Dragons and Source Mountain, a significant distance without transport.

It would be so much easier with Wilhelm there. They could have just stolen whatever would take them north and then left Endinfinium together.

Another pang of guilt clenched like a fist in his stomach.

In time, his friends would forget about him. After all, he had been here only a short time, and without him around to stir up the Dark Man, they would invariably be safer.

It was better for everyone if he left. Or ... or...

Died trying.

The idea had slipped into his thoughts before he could block it out. The possibility was really there. Most here had made peace with their predicament, though they all shared a common ground that Benjamin didn't. Almost everyone he talked to had come from an unloving background and had no desire to go back home. Wilhelm had grown up in an orphanage, while Miranda was a clone, having been built and raised in a laboratory.

Too many things still mystified Benjamin about Endinfinium to ever trust it enough to want to stay, not when he had loving parents and an adoring kid brother waiting for him back in Basingstoke.

For one, there were hardly any adults. The school wasn't exactly overflowing with pupils, but other than the teachers, he could count on one hand the number of adults he had met. He had been across the Great Junk River briefly, travelling right to the foot of the High Mountains, but he had seen no towns or villages. Where were the people? Where did they go when then graduated?

Many of the teachers had told him Endinfinium's history went back further than anyone realised. The nearly mindless cleaners who wandered the school were the reanimated corpses of the dead, while the ghouls of the Haunted Forest who rose up to do the Dark Man's bidding were discontented spirits fused with reanimated objects.

No, the dead provided ample evidence that over the years, many people had grown up, lived, and died here.

But where were they now? What had happened to last year's graduates, and those of the year before? No one ever talked about it, as if no one knew.

Benjamin wasn't so sure he wanted to know. Already, he had seen enough terrifying things to last a lifetime. The kids who graduated, though, certainly didn't go back to their homes in England or wherever they came from. If they did, that would be all anyone would talk about.

Maybe if I leave, I can come back and help everyone else.

Again, conflicting emotions. How many would actually want to leave? Wilhelm claimed to love Endinfinium, even though he constantly ribbed on it, so Benjamin felt like the only truly lost boy in Neverland.

A gentle laugh made him look up. Cuttlefur had just cracked a joke, and Miranda was chuckling with one hand on his shoulder. She looked so happy.

Benjamin frowned.

What was it Wilhelm claimed Cuttlefur had said? That he knew of a way for them to leave?

A tickle of unease ran down his back as he remembered Cuttlefur's almost-imperceptible smile at their public shaming. And Wilhelm claimed Cuttlefur had looked up at Rick's camera and waved.

He had only just shown up, and he was claiming already he knew of a way to take them both back home?

Perhaps Wilhelm was right and Cuttlefur was up to something. With Wilhelm stuck at the school, there would be no one to look after Miranda should he go looking for

Source Mountain. Cuttlefur might just be a typical older kid, playing with her affections, but what if he were something else?

What if he were dangerous?

Benjamin gripped the edge of his trouser leg and squeezed as tightly as he could, trying to stop himself from screaming.

He was still struggling with indecision when some of the other kids let out a whoop, and began waving their hands in the air. A shadow fell across them, and Benjamin looked up as, to the utter horror of Ms. Ito and Professor Eaves, his old friend, Lawrence, the reanimated train, crawled over the top of the school and down the front of the main entrance.

'Caspian, you utter cad!' Ms. Ito hollered in her familiar piercing voice, sharp enough to cut glass. 'Have you no respect for history?'

'What happened to the airship?' Professor Eaves added, giving his stomach a quick rub. 'I don't mind airships. That thing ... I mean, just look at it.'

Lawrence—his current shape comprising five train carriages that had reanimated into a rough lizard-shape, with huge, metal hind- and forefeet that propelled him over rough terrain his manic spinning train wheels couldn't handle—was, for all intents and purposes, Edgar Caspian's pet. A few months earlier, Lawrence had taken Benjamin, Miranda, and Wilhelm to the High Mountains, where they had found the Dark Man's waiting army, and with Lawrence's help, they had gotten back to the school in time to warn the teachers. In the process, Lawrence had lost half his length and nearly lost his life, and after a bruising encounter with a cruise-shark, ended up more of a lizard-train than a snake-train, but the power of reanimation had brought him back.

A door in Lawrence's locomotive head opened, and Edgar Caspian leaned out.

'Airship sprang a leak,' he called to Ms. Ito, who glowered like a fire in the dark. 'All aboard. We haven't got all day, have we?'

'If the damned thing makes me nauseous, I'll be opening up your suitcase as a sick bag, Caspian!' Ms. Ito snapped.

As they climbed on, Benjamin looked at Miranda, nostalgia for their last adventure flooding back, and he saw her sit down near the back of the first carriage, Cuttlefur beside her. Benjamin stared in horror at the free seat beside him, then peered up as a shadow fell across his lap.

'Is this seat free?' muttered Snout. Benjamin frowned as the unofficial most-boring-boy-in-the-school stood awkwardly in front of him.

'Um, well....'

'Of course it is,' snapped Ms. Ito, her leg cast swinging around to connect with Snout's behind, knocking him into the seat. 'Belt up, boys. We're not travelling in the luxury I was anticipating.'

'I really like the beige colour of these seats,' Snout droned as Lawrence growled and lumbered forward. Benjamin gave Snout a polite acknowledgement, then hurried to fasten his own seatbelt. Around him, the other pupils whooped and cheered as Lawrence dropped over the cliff-face edge, dramatically pausing vertically downward, then spun his back end around and bounded back up again.

'Caspian, you're sharing a room with the kids for this!' Ms. Ito barked from the back, but her voice was almost drowned out by a collective cheer.

Lawrence, at times rolling like a train and at others running like a lizard, twisted and wound inland toward the

Great Junk River, then turned north. Benjamin glanced back. Ms. Ito had pulled on an eye mask, clutching the back of the seat in front. Other pupils had ignored the call to wear their seat belts and now hung off the luggage rails overhead, while Dusty Eaves, one hand gripping his stomach, shouted for order.

The hills rose and fell, a carpet of green mixed with patches of scrub and woodland. The river remained to their left, occasionally visible in the distance when they crested a hilltop. The further north they went, the more the land became undulated, as if the world was getting squeezed up by some distant obstruction.

By the time he turned back toward the coast, Lawrence had slowed down a little. Some of the pupils were sleeping, others had taken to playing trumps or I-Spy. Snout was muttering something about the possible nutritional value of breakfast when Edgar stood up at the front and turned round.

'Well, everyone, we have arrived! I hope you had a pleasant journey, but it's almost time to get off. Welcome to the Bay of Paper Dragons!'

PART II

THE BAY OF PAPER DRAGONS

20

BREEDING POND

'I can't see any dragons,' one of the second-years moaned. 'In fact, I can't even see the sea yet.'

'Be quiet, fool boy,' Ms. Ito snapped. 'A case can be made for turning some of you into fish food. We're overpopulated already; few of you would be missed.'

Benjamin climbed stiffly out and shook the aches from his joints. Lawrence, despite his origins as an Italian express train, had provided a more theme-park-style of a journey. Though Professor Eaves had somehow managed to sleep through most of it, Ms. Ito, whose face was practically green, had suffered worst of all. Benjamin glimpsed her stumping to the nearest bushes, followed by a noise like someone emptying out a pot of soggy mashed potatoes onto a concrete floor.

Lawrence had stopped at the top of a narrow, forested valley, and Benjamin hadn't prepared himself for how the landscape might have changed this far north of the school. Instead of the bare headlands, with their couch grass and wind-hassled patches of gorse, the land sloped down to a triangle of sea occasionally visible through the trees.

Craggy outcrops of granite poked up out of the foliage, all dark greens and browns.

'Right, everyone, this way,' Professor Eaves said, waving his arms to herd the children toward him. A few had already wandered off, and he sent a couple of the second-year prefects to go look for them.

'We have to walk from here,' he said. 'The Bay of Paper Dragons is about a mile further on. Stay close, please. While we've been assured there's nothing of danger in these woods, it's better to be safe than sorry.'

'We'd hate to lose one of you so soon,' Ms. Ito grumbled, stumping out of the bushes to stand beside him. 'Hurry up. In pairs, please. The path is pretty narrow, and in a couple of places there are small streams running alongside. Endeavour to stay out of them, please.'

Benjamin found himself walking beside Snout again. Miranda strode up ahead, practically glued to Cuttlefur, his blue head bobbing along like part of the sky had fallen to play among them.

'Do you think they prune it with clippers or just hack it back?' Snout said, pointing at the path's cut-away foliage.

Benjamin suppressed a sigh. 'I have no idea,' he said.

Twenty minutes later, they came around a corner to find themselves face to face with a building that sat in amongst the trees back from the beach and announced itself, on a signboard, as the Paper Dragon Bay Guesthouse. Benjamin blinked. Over the last few days, he had built the building up in his mind to be one of a number of things. In the absence of any photographs, he had been left to conjure up an image for himself, piece by piece, like a made-up jigsaw puzzle. One view had the Paper Dragon Bay Guesthouse as a dull, stone building like part of the school, a relic from a more populous period of Endinfinium's history, while another image was of a wooden shack similar to their dormitory, a tumbledown near-ruin ready to slide into the water and be devoured.

What he hadn't expected, though, was something out of a dated carnival—a lavishly designed explosion of faded colours: flames of red and yellow and purple racing up the side of a building so ornate with alcoves and balconies, it was impossible to be sure where the walls began and the balconies ended. It rose out of the ground like an oriental flower that had sprouted in a sudden rush, bursting up through a pallet of paints, stretching in a series of colourful viewing platforms, overhanging balconies, and protruding galleries for the sky.

'That looks architecturally unsafe,' Snout muttered beside him.

Benjamin gave the other boy a grim smile and quickened his pace, heading towards Ms. Ito and Professor Eaves, who led the line meandering along a cobbled path of colourful ovals of stone that arced back and forth around collapsing walled flowerbeds with faded wooden labels indicating what the original seedlings in each might once have been.

'Looks like old Barnacle has let the place go,' Professor Eaves muttered. 'I remember when we came here all those years ago. You could see the water through the trees.'

'I told Loane to send someone up to check,' Ms. Ito replied. 'Fool sent a couple of cleaners and one of his idiot secretaries. We vote him down next time, Eaves.'

'You'd rather look after them?' Professor Eaves said.

One side of Ms. Ito's face lifted unnaturally far as she glanced at him, which Benjamin guessed was a rare expression of amusement. 'All right, vote him in again,' she said.

'It looks even less safe than I remember,' Eaves said a

few steps further on. 'I mean, the wing that collapsed has been rebuilt, but the rest of it looks about to go.'

'We can hardly make them camp in the bus,' Ms. Ito said, presumably referring to Lawrence. 'Not much of a school trip, is it? A bit of danger never hurt anyone, Eaves. And if it does'—she gave him that half-face smile again—'they'll just come back. Not like we can escape them, is it? Damned brats come back one way or another, don't they?'

'I'm not worried about it killing them,' Professor Eaves said. 'I'm worried about it falling down and trapping us in there with them. Gubbledon said some of their rooms stink in the morning when he goes to wake them up for breakfast. No windows open ... all that cabbage for dinner ... you want to get stuck in a dump like this with that for several days?'

'Perhaps *we* should camp in the bus.' The absence of Ms. Ito's creepy smile meant she was serious.

'And leave Caspian in charge of the kids? I don't think so.'

Ms. Ito sighed. 'Another of Loane's stupid ideas. Perhaps we should vote him down after all?'

'I will if you will.'

As they continued to gossip and grouse about the other teachers, Benjamin slipped back a few places. The Paper Dragon Bay Guesthouse, which had seemed quite close at first, appeared to recede up the valley as they followed the winding path. It had to be far bigger than it looked from a distance, and some of the other kids were now huffing and complaining as they dragged their suitcases over the lumpy stones. The main topic of conversation was the lack of any visible dragons, with the lack of any visible bay hot on its tail. Only as the trail steepened did Benjamin notice the stuffy heat. Just this morning, they had been standing on a blustery clifftop with jackets to ward off the chill. Now, pupils were slowly stripping off their coats and sweaters as the temperature rose with each step.

And then they stepped out from the foliage to find themselves on a stone causeway leading straight out across an open area of deep green water to a rock buttress. There, it dipped under shadow before jagging back into the trees for a final climb up to the guesthouse.

'Wow!'

'Look at that!'

'Oh, my!'

'Dragons!'

Benjamin looked to where several pupils pointed. The stone causeway encircled a wide pond fed by a stream that trickled over rocks and out from the forest. In the very centre of the swimming-pool-sized pond swam a group of strange creatures, ducking and diving in and out of the water.

They were elongated like serpents, yet segmented, and bright red with wide, square faces and snapping jaws beneath yellow-and-black eyes. Strange, shimmering wings protruded from their sides, shining gold-and-silver.

Most Benjamin could see were about twice the length of a man, but each was surrounded by a couple of dozen miniature ones that followed the larger ones everywhere like ducklings.

'The breeding pond,' Ms. Ito said, turning around to address the pupils. Then she grunted and stumped on, as if that had been enough explanation, Professor Eaves following at her side.

Benjamin and several others stopped to look at the creatures, which swam with languid grace, though their bodies had an unusual flexibility as though constantly stretching and retracting.

Then, to a series of gasps from the pupils, one emerged and came to rest on top of a wide, floating lily leaf. The leaf was the size of a coffee table, and the dragon first curled around the outside to steady it, then made a space in its body for its young to jump up and nestle in the middle.

'It's really made out of paper!' someone shouted.

Benjamin gasped. It really was. As the sun caught its body, the dragon's colours began to lighten, as if it were drying out. Nestled in its protective coil, several of its young had already turned a colour that made their ephemeral little bodies nearly invisible against the forest's backdrop.

The paper dragon opened its mouth, then clacked its wooden teeth together. Its head bobbed and weaved, as though nodding a greeting to the watching pupils. Only when Ms. Ito barked for everyone to hurry up was its hold over them broken.

As they crossed over the causeway and back into the forest, Benjamin glanced back to catch one last glimpse of the paper dragon, its colours now so faded, it was like an old T-shirt that had been left out in the sun.

'Carnival dragons from China,' someone said a couple of places in front of him. 'My dad brought one back from a business trip once. They were like hand puppets. You put your hand inside and you snap its mouth together. Bit smaller than that one, though.'

'I thought we were going to see real dragons!' shouted one of the second-years, a fat kid called Adam, who was always complaining about the size of the lunch portions even though the cleaners would, with as much enthusiasm as a mindless, reanimated corpse could muster, gladly refill your bowl upon request. 'That's not a dragon. It's a stupid kids toy.'

Without Adam noticing, Ms. Ito had stumped back down the line to stand behind him. As he started to clap at the creature curled up on the lily, she swung her leg cast and knocked him face-first into the water.

Adam went under, screaming and flailing in water far deeper than Benjamin realised, and the paper dragon uncurled and dived in, its brood following.

Like a homing missile, it powered through the water toward its prey, its upper lip above the surface, water splashing off its wooden teeth as its long, colourful tail swished back and forth.

'Someone grab him!' one of the second-years cried at the exact moment Ms. Ito shouted, 'Let him learn the error of his fool ways.'

The paper dragon closed in fast, and Adam couldn't get a grip on the causeway's edge because the stones were as smooth as glass. Benjamin felt strangely excited about the impending bloodbath, when the pupils suddenly separated as Cuttlefur came pushing through.

'Here, take my hand!' he shouted, lying flat-down on the causeway and stretching out both arms toward the floundering second-year.

The dragon was just feet away when Adam surfaced like a dying whale and spewed a geyser of slimy green water over the nearest huddle of excited pupils. They squealed in disgust and stumbled back as Adam found Cuttlefur's hands, and the blue-haired boy jerked him up out of the water with surprising strength just as the paper dragon's wooden jaws snapped down where Adam's head had been. As the fat boy lay wet and gasping on the glistening stones, the dragon did one aggressive circle, teeth clacking, then retreated back to the lily pad with its brood in pursuit.

'Th ... th ... thank you!' Adam gasped, picking bits of

green slime off of his soaked school uniform. 'I thought I was lunch!'

Cuttlefur looked up at Ms. Ito, and the rest of the pupils fell silent as his eyes narrowed. No one ever glared at Ms. Ito. Benjamin had heard legends of ten thousand cleans just for back-talking her in class.

'You tried to murder Adam,' Cuttlefur said. 'That's not a very good way to behave, is it?'

Ms. Ito met his gaze, nostrils flaring. 'Watch your tongue. I've taken them out for less.'

'You can't murder the pupils.'

'One day, if you live long enough, you'll learn that not all lessons are taught in a classroom, boy.'

And before Cuttlefur could reply, she turned and stumped off toward Professor Eaves, muttering, 'It's got wooden teeth, for the sake of the two suns. Are all of our pupils utter cowards?'

Adam tried to pull Cuttlefur into a hug, but Cuttlefur stepped back out of range, holding up his hands in protest that 'thanks' was enough. Behind him, Miranda touched him tenderly on the shoulder, while other pupils gazed at him as though a god now walked among them. Benjamin, who had drifted back to where Snout and his bumbling inanities waited, wondered what Wilhelm might have thought about all of this.

Before he could start to pine for his absent friend, though, a booming voice echoed down the path.

'Welcome! Welcome, one and all! Welcome to the Paper Dragon Bay Guesthouse!'

21
BARNACLE

The man was so big, he made Fat Adam look svelte. Encased in a white flannel one-piece partially hidden by a dirty, brown apron that hung right to his knees, he wobbled from side to side as he walked, nearly dropping over one or other of the causeway's edges with each step. Only a casual familiarity with his surroundings protected him from a coating of the same green slime that had soaked Fat Adam.

Up ahead, the teachers—Ms. Ito looking slightly sheepish after her attempted murder—had paused by a section of neatly mown grass adorned with several wooden picnic tables.

'Glad you made it at last,' the fat man said. He attempted to engage Ms. Ito in an embrace, but when she twisted away from his grip, he instead zeroed in on Professor Eaves. Caught between the fat man and the resolutely immovable Ms. Ito, Professor Eaves had no choice but to grimace as the newcomer appeared to fairly absorb him into his body, encircling him with arms as thick and as soft as a beanbag.

'Barnacle,' Eaves said, managing to survive with only a partial hug. 'You've … grown since we last met.'

'Yes, yes, outwards and upwards,' Barnacle said, and as he stood still, Benjamin figured out what gave Barnacle his name. Out of the sides of his face grew warts which, on closer inspection, turned out to be small barnacle shells. He scratched at them with one fat hand, making most of the girls cringe.

'He should put some cream on those,' Snout said.

'A late lunch has been prepared,' Barnacle said. 'You can leave your luggage in the entrance lobby. I'll have the cleaners take it up to your rooms.'

Then he began the ponderous effort of turning around. While Ms. Ito and Professor Eaves waited patiently, the pupils queued up behind them. Fat Adam was still complaining about his head-to-foot coating of slime, while Miranda shot daggers at a couple of second-year girls giving excessive attention to Cuttlefur's blue hair.

With Barnacle in the lead, everyone continued up the slope to the guesthouse, which was set back into the hillside and surrounded above and below by a thick tropical forest, with a cleared area at the front where vehicles could park. The car park was currently empty, but a road angled behind the huge, gaudy guesthouse and out of sight into the forest.

'Take a look, kids,' Barnacle said as they reached the car park. He turned away from the guesthouse and gestured out to sea.

A series of 'wows' and gasps greeted the view. Benjamin wandered to the edge of the car park, where the hill sloped away to a beach. Far below spread out a U-shaped bay enclosed on either side by thickly vegetated headlands that circled around to almost touch each other. A sand bar made a natural gate against the sea, and the bay was a larger version of the breeding pond, its dark green water punctuated by rock stacks sticking out like blunt pencil heads.

And there, in the water, were the dragons.

'They're huge!' Miranda gasped.

Several gaudily coloured paper dragons the length of a school swimming pool circled in the water, occasionally bobbing up or diving below the surface. Several more lay curled around the rock stacks like rainbow-coloured streamers.

'Why are they so big?' Miranda asked, turning to Barnacle. 'The ones in that pond were tiny.'

'Big ones,' he said. 'Males.' His fat face widened into a grin that pushed barnacles up to nearly cover his eyes. 'You'll be going on a tour tomorrow. My assistant is an expert on them.' Miranda opened her mouth to ask another question, but Barnacle clapped his hands together and turned away. 'Now, everyone, let's eat!'

The second-years rushed up the path to the guesthouse doors. Having been around long enough to see plenty of bizarre animals, they weren't as interested as the first-years. As the rest of the first-years—Benjamin, Snout, and Miranda among them—stared at the elegant creatures drifting through the water, Ms. Ito stuck out a hand to turn them away.

'Come on, hurry up,' she barked. 'Not got all day.'

'Give them a minute,' a familiar voice said, and Benjamin turned to see Edgar striding up the path. The old wizard wore a jovial smile that made Ms. Ito scowl like an angry vulture.

'I'll look after them,' he said.

'Food's gone, you starve,' Ms. Ito spat, then she turned and stumped toward the guesthouse.

Edgar just shrugged. 'Quite a view, isn't it?' He glanced

at Barnacle, who examined the backs of his hands as if he had never seen them before. 'Oh, hello, Alan. Been a long time. How's business?'

Barnacle looked up. 'Oh, great. Don't get as many travelers as we used to, but not bad. You are?'

Edgar frowned. 'Don't you remember me? Professor Caspian. I brought you here on a school trip thirty-odd years ago. You never wanted to leave, and I see you didn't.'

'Oh, right.' Barnacle tapped the side of his head. 'Brain's not what it was.' He flashed Edgar a wide grin. 'Must be the humidity. Right, lunch. Don't let it get cold; there's nothing else until dinner.'

Cuttlefur, Miranda, and Snout also started toward the entrance, but Benjamin hung back with Edgar, feeling for the first time like he was close to a friend, despite Edgar being as old as his grandfather.

'He's a little strange,' Benjamin said.

'Huh. You don't know the half of it. He lives off the algae growing in the water that stops the dragons from disintegrating. It's got a high natural fat content that coats the dragons' skin. But you don't want to eat too much of it, or you'll swell up like a balloon. Always did like his seafood, that boy.' He grinned. 'Was always first in line for a second portion. Strange how he didn't recognise me, though.'

'You used to teach him?'

'Alan Barnes—now, affectionately, Barnacle—was the biggest swot I ever had,' Edgar said. 'Couldn't keep his hand down in class. So keen I wanted to send him to the locker rooms just so other pupils could have a chance to answer questions. Hmm. Strange that he doesn't remember me....'

'We'd better hurry up and get to lunch,' Benjamin said. 'Just in case he's still got the same appetite.'

On the guesthouse's bottom floor, a series of trestle tables filled a gloomy cafeteria, and Benjamin sighed as he sat down, hearing Snout trying to discuss the spiral design on his fork's handle with anyone who had no choice but to listen. When he looked down at his plate, though, his eyes lit up.

Amidst a circle of the same kind of vegetables as Endinfinium High's lay a neat triangle of pink meat.

'Is it really salmon?' he said, looking up, finding no one but Snout to talk to.

Snout shrugged. 'Looks like it. Tastes … more or less like it.'

'Endinfinium salmon,' proclaimed a voice from so close behind Benjamin, he almost fell off of his chair. He looked around to see a smiling, middle-aged man wearing a chef's hat that flopped over one side of his face, which was thin, the hair around his ears grey, but when he smiled, his dark blue eyes sparkled as if a current of electricity ran through his visage. He held up a wooden bowl and a ladle. 'Sauce? Of course you do.'

Benjamin leaned sideways to avoid getting burned as a boiling cascade of green slime with the consistency of custard splashed all over his plate. As he looked up in despair, the chef stepped back with an extravagant bow.

'Chef Jim Green at your service,' he said. 'That's "green," like my cooking. Eat up, now.' And he was gone, weaving around the tables to ladle out scoops of slime into bowls, whether it was asked for or not.

'Tastes better than it looks,' said Adam, sitting a few seats down on the other side. He had found time to change out of his wet school uniform, now wearing brown overalls that, by their size, had been loaned from Barnacle. He grimaced. 'At least, warmed up, it does.'

Benjamin glanced at the teachers' table where Ms. Ito

and Professor Eaves held an animated conversation while pointedly ignoring Edgar. Barnacle circulated among the tables, huge hands on his hips, lines of sweat dripping down his brow. Despite the big grin he had given them upon arrival, he now looked distinctly unsettled by their presence. Benjamin hadn't realised he was staring, until Barnacle abruptly turned in his direction, and their eyes locked. A shiver of unease tickled down Benjamin's back as the rotund innkeeper's eyes held his own gaze for far too long to be casual, and Benjamin felt a hint of something that scared him just a little.

Recognition.

22

ABSENCE

The boys' rooms and girls' rooms were separate, with the places in each three-person room decided by drawing lots. While Benjamin was relieved to have avoided sharing a room with Snout, he instead found himself sharing a three-bed room with Fat Adam and Cuttlefur. Adam's mouth was as big as his stomach, and Cuttlefur sat politely while Adam flapped a paper leaflet like a fly swatter, prattling on about how close he had felt to death when Ms. Ito pushed him into the breeding pond.

'Surely there's a rule about that sort of thing,' he said. 'I mean, if there were courts or police, I could call them and have her arrested, couldn't I?'

'Not really possible, is it?' Benjamin said.

'I'm saying, but if it was. I mean, she tried to murder me.'

'I think she was teaching you a lesson.'

Cuttlefur laughed. 'I don't think she cared one way or another. That's why she's so scary.'

'But you stood up to her! I mean—wow! You took on Ms. Ito!'

'I didn't take her on. I just told her the truth.'

'I bet she hates you now.'

'I think she's more likely to respect me.'

As he listened to the exchange, Benjamin slowly warmed to Cuttlefur. The boy was easy to like, despite Wilhelm's protests, and no wonder Miranda and he had become practically inseparable.

Did Cuttlefur really have a way to leave? Perhaps he also knew about Source Mountain and had planned to take her there.

Might be easier if they tried to escape together.

Benjamin hadn't had much time to figure out how he would actually get to Source Mountain and what he would do once he got there. He hoped Jeremiah Flowers had left behind some sign he could follow, but if not, there was always his magic.

He hadn't used it in weeks. Part of him was afraid it would begin to tear apart his body like it had done before, when he drew the power from himself rather than from the earth like Grand Lord Bastien had taught him. At the same time, though, he felt like he was saving it for one huge blast, something that would either help him or destroy him. Could he blast his way through the culvert to the world on the other side, or didn't it work like that?

Today was Tuesday, and they wouldn't be returning home until Friday morning. Until that time, he was prepared to sit and wait for his chance.

In time, it would come. He just had to be patient.

'Toilet,' he muttered, getting up and going out, leaving Adam to bend Cuttlefur's ear with his plans for Ms. Ito's eventual demise.

Despite its colourful exterior, the guesthouse's rooms and corridors were gloomy, narrow, and poorly lit. Wanting to be alone, Benjamin took the first unlit corridor he came to and wandered through dreary corridors of closed doors with dusty handles, past prints on the faded, water-damaged walls. At one point, he ended up in a dusty ballroom with tables and stacked chairs covered by dirty sheets. Unlike the school, none of it seemed to be reanimated, as if things here were truly dead. He put his hands on a wooden doorframe, feeling for the familiar warmth, though he only sensed the slightest residue heat, nothing more. When he leaned close and smelled the wood, he thought he understood why: a faint smell of ancient chamomile lingered, as though the walls had once been painted with the stuff and had been dormant ever since.

At the end of another corridor, Benjamin stopped at the bottom of a metal fire escape, and in the light of a skylight far above, he saw a single set of footprints in the dust.

They were petite, like those of a girl's.

Quietly, wincing at each creak of the steps beneath his feet, Benjamin climbed up to the roof.

At the top, the door was slightly ajar and led onto a bare veranda. It faced away from the bay, back to the hills. The yellow sun had already begun to set, leaving the veranda in shadow.

Even in the gloom, Benjamin recognised Miranda's bright red hair. She was facing away, back toward the hills that rose above them and blocked their view of inland. Her hands were spread, fingers wide, and she pushed them forward and back as if trying to bounce an invisible basketball.

He closed his eyes, feeling for her magic. Edgar had taught them that Summoners like himself, Channellers like Miranda, and Weavers like Wilhelm could sense each other if they understood how the sensation felt.

It was a kind of tingly warmth, like when you warmed your hands at a crackling fire, though you didn't feel it with your skin, you felt it from the inside out, as if the magic were a magnifying glass focused on your own heart. Subtle and as difficult to miss as a simple temperature change, but with practice, you were able to spot it. After Grand Lord Bastien had explained the feeling to Benjamin, he had gone with Miranda and Wilhelm to an unused classroom, where they had sat in a circle and practiced guessing whether or not one of them was pulling on their magic. It had proved quite an experience, until Captain Roche had caught them at it and sent them all to the locker rooms for a thousand cleans for going into an off-limits room without permission.

When Benjamin opened his eyes, Miranda was still standing with her back to him, shaking her hands out, becoming increasingly agitated. She was a Channeller, able to draw on the reanimation magic at will, using it to reanimate and deanimate at her choosing. But as Benjamin felt for it, he shook his head. There was nothing.

'Miranda.'

He stepped out onto the roof. She spun round, and her hands came up, ready to unleash her power on what she thought was an enemy, though with none of the warmth that should have come with it.

'Benjamin … what are you doing here? Did you follow me?'

'No. I was just exploring. I saw your footprints.'

'What do you want?'

The unfamiliarity in her voice was heartbreaking. Until Cuttlefur had shown up, they had been best friends, nearly inseparable.

'What are you doing?'

'Nothing. I'm just—'

'I can't feel your magic. Perhaps you should speak to Edgar?' He shrugged. 'Maybe you're tired or something?'

Miranda's eyes widened, her lips curled back, and Benjamin started. The Miranda he knew was fiery, but the look on her face was devilish, almost evil.

'It's not gone!' she shouted, throwing her hands up as though to shove him back against the wall. Nothing happened.

Benjamin shook his head. 'Just calm down. I'm sure it'll be back in a bit. Try not to panic.'

'Shut *up!*'

She marched toward him. When he didn't move aside quickly enough, she shoulder-barged him out of the way, then broke into a run to the door. He watched her, heart thundering.

'Miranda, please! Come back!'

'You're not my friend! You're on *his* side!'

Benjamin could only assume she meant Wilhelm, but before he could ask, she was gone through the doors and down the steps.

As the sound of her footsteps died away, he forced himself not to give in to the despair building up inside him.

The source of the Great Junk River was so close, he could almost reach out and touch it, and though he had no intention of giving up on his escape attempt, he had hoped to leave on good terms with his friends.

Miranda, though, was hurting. And he didn't know what he could do to help.

23

HOPELESS

Miranda stomped back through the corridors to her room with a thundercloud over her head. Her magic had gone, and her friends didn't care, so no, everything would not be okay. She had lost the only thing that made her feel safe, and without it, she felt helpless. What was Benjamin talking about? Edgar couldn't help her. The old wizard could tell her how to use it, but he couldn't bring it back once it was gone.

When she reached a quiet corridor far enough away from Benjamin, Miranda stopped, cupped her face, and cried until her eyes hurt and her stomach knotted. Then, she wiped her eyes and spent a couple of minutes calming herself. It did no good to cry about it, but she did feel a lot better. Her magic was gone, but what did it matter? She and Cuttlefur would be gone soon, too, and back in England, with a real family. She wouldn't need her magic anymore.

She undid a top button on her shirt and put a hand inside, searching for the necklace Cuttlefur had given her, and when her fingers closed over the red stone, an overwhelming sense of relief washed over her as if he was protecting her, even when he wasn't there. The stone, too, felt warm, as though it had sensed her distress and was trying to bring her comfort.

It didn't matter that her magic had vanished when she had such a wonderful gift. Cuttlefur was just too kind, not like Benjamin and Wilhelm. She couldn't believe she had considered them friends. All this time ... and it had taken Cuttlefur to show her the truth.

They weren't her friends, weren't on her side at all. Cuttlefur was the only one who could protect her, and she needed to find him now. He was sharing a room with Benjamin, but if she hurried, she could get to their room before Benjamin found his way back and created an awkward scene.

When she got there, though, neither Cuttlefur nor Benjamin was there. Only Fat Adam, sitting on the bed farthest from the only window, flicking through a picture book of old cars.

'Cuttlefur went off somewhere,' Adam said. 'Not sure where. Benjamin went to the toilet about half an hour ago, too. Didn't come back. I hope he's not sick.'

'I'm sure he's fine,' she said, trying to be civil. She secretly wished Benjamin was sick enough to be glued to the toilet. It would serve him right. 'Which way did Cuttlefur go?'

'Don't know.'

She resisted the urge to berate Adam and went out. The corridor led away left and right, so she chose left, back to the entrance. Cuttlefur was more likely to have gone outside than into the dark, unused corridors at the back of the guesthouse.

On the way, she had to go past her own room near the end of the corridor. She was sharing with Amy and

Cherise, two second-year girls who wanted little to do with her, both because she was a lowly first-year and because she was friends with Cuttlefur. By default, she had been given the dirtiest, springiest bed, and Amy and Cherise had then paired up for girly chats on Cherise's bed, with two snotty glares when Miranda asked a simple question about lunch, which was enough to tell her she wasn't welcome.

Neither were in the room now, though, so she went inside and stood nervously in the centre. Had they gone off somewhere with Cuttlefur, perhaps? Or had she missed something on the scheduled itinerary that the teachers would now be spitting fire about? Above Cherise's bed, a window overlooked the car park below, so Miranda climbed across the bed to look, letting the dusty sole of her shoe brush Cherise's pillow on the way.

The window also overlooked the bay. The red sun was now hidden behind the twin headlands that almost turned the bay into a lake, while the yellow sun hung just above, stretching long shadows from the trees across the car park to the doors of the guesthouse.

Miranda shivered. For a moment they felt like the Dark Man's claws, reaching out for her. Then something behind her fluttered.

She turned. The box she had slid beneath her bed shifted. Rick, Wilhelm's pet Scatlock, was inside.

Anger surged. Wilhelm called himself her friend, yet he had spied on her. And she had told him she would keep Rick until he proved himself her friend again. But that would never happen.

She ran over to her bed, pulled out the box, and carried it over to the window. When she ripped it open, Rick fluttered his wings as if in greeting, but all Miranda saw was the camera still tied around his neck, the one that had started all the trouble. Maybe that was why Cuttlefur wasn't in his room. He was avoiding her, afraid of the camera she had brought.

Feeling a surge of hatred, both for Wilhelm and for his stupid pet, she grabbed hold of Rick's wings, slid open the window, and flung him out. If Wilhelm had been here, she would have flung him out, too.

Only as she did so, she realised what an idiot she was. Rick was a Scatlock; he could fly.

Angry with herself, she stood up on the bed to lean out the window. To her relief, Rick was a couple of floors below her, one wing severed by a window frame's metal strut that had broken loose. Without the wind currents to aid him, the weight of the camera had sent Rick falling straight down. He was stuck, and the camera pointed inwards at the dark windows of an unused floor.

Good. No one for Wilhelm's silly little camera to spy on.

She shut the window and climbed down, grunting, satisfied by the dust her shoes had left on Cherise's duvet. She rubbed it into the material a little so it was less obviously a shoe print, then returned to her own bed and rifled through her bag for the itinerary.

7 p.m.—barbecue and campfire in the car park, with ghost stories and an organised ghost hunt in the forest.

Miranda rolled her eyes. She could hardly wait. The sooner she found Cuttlefur and they escaped from Endinfinium, the better.

24

CLEANING TIME

So far, the toilet block of the old gym had lived up to its reputation. Wilhelm, wearing a plastic face mask and decked from head to foot in protective waterproof clothing, grimaced as he held a plastic hose that sprayed out a liquid which smelt only marginally better than the urine it resembled. In front of him, a line of angry urinals clacked their reanimated mouths and tried to break away from the pipes holding them into the wall. Chips of masonry flew everywhere, the pipes clanged on other pipes deeper in the wall; the dank, dirty toilet room had filled with a cacophony of discordant ringing sounds like a Halloween carnival.

Beside him, one of the cleaners gave a long, high-pitched wail as a plug hole in the middle of the floor burst upward, wrapping a dirty, plastic pipe around his leg. The pipe jerked backwards, and the cleaner slipped to the floor, splashing brown liquid over the wall. His hose fell loose, and for a few seconds until he was able to kick it away, Wilhelm was hit in the front of his mask by a torrent of cold chamomile tea.

'Break! Break!' came Captain Roche's gruff shout as he supervised the clean-up operation from outside the toilet door. The huge gym teacher, too wide to get through the opening—even sideways—had assumed a typical management position, as Wilhelm saw it: all talk, no action. While he and the group of docile cleaners had spent the morning fighting off several dozen angry toilet fittings, the captain had sat on a bench and shouted encouragement while snacking on vegetable fritters brought up from the kitchens.

Wilhelm tossed the hose to the ground, and the nearest urinal snapped at it, porcelain teeth closing over air just inches away. A final squirt of cold tea struck it, and it shrank back, whimpering as though slapped. Wilhelm sighed and joined the line of cleaners filing out.

'Good work, everyone,' Captain Roche said, standing up with the kind of groan that suggested he'd become accustomed to doing nothing. 'Good work done in there. Get something to eat.'

Other cleaners had brought up trays of other vegetable-based snacks, and Wilhelm was amused to find the food a step up in quality from lunch and dinner. Without his friends, though, the company—nine solemn cleaners who neither spoke nor attempted to eat as they sat around him in a circle—was somewhat lacking.

'So, you know, do you have any hobbies?' he asked the one nearest, a man who had probably once been in his forties, but had reanimated entirely in shades of grey, like a character in a black-and-white television drama. Eyes flicked toward him, looked him up and down in a suggestion of basic intelligence, but the cleaner, who sat patiently with his grey hands on his knees, otherwise made no reaction.

'Do you like vegetables, or would you prefer a bit of

bacon from time to time?' he asked the cleaner, picking a vegetable fritter off of a plate and popping it into his mouth. 'Ketchup or brown sauce?'

'Aren't you ever quiet, Jacobs?' Captain Roche said. 'It's a wonder you don't run out of things to say.'

'You have to talk more when you're speaking for two, sir,' Wilhelm said. 'I bet these guys don't make much of a chorus club.'

The cleaners could, in fact, produce sounds, as Wilhelm had discovered when one had been caught by the plughole pipe, though the sound was more to alert someone to its presence, rather like a car alarm. As soon as the pipe had slithered away, the cleaner had continued to work as if nothing had happened.

'Don't they, like, get bored of basically being our slaves?'

Captain Roche sighed, as if conversation was a terrible chore. 'We're not forcing them to do anything,' he said. 'Once a month, we send a foraging mission across the river to the Haunted Forest. We pick up any who have wandered down to the waters' edge and bring them back to the school. We don't even tell them what to do. Some of them wander off again, others slot neatly into a role within the school.'

'What happens to the ones that wander off?'

'I don't know. Same as happens to the ones we don't pick up.'

'Eaten by ghouls?'

Captain Roche groaned. 'You kids and your fairy tales. We don't know. Maybe. Maybe they have whole communities in the middle of the forest. Jacobs, don't you tire of asking questions?'

'Not when there aren't enough answers.'

'No wonder you and Forrest get on so well. Right, back to work.'

At the mention of Benjamin, Wilhelm thought about the trip the rest of the pupils had gone on. What were they up to now? Had Miranda finally gotten tired of that idiot, Cuttlefur?

He wished he could find out, but Miranda had taken Rick, and his computer was broken—

Or was it?

If dead things could reanimate, wouldn't his computer fix itself?

'Sir,' he said, as he stood up, 'how long does stuff take to reanimate?'

'How long's a length of rope, Jacobs?'

'Depends.'

'There's your answer, then.'

'Well, is there some way to speed it up?'

'I teach gym, Jacobs. How would I know?'

Wilhelm closed his eyes and concentrated. Yes, it was there, just as he'd known it would be: the subtle heat of Captain Roche's magic. With the exception of Edgar, the teachers maintained a line that Endinfinium's magic wasn't real, and they refused to use it in view of the pupils. They all possessed versions of it, though, and the little tingle of heat Wilhelm could feel where there should have been none meant Captain Roche was keeping his ready, just in case.

'Do you remember much about life before you came here, sir?'

Captain Roche groaned again. 'Jacobs, if the rest of you worked as hard as your mouth does—'

'Just wondering, sir. I quite like it here. Not many people talk about where they came from.'

'Perhaps that's because there's nothing much to tell.'

'The cleaners, though. They were all pupils at the school once, weren't they? Why did they die? What happens when you graduate?'

'You find somewhere to best utilise your skills, Jacobs. For you, I imagine there are plenty of toilet blocks that need cleaning. And on that thought, how about we get back to work? If you're done before Friday, I'll let you have the rest of the time off until the others get back.'

'And if I'm not done?'

'You'll be coming after classes for as long as it takes.'

Wilhelm sighed. 'Yes, sir.'

The rest of the afternoon passed in a haze of smelly chamomile and angry toilet fittings. Several enthusiastic shower heads caught up one of the cleaners like a fly in a spider's web, but Wilhelm managed to avoid any drama of his own, and by the time Captain Roche had called a halt for the day, he was aching from head to foot.

As he trudged back to the dorms and a depressing evening of playing trumps over dinner with Gubbledon, he wondered again how the others were getting on. Despite the harsh words that had passed between them, he missed both Benjamin and Miranda. He had always considered himself a bit of a loner, and in fact, back in the orphanage, he had shunned contact with others. Since arriving here, though, he had grown to like it.

The computer tablet connected to Rick's live video stream sat on his bed where he had left it. The screen was still broken, but the hint of an obscured picture had come through the shattered glass. It felt slightly warm, as if it had begun to reanimate, but how long would it take to fix itself? It was impossible for him to fix it. Even if he found a similar one among the junk in the locker room, he wouldn't know how to fit in a replacement screen without breaking it. No, he would have to wait for it to reanimate, which could take days, or even weeks.

If only the process could be sped up. He thought about the way they cleaned, using chemicals made from chamomile or even the tea itself, piped straight from a huge vat in the kitchens. Chamomile generally relaxed people when they drank it, and that's why old ladies liked it, wasn't it? And it was always served inoffensively warm.

If warm chamomile calmed reanimated objects, then to speed up his computer's reanimation, he would need something completely opposite. Aggressive, hot.

He smiled.

The answer was obvious.

Fire.

25

SECRETS

The figure in the hood crept through the dark corridors of the guesthouse, one hand on his pocket, holding the device the man in the woods had given him. If someone discovered him ahead of time, he was to use it immediately, squeezing and throwing simultaneously, and he would no longer have to worry about them.

So, if he wanted to complete his mission and return home, it was imperative he continue undiscovered. He had made contact with the innkeeper earlier, and a few whispered questions had established a meeting time and place.

He turned a final corner and rapped on a door labeled STORAGE.

'Is that you? Come in.'

He kicked the door, and it swung open through a carpet of dirt. The innkeeper stood in the centre of a dusty but empty space, holding a candle in front of him. A single, small window was at his back, giving a dirty view of the distant horizon and a yellowish tint of a sunset that never quite happened.

'You knew I was here?'

The figure in the hood nodded. 'Of course. He taught me well. I could feel you halfway back down the corridor. You should be careful with the teachers around.'

'Well, let's go through the plan before we're discovered.'

Cuttlefur pushed back his hood, and his blue hair flopped around his shoulders. He shook it irritably. He looked forward to the day he could cut the damned stuff off, particularly as his natural brown was starting to show through in the roots. The stupid girl would notice soon. Not for a few days at least, though; far longer than was needed.

'Have you heard from him?'

The innkeeper shook his head. 'Only as … thoughts.'

'Then let's make sure we're on the same page, shall we? Can you imagine if we end up stuck here in this hellhole forever?'

The innkeeper shook his head. 'We won't.'

'Let's make sure of that. So, two days from now…'

~

The incinerator room was baking hot. Wilhelm, with a towel wrapped around his face to deflect the waves of heat, crept as close as he could to the roaring furnace where all of the school's disposable waste was dumped, and placed the computer down onto a rock. The air felt hot enough to melt the plastic casing, but if it hadn't melted him, then the computer would be all right. He retreated a safe distance to watch.

At the back of the cavern, he crouched down in an alcove out of the direct line of the fire. He'd heard stories of the incinerator rooms and had no intention of being eaten by the monster when it appeared. There was less food waste today than usual, but as always, whenever a dump of waste came down from the kitchens, things could get risky.

A roar filled the cavern and, despite his best intentions to stay out of sight, Wilhelm glanced out as something huge and distorted lumbered up out of the waste pile and staggered a few steps in his direction. It looked like a bear made out of fire and trash, a constantly evolving, amorphous thing shifting and transforming with each step it took. It stumbled toward the entrance, then paused as it caught sight of the computer. A flaming paw scooped it up, and Wilhelm tried not to cry out, terrified the creature would take the computer back into its den, until it grunted and flung it away. The computer bounced across the ground near Wilhelm's feet.

Again he looked up at the rubbish monster that had started to disintegrate as the flames chewed through its temporary body. Wilhelm counted down from three, then raced out of cover, scooped up the computer, and bolted for the door, reaching it just before a hail of flaming foodstuffs struck the wall beside it.

He slammed the door shut and leaned his back against it, taking a deep breath. Sweat streamed down his face, and his skin felt sore. The cuffs of his school uniform had been singed, and while damage to school property was worth a spell in the locker room, he felt happy enough to have just escaped with his life. Going into the incinerator room while the rubbish monster was reanimated qualified you as a disposable foodstuff by default.

He waited until he had returned to the lobby before he inspected the computer. He had wrapped it into a rag and now, as he pulled away strips of charred cloth, he had little hope that his plan had actually worked. But when he touched the first corner of revealed casing, he gave a little gasp.

During his retreat up the steps from the basements to the lobby, the metal should have cooled. It was still hot to the touch.

And when he turned it around, he saw the screen had reanimated and knitted itself back together.

'Yes!'

He switched it on, waiting for the video to reconnect. He fully suspected Miranda had put Rick into a box and probably covered him with a towel or something. But even without a visual link, he might be able to pick up nearby conversations.

The view continued to lighten as the camera adjusted its light filter to deal with a dim background. It was evening now, of course, but he had expected Miranda to keep Rick inside.

As he turned up the volume to maximum, he heard the creak of a tree, and the camera drifted left as if caught in a breeze. Wilhelm saw the branches of a small bush growing out of a crack in the wall of a building. The camera drifted back right, and he saw Rick was pointing into a gloomy window.

Miranda must have thrown Rick away, though it looked at least like Rick was still alive. If only there was some way to contact Benjamin, Wilhelm could ask him to retrieve Rick and bring him back—

'No!'

A flash of blue hair appeared on the computer screen as Cuttlefur leaned against the glass and peered out, eyes scanning some unseen area below the camera. A moment later, a huge, ugly man appeared behind him, patting him on the shoulder.

'No one can hear us,' came a hissy rumble from out of

the speakers turned up to maximum. 'Let's make sure we're on the right page about how we capture the girl.'

'I'll be glad to see the back of her,' Cuttlefur said. 'The sooner the Dark Man has her and we can get rewarded, the better. She's driving me crazy with her stupidity. I'd be happy to finish her off myself, but I know he wants her alive so Forrest will be stupid enough to try to save her.'

'He was right about you,' the fat man said. 'You're a nasty piece of work.'

Cuttlefur turned, and his face broke with a sadistic grin that made Wilhelm shiver. 'You don't know the half of it,' he said. 'And that stupid girl has no idea. Come on, let's go over the plan.'

They retreated from the window, gradually fading to shadowy nothings as the last of the evening light died away. Wilhelm turned up the volume, but it was now impossible to hear what they were saying.

What was certain, though, was that Miranda was in danger. Maybe Benjamin, too. And no one but Wilhelm, who was stuck back at the school dozens of miles south, knew anything about it.

26

DRAGON

'Lawrence? Are you awake? I need a favour.'

The huge snake-train opened one massive eye so close to where Benjamin stood, he jumped back. The eye that also served for a headlight caught him in a circle of yellow. Benjamin glanced over his shoulder, afraid the bright light would be visible from the guesthouse in the valley below.

'What's your destination?'

Benjamin cringed. Lawrence's booming announcement-style voice was loud enough to make the trees around him rustle.

'The source of the Great Junk River.'

'Climb aboard. Where?'

Benjamin jumped through the door as it slid open. 'I'm not quite sure. Northwest, I think.'

Lawrence uncurled and began to meander through the trees, following the trail of an old dirt road. Over the months Benjamin had spent in Endinfinium, he had developed a fear of the nighttime forest, so he sat by the windows, searching through the dark for the orange glow that would indicate the presence of ghouls, the reanimated part-human, part-machines who served the Dark Man. The Haunted Forest beyond the Great Junk River was alive with them—hence, its name—but the Grand Lord had told him that for ghouls to appear in most parts of Endinfinium, this required an influx of dark magic. While some pupils—Snout, for example—had the unfortunate ability to draw them out of the ground, ghouls were rarely seen outside of times of danger.

A strange sound came from Lawrence's engine, like a machine's version of whimpering.

'Are you all right, Lawrence?'

'Yes, fine, Master Benjamin.'

'Are you sure?'

'Yes.'

Obviously, Lawrence wasn't sure. As they broke through the trees along a ridgeline, with the river shimmering in the valley below them, Lawrence began to whimper louder.

'There,' the snake-train said, pausing for Benjamin to take in the view. 'Source Mountain.'

Benjamin gaped. Never had he seen anything quite like it, but whatever it was, it wasn't natural. Basic rules of geography suggested a river's source should be nothing more than a trickle of water. Here, the Great Junk River was still at least a hundred meters across, flowing down the centre of the valley—an arc of glittering silver with junk bobbing in its waters.

To the south, it disappeared into the forest. To the north, however, stood something Benjamin could barely believe.

At the northern end of the valley, a towering volcano cone with a flattened-off peak rose up out of the ground, and through a cut in its southern edge gushed millions of tons of water. Rather than dropping straight down the side of the cone, though, it swung in a tight arc, wrapping around the mountain in a descending spiral before plunging into the river channel.

Benjamin smiled, mischievousness bubbling up to the surface. If it was cleaned up a bit, it would have made the mother of all waterslides.

'That's it?' Benjamin whispered. 'The source? Up on top of that mountain?'

Lawrence's locomotive shook up and down in a nod. 'The source,' he boomed.

'Can you take me up there?'

This time, the great locomotive shook from side to side, and Benjamin grabbed on to the back of a seat to avoid being thrown to the floor.

'The source is not life,' Lawrence said. 'It's death.'

'Can't you just drop me off halfway?'

Lawrence began to uncoil. 'We're too close,' he said. 'We should leave.'

'Wait!'

But Lawrence wouldn't be stopped. He slithered off the hillcrest and headed back the way they had come. For the first few minutes, Benjamin tried to protest, but after a while, he gave up and sat back in his seat to watch the night flash by. He was frustrated, though at least now he knew what the challenge was.

With his excitement gone, it took longer than he remembered to get back, and once there, Lawrence curled up in the same parking area as before, then wished Benjamin luck. Benjamin smiled as he waved goodbye, but he felt no happiness. He was no closer than before to figuring out how to escape from Endinfinium.

Lost in thought, he had gone deep into the thick forest before he realised he had somehow taken the wrong path; instead of meandering through to the breeding pond, his path cut through tall pillars of rock in the direction of the beach.

Benjamin decided to continue. He didn't really feel like sleeping, and even though dawn was still some way off, the red sun had already begun its circuit of the world and was casting enough of a glow over the land for him to see by. According to the schedule, they were due to take an excursion in the morning out to the southern headland. Perhaps if he cried off sick, he could make another attempt to get to the top of Source Mountain, and perhaps if he could convince Lawrence to let him out near the bottom of the slope, he could climb the rest of the way himself.

Up ahead came the gentle splashing of waves breaking on the beach, and he felt a sudden thrill of danger, of being alone down here with the dragons circling in the water. Had that dragon really been about to attack Fat Adam? He wasn't sure he wanted to find out.

He stepped out of the trees and onto the beach. With the water so calm, it reflected the swirling colours of the sky, and he had a sudden urge to run across the gentle sand dunes and splash through the pools of water caught by the tide. As his feet carried him up the nearest dune, he felt free and alive like he hadn't in weeks. All alone on a deserted beach before dawn, he felt like a normal boy again, and that this wasn't some strange world where trash came back to life, but a simple beach in England.

As he crested the rise of the last dune before the shoreline, he stretched his arms up into the air and looked down over the beach. He opened his mouth to shout out something irrelevant to the sky, then snapped it shut at the sight of a figure standing by the water's edge, barely twenty paces in front of him.

He dropped to the sand, pushing back from the edge of the dune, then slowly lifted his head to look.

Cuttlefur.

The blue-haired boy stood by the water, gentle shore breakers lapping around his feet. A strange sound came from his throat, and Benjamin took a moment to recognise it as laughter, because there was no mirth in it, only sadism and bitterness. As Benjamin watched, Cuttlefur lifted his hands high over his head, waving them back and forth as if signaling to a plane.

A massive black shadow rose up off the rocks in the narrow gorge between the headlands, made a quick loop just above the water, and then dropped out of sight beyond the distant cliffs.

Benjamin slapped a hand over his mouth. By the shoreline, Cuttlefur gave the vanished shape a sarcastic wave, then turned back to the dunes.

Benjamin pushed himself back until Cuttlefur was out of sight, then he turned and ran, bolting back across the sand to the path and then through the forest, past the breeding ponds and back through the rear entrance to the guesthouse. Gasping, he ran straight up to his room and dived under the covers, listening to his heart gently slow over the sound of Adam's breathing, as the chubby boy snored lightly, a grin on his face as though dreaming about breakfast.

He wasn't sure how long he lay there before he heard the door open and Cuttlefur come in, the blue-haired boy humming a happy little tune to himself. With his eyes closed to slits, Benjamin saw Cuttlefur aim a kick at Adam's schoolbag, then climb into bed, a wide grin on his face.

Only an hour was left until the wake-up call, but Cuttlefur had fallen straight asleep, snoring lightly.

Benjamin couldn't sleep. He lay awake, his hands cupped under his face, thinking about the thing he had seen and wondering if Wilhelm was right.

The thing that had detached from the cliffs had looked like a great black dragon.

And it appeared Cuttlefur could control it.

27

BROKEN WHEELS

The front wheel fell off of the bicycle. Wilhelm managed to jump clear as the bike slumped forward, landing in the wet grass as its wheel rolled away down the slope, then he rolled over to look back at the school's uppermost towers still visible over the rise.

He had gone perhaps five miles. No way he would ever get to the Bay of Paper Dragons in time to warn Benjamin and Miranda about Cuttlefur and the innkeeper's plans. Before he was even halfway, they would be dead, or worse.

It had crossed his mind to go straight to the teachers. After all, he and his friends had saved the school once. But in the corridors of an educational facility, good deeds were quickly erased by the bad, even here in Endinfinium. No one except for Grand Lord Bastien would believe him, and ever since the Dark Man's attack, the Grand Lord had stayed in his tower, unavailable and unseen, doing whatever it was Grand Lords did. Of the other main teachers still at the school, that left Captain Roche and Professor Loane, neither of whom liked him much, and both of whom were highly unlikely to believe him if he made any accusation against Cuttlefur.

So, he had no choice but to attempt to get to the Bay of Paper Dragons by his own steam. He had gone first to the school's garage, where a number of old cars, motorbikes, and bicycles stood lined up, collecting dust. Unable to locate a key for anything motorised, he was stuck with the least water-damaged of the school's bicycle fleet.

Considering the harshness of the dirt-and-rock paths meandering through the hills to the north, south, and west of the school, the bike had done quite well just to get him this far. Unfortunately, it would go no further.

He hefted the bag of provisions he had poached from the kitchens on his own special kind of long-term borrow and struck out along the track. He had gone no more than a few steps, though, when he turned his ankle on a loose rock.

'Waste of time!' he shouted and, sitting down on the turf beside the path, threw his bag aside, rubbing furiously at his throbbing ankle.

He had to return to the school, tell the teachers what he had overheard, and hope they believed him.

'Might as well just bang my head against a brick wall,' he muttered.

A few spots of rain appeared, and Wilhelm scowled, then climbed off the path and headed for a stand of scrubby trees in a hollow a short distance inland. He had enough food for a week's expedition, a torch, and a handful of comic books to keep him entertained when he stopped for the night, but he hadn't thought to bring an umbrella or any kind of jacket. As the rain began to get heavier, he realised how useless the nearly leafless branches of the wind-bent trees would be for shelter. Faced with no choice, he jammed himself into the space between the thickest of the crooked trees and tried to pretend he wasn't getting soaked. His bag wasn't waterproof, either, and while his food was well wrapped up, his comic books would get wet. Frustrated, he stared at the ground in disillusionment.

The wind was getting up, too. Benjamin always thought bad weather was a sign of the Dark Man's presence, but Wilhelm had been around a while longer than his friend. The weather had a mind of its own, swinging in for an attack whenever someone was most vulnerable. As he sat shivering and soaked, Wilhelm looked up at the trees' branches, wishing he could weave them into some kind of net to keep out the rain, glaring at them as if to bend them to his will by thought alone.

'Huh? What's that?'

Something under his knee was warm. He shifted to reveal a piece of old wood partly covered under the sod. With desperate hands, he scrabbled away the dirt and lifted it up.

It looked like any other piece of broken branch—a couple of leafless twists off of a thicker, central piece—and now that he held it in his hands, it was cold and lifeless. Strange. He was sure he had felt…

He closed his eyes, feeling for the warmth with his mind. And there it was, right in front of his face; not physical warmth, but the warmth of magic.

How could a piece of old branch have any reanimation magic?

The stand of trees was part of a dry gully through which occasional streams would pass when the Great Junk River was high. Its level rarely changed, except for when his friends had diverted it to wash away the Dark Man's army. On that occasion, though—

Wilhelm clicked his fingers. 'Of course.'

The river had been diverted through the tunnels below the school, but the volume had been too great, even for them, and much of the water had flooded out overland through long-dry tributary channels like this one, taking with it much of what had been left behind in the tunnels.

'Fallenwood.'

He and Benjamin had enlisted the help of their new friend to save Miranda; Fallenwood's reanimated twig army had built them a tunnel into the caves.

And this little piece of wood had broken loose and been washed out.

Fallenwood refused to leave the forest around the abandoned botanical society building in the woods a few miles south of the school, but this was a matter of life and death. Wilhelm gripped the twig, held it against the side of his face.

'Fallenwood, can you hear me? It's Wilhelm. I need your help. Benjamin and Miranda are in great danger. I need to get to the Bay of Paper Dragons. If there's anything you can do to help me ... please. I'll never forget it. I'll be in your debt forever.' He smiled. 'I'll even come clean up your home for you. I'll do ... anything.'

He closed his eyes again, feeling the heat of the twig's reanimation magic. In such a small piece it was slight, but it was there. If Fallenwood could speak to his people, perhaps he could hear Wilhelm.

With a sigh, he sat back, giving up on trying to stay dry. He could do nothing now but wait.

And hope.

28

EXCURSION

Breakfast was actually rather good, even though everything tasted like varying shades of indecision. Benjamin had been squeezed onto the end of a trestle table beside Fat Adam, who was monopolising a platter of fish fritters, loading them one by one onto his plate while using his big elbows to deflect other forks making any attempt to infringe upon his domination. As he fought off a surprise sideways attack from a small first-year called Tommy Cale, Benjamin tried to catch Miranda's eye. She sat a few places down on the other side, with Cuttlefur on her right, and Cherise, her second-year roommate, on her left. As Cherise tried to talk past Miranda to Cuttlefur, Miranda gripped her fork like a potential murder weapon. Benjamin relaxed and felt for her magic, but there was nothing. He felt a slight warmth from several other pupils around him, many of whom had no idea of the existence of their own magic, but Miranda was as cold as the rocks down by the beach after the yellow sun had gone down.

From her expression, a crimson-flushed wall of anger painted with a light dusting of despair, she knew it, too.

'So, I heard we have to make groups of three today,' Cherise was saying to Cuttlefur, as Tommy finally managed to spear one of the fritters, much to Fat Adam's dismay. 'Professor Eaves said they have to be mixed. You can work with me and Amy, if you like.'

'I was planning to make a group with Miranda.'

Benjamin cringed at how Miranda's face lit up, like she was under some kind of spell.

'Well,' Cherise said, not to be put off so quickly, 'how about her, me, and you? We can let her join us if she wants. I mean, who else are you going to work with?'

Fat Adam had pushed Tommy off of his chair while Ms. Ito stumped over with a face like thunder. Benjamin was torn between making a play for a fish fritter and listening in on the rest of Cherise's conversation.

'Forrest,' Cuttlefur said suddenly, and Benjamin's head snapped up. Miranda made to protest, but as soon as Cuttlefur opened his mouth, she closed hers. 'We have to be in mixed groups,' he said. 'Didn't the professor tell you that? Forrest doesn't have anyone to work with so, you know, I thought we could do something nice for him.'

He turned to give Benjamin a stare that made Benjamin shiver. His eyes said so many things, one of which was: *I know you saw me on the beach this morning.* Benjamin looked away, even as Ms. Ito loomed over them, black-and-white hair shimmering, mouth expelling a series of rapid-fire threats of locker rooms, long walks home, and nothing but stale cucumbers for lunch until the end of eternity.

'I was planning to work with Snout and Adam,' Benjamin said, defiantly meeting Cuttlefur's stare.

'They're both boys,' Cuttlefur said, 'despite the rumours I've heard about Snout.' A couple of boys further down sniggered. Snout, examining the embroidery of the tablecloth with his fork, didn't appear to have heard the comment. Benjamin felt like thumping Cuttlefur, but as it was an opportunity to keep an eye on both of them, he forced a smile.

'It seems you're right. Since you offered, I'd be happy to join you.'

Miranda glared, though she seemed less angry than he might have expected, perhaps happy to trade working with him in place of having to spend the day deflecting Cherise's attention from Cuttlefur. She flicked her hair, then speared a fried potato so hard it broke in half. She scooped up the battered remains and tossed them nonchalantly into her mouth, glaring at Benjamin as she chewed, as if imagining she was crunching on his charred, bleached bones.

'You have ten minutes to assemble outside in groups of three,' Ms. Ito hollered, pulling a forearm-sized egg timer from a big pocket of her jacket. 'Each minute of lateness will accumulate fifty cleans upon your return to the school.' With a grunt of finality, she upended the timer on the tabletop with a loud crack.

The dining hall immediately descended into chaos as pupils rushed to make groups, then make it back to their rooms for their packs before Ms. Ito's timer ran out.

Benjamin had brought his pack with him, having temporarily shelved his plan to climb up Source Mountain. Miranda had already left with Cuttlefur, so he trailed some other pupils down into the car park, where Miranda and Cuttlefur waited.

'Welcome to our group, Forrest,' Cuttlefur said, and he reached out a hand Benjamin had no choice but to shake. Miranda, however, said nothing, while Cuttlefur wore a mischievous grin that immediately put Benjamin on edge. But he didn't have time to worry about it. The chef, Jim

Green, had reinvented himself as a green-clad expedition guide and was now waving them toward the path. Dusty Eaves walked beside him, with Edgar at the rear to shepherd any stragglers. Ms. Ito, due to her permanently casted left leg, had chosen to remain behind at the guesthouse.

'Stick close to the path, would you please?' Jim Green shouted back down the line. 'No more episodes like yesterday, if you can help it. Some of the dragons aren't quite so forgiving.'

They headed into the forest, and as they walked, Jim Green pointed out various plants and animals that appeared in the undergrowth to either side.

'Over there we have a Brazilian hotrod,' he said. 'See the red stalks that look like fire pokers? Don't touch the tips. Very sharp. No idea how they ended up here in Endinfinium, but like most things, they were probably accidental. Some seeds left in an old box or caught in the tread of a discarded shoe.'

Of course, half of the kids immediately behind him reached out to test the plant's sharpness on the palms of their hands, with Fat Adam bursting into tears and snapping the head off of one plant in frustration.

'A hundred cleans in your bank,' Professor Eaves grunted, pulling out a notebook and jotting down something that only made Adam wail more.

'And you see those in there?' Jim Green continued. 'They're fan-flowers.'

Gasps came from the pupils nearest to the front. Benjamin craned his neck to see what the fuss was all about, and he gasped too at a large assembly of what appeared to be electric fans that had reanimated and grown petals. Now, they stood pointing outwards in a circle on top of a little knoll, in an array of vibrant colours, their old rotor blades gently spinning in the breeze.

'Where do they all come from?' asked Tommy Cale.

'Well,' Jim Green said, 'that's the great mystery, isn't it? They've been here quite some time, for certain, because some of the species have actually learned how to breed.' He pointed at a cluster of tiny fan-flowers no bigger than Benjamin's thumb. 'It is believed that none of this section of forest is natural; that everything was collected by the great botanist of Endinfinium, Jeremiah Flowers.'

Benjamin's ears pricked up.

'Who?' Fat Adam asked. 'Never heard of him.'

'Oh, he's long dead,' Jim Green said. 'Supposedly, at least. He disappeared. No one is sure what happened.'

He escaped, Benjamin wanted to shout. But he kept quiet. Instead, he inched away from Cuttlefur and Miranda, getting closer to the front as Jim Green started walking again.

'Jeremiah Flowers was a great man in Endinfinium,' their guide explained to a rapt group of boys following at his shoulder. 'He founded the Endinfinium High School Botany Society, but after a few years, he became tired of it and went off in search of more unique species of flora and fauna, eventually settling here in the Bay of Paper Dragons, where it is believed he was responsible for collecting all of the species you see around you, as well as protecting the nature of the dragons themselves.'

'Where did he go?'

Jim Green shrugged. 'Well, there's the realist belief, and the romantic one. In those days, the Bay of Paper Dragons was a remote outpost, rarely visited by people from the school, mostly forgotten about. Where the guesthouse stands today was Jeremiah's home—a small shack set halfway up the hill from the beach. When one day messengers came looking for him, he was nowhere to be found.'

'He must have left something behind, right?' Snout asked. 'Evidence?'

Jim Green nodded. 'Oh, he did. Piles of papers were found in his possession—hundreds of pages of notes on the flora and fauna of Endinfinium, and his own crude drawings. Many were made into books, which I've heard are collecting dust in the school's library.' He grinned. 'Have any of you ever been in it?'

A few snorts of laughter rose up, and Professor Eaves glared at a couple of boys, lifting his notebook out of his pocket in a threatening manner, which made them immediately clap their hands over their mouths.

'And there was one more thing,' Jim Green said. 'He left behind a diary of his day-to-day life. Most of it was inconsequential stuff about his daily chores and the dragons, but there was a final passage about going off to find the ultimate starting point of all life in Endinfinium: the source of the Great Junk River.'

'Where?'

'About twenty miles northwest of here is the river source. It flows straight up out of the ground, but quite why is a mystery, because we have neither the means nor the technology to figure it out.' He grinned. 'Some people say it's magic.'

'There's no such thing,' Fat Adam shouted, even though from the warmth his body gave off, Benjamin knew he had a latent Weavers' skills.

'In any case, we know it's there, but not why. Jeremiah, it seems, wanted to know. Unfortunately, that's where the diary ends, and Jeremiah was never seen again.'

'Perhaps he actually found out,' Fat Adam said, 'and it was so awesome, he decided to stay.'

'Ah, but it would have been impossible. The water is coming out, not going in. It would have brought him—or what was left of him—back out, and he would have eventually reanimated into a cleaner or a ghoul, like everyone else.'

At this, the children descended into whispering huddles, and Professor Eaves groaned. 'Don't fill their heads with such nonsense, man.'

'How do you know it's nonsense?' Jim Green said, eyes twinkling. 'We all share enough of the mysteries of this land to know there are a thousand things we don't understand about it.'

'Got to make your peace with any situation,' Eaves said. 'We've all learned that. Shouldn't we be moving on?'

Jim Green gave the pupils a conspiratorial smile, then turned back to Professor Eaves. 'Quite, quite. The dragons are waiting. This way, please.'

Up ahead, the front of the line emerged through the trees, onto the head of the beach, and Benjamin shivered as he spotted the dune from where he had watched Cuttlefur just a few short hours before.

'This is the main bay.' Jim Green waved his hands in both directions. 'According to the writings of Jeremiah Flowers, they used to be found only in the small lake we now call the breeding pond. Jeremiah allegedly used explosives to reduce the distance between the two headlands in order to protect the dragons from the tide's drag and any large predators. After that was achieved, he released several dragons into the bay, and the results were astonishing.' He motioned to a great swirl of colour curled around an outcrop a stone's throw offshore. 'I don't know if any of you ever kept goldfish?'

A few pupils murmured yes or no as Professor Eaves snorted. 'Of course you did, didn't you? Answer the man!'

'Jeremiah found that dragons grew in the same way as goldfish did: according to the size of their environment. And because they no longer have any natural predators nor fear from the elements, here in the Bay of Paper Dragons, they continue to grow. The only restriction is their own size.'

'Are they actually made from paper?' Tommy Cale asked.

'Lacquered papier-mâché, as far as we can tell. The lacquer is old and cracks as they grow, giving them their slightly grainy appearance. Water can then get in, so they have to surface or bask on the rocks every few hours to dry out again.' He gestured along the beach toward a pair of small fishing boats moored just offshore. 'Every few weeks, Barnacle and I sail out and attempt to paint them as they lie on the rocks. Like any other animal, though, they don't understand we're trying to help them.'

'What happens if too much water gets in?' Snout asked.

'Bits break off and sink. If too much breaks off so the dragon can no longer swim, the rest of it sinks to the bottom.'

'And dies?'

Jim Green laughed. 'They can't die, not in the way we know it. What they can do is dissolve until there's not enough left in one piece for the creature to be considered alive. That's why the water has a rainbow tint. It's the colours of the dissolved dragons.'

'So the whole bay is alive?' Snout said.

Jim Green looked at the boy for a long time before he answered. 'The whole of Endinfinium is alive,' he said, eyes twinkling. 'Every last inch of it.'

29

DREAMS AND HOPES

Miranda sighed. Up ahead, Jim Green continued to talk, holding the group of pupils around him rapt by his knowledge of the lore of the Bay of Paper Dragons. She stared at the back of Benjamin's head, feeling bad about how she had spoken to him recently, and she willed him to turn around and smile at her, but he was only interested in Jim Green's story.

Something warm touched her hand, and she felt Cuttlefur's fingers lock over hers. 'He has a lot to say, hasn't he?' Cuttlefur whispered, leaning close.

Heat rose up Miranda's neck. She tried to hold his hand back, but it felt so embarrassing and awkward, she just let her fingers hang limb while his encircled them. And what if Cherise or Amy saw? They'd be so jealous, they would tease her half to death when they got back to the guesthouse.

She was almost happy when the group started moving again and Cuttlefur had to let go. Benjamin was still up near the front, and Miranda slipped a few spaces back down the line, hoping to get near Edgar, who was trying his best to stop a group of the rugby kids from pulling the heads off of all of the flowers. Jim Green led them on a path headed west around the beach to a rockier area where the cliff was steeper and closer to the shore.

Finally, when the cliff was nearly overhead, they came to another stop. Jim Green turned to Professor Eaves. 'Right, here we are. We'll stop here for about two hours, then move on up to the headland for lunch. Over to you now.'

Professor Eaves cleared his throat. 'Okay, now I want you to split up into your groups,' he said. 'You'll find several of the dragons basking on the rocks just offshore. I want you to find one that interests you, sketch it, then write me a detailed description. Include speculation if you want; for example, how old you can guess it to be, what its use might have once been, how intelligent you think it is. Don't forget, I expect thorough reasons. This is science class, not English.'

Several pupils groaned.

'Oh, and you have two hours to finish it. Otherwise, you can do it tonight in the guesthouse common room. Ms. Ito will be supervising.'

Groans were quickly drowned out by a scramble of activity as groups split away to hunt for a paper dragon worth examining.

'That one'll do,' Benjamin said, pointing to a fifteen-foot-long dragon curled around a rock about a car's length offshore. Most of the other groups had headed for a bigger one a little further along the beach, but this dragon seemed unconcerned by its lack of popularity.

'I don't think so,' Miranda began on autopilot, as though rejection of Benjamin's ideas had become prerequisite, until she realised it really would, in fact, do.

'Sure,' she said, turning to seek Cuttlefur's approval. 'It's fine.'

Cuttlefur, though, wasn't looking at her, his eyes transfixed on a point somewhere midway between the two headlands facing each other like the pads of a vice. Feeling an uncomfortable jealousy of his misplaced attention, Miranda followed his gaze, but saw only the rippling of water and the occasional surfacing of a gliding paper dragon, its upper teeth clacking down on the surface.

'Not quite what I was expecting,' Benjamin said, pointing at the creature that regarded them calmly, its lower jaw bobbing up and down as though attached to the rest of its head by a string. 'I mean, I was expecting giant, winged things that breathed fire.' He gave the distant headlands a sudden suspicious glance, then quickly looked back as if embarrassed about being caught.

She didn't want to talk to him. He was her friend, and he had let her down, but she found the old conversations appearing on her tongue as if by magic.

'They're pretty unique, aren't they?'

Cuttlefur scowled at her as if she was making friends with a teacher. 'I think they're kind of useless. I mean, they don't do anything. What a waste of everyone's time.'

'Just because they're not doing anything right now, doesn't mean they can't, or won't,' Benjamin said.

Miranda stared at him as he watched the dragons with that otherworldly look suggesting his mind was elsewhere. She knew how much harder it was for him to be here, after his brother had been in the Dark Man's clutches, only to be snatched back to England, leaving Endinfinium forever.

She didn't fully understand it, only that, for a while, David Forrest had been part of both worlds until a choice had been made for him.

'How about we make this interesting?' Cuttlefur said.

'Forrest, why don't you go in and see if you can wake it up? It looks like it's asleep.'

Benjamin shook his head. 'Not after what happened to Adam. No way.'

Cuttlefur scowled. Miranda frowned. In the last couple of days, Cuttlefur had begun to change. When they were alone, he was charming and kind, but with other people, an undercurrent of contempt bubbled up like a hot spring. She was still mad at Benjamin, but they had been friends for a long time, and if Cuttlefur and she would soon leave Endinfinium, she didn't want to part on bad terms. Even if she was still angry at him, would it be so bad to try to smooth things over before she left?

'Are you all right?'

Cuttlefur was looking at her. Miranda shook her head, then nodded, letting him make up his own mind. 'Let's just get this done,' she replied. 'Can either of you draw? I suck, so I'll do the description. Benjamin?'

'I'll draw.'

'Cuttlefur—'

'I've got a better idea,' he interrupted and, hefting up a fist-sized pebble, cocked it over his shoulder.

'No—'

'Cuttlefur, don't—'

Too late. The blue-haired boy flung the stone at the paper dragon. Miranda wasn't sure what she had expected to happen, but it wasn't for the rock to strike it, then pass through its body with a muffled clump that reminded her of a hole-punch from the classrooms back at the school, leaving behind a visible, fist-sized hole as it plopped into the water beyond.

The dragon, still curled up on the top of the rock, made no reaction to the new hole halfway along its multi-coloured abdomen. It continued to stare in a rough southwestern direction, its lower jaw bobbing like the tongueless mouth of a rather excited and extremely colourful dog.

'You shouldn't do that,' Benjamin said.

'Look, it's fine,' Cuttlefur said. 'They can't feel pain like we can. Watch.'

He picked up another rock, glanced at Miranda, and flashed her a smile. Then he lifted his arm to throw.

'Don't!'

As Benjamin's eyes narrowed, the rock popped out of Cuttlefur's hand and exploded into dust. Cuttlefur himself was flung through the air by an invisible force to land on his back in the soft sand of the upper beach a short distance back from the shoreline.

In an instant, his surprise was gone, and he glared at Benjamin. 'That the best you've—'

'What's going on here?'

Professor Eaves strode up the beach, pointed at Cuttlefur, then Benjamin, and then turned to Miranda as if he expected her to explain.

'He ... pushed me,' Cuttlefur said. 'Didn't he, Miranda?'

'You liar!' Benjamin shouted, kicking sand at Cuttlefur. 'You threw a rock at the dragon.' He was shaking one hand, as though his magic had hurt him. Miranda remembered the way it had left cuts all over his body, and it looked like he still struggled to control it.

Professor Eaves glanced from one to the other again. 'Is this true?'

'Look!'

Benjamin turned to point at the dragon. Miranda gasped. The dragon had already gone, having slipped off the rock, and was now gliding away from them with only the back of its head visible above the water, a surface ripple the only indication of its long tail snapping back and forth beneath.

'I suppose we'll never know, will we?' Professor Eaves said, reaching into his pocket as he looked at Benjamin. 'You've been spending too much time with young Master Jacobs, and even in his absence, it seems his influence holds strong. You've been warned about this. Two hundred cleans for you when we get back to the school.'

'But—'

'I'll reduce it by fifty if you show a marked improvement in your behaviour for the rest of the trip.' Professor Eaves smirked. 'Our boots will need cleaning after getting back from this dirty beach.'

Benjamin scowled as Professor Eaves marched on up the beach, climbing awkwardly over rocks and stumbling every few steps on hidden bowls in the sand. Miranda glared at Cuttlefur, who hummed to himself as he stood and brushed himself down. She went over to Benjamin and reached out for his shoulder.

'Benjamin—'

'Leave me alone.'

He kicked out at the sand, then walked off down the beach in the direction they had come. She stared after him, an ache in her chest.

'Sorry about that,' Cuttlefur said. 'I suppose I'll have to draw the dragon, won't I? Come on, let's go and find another one.'

She turned on him. 'You're a pig.'

His vindictiveness faded and the Cuttlefur she liked smiled back. 'Look, I'm so sorry. That was out of order. I just, you know, find it hard to be nice to Benjamin after he and Wilhelm spied on us and then attacked me. It's like he betrayed a trust I can't forgive, no matter how hard I try. I don't think we're destined to be friends, you know?'

'You could try.'

Cuttlefur nodded. 'I will try, just for you. I'll apologise when we get back and tell Professor Eaves that everything was my fault.' He spread his arms and grinned. 'I'll even clean the boots! Look, are we friends again? It won't be long now until we can leave Endinfinium and go home anyway. Just another couple of days. You'll be so happy to have a real family at last.'

Miranda nodded. *The magic of words*, she thought. More powerful than anything else. Her anger and suspicion still stood like the silhouettes of two horses on the horizon, but they were no good to her now. Cuttlefur's words had woven a spell more complex than she could understand, and even though she could see its threads swirling and coiling around her, she could do nothing but smile and nod, and to think of all of the goodness he promised and to let her dreams take over.

'I can't wait to meet my family,' she said.

30

HOPES AND FEARS

The guesthouse appeared to be deserted. Jim Green was down on the beach with the pupils, of course, but there was no sign of Alan Barnacle. A couple of stumbling, vacant-eyed cleaners moved through the lower floors, picking up trash and organising tables for the evening meal, though none paid Benjamin any attention as he went up the stairs to his room and packed a few clothing items into a small bag he had found in one of the unused rooms.

Then he went down into the kitchens to rummage through the cupboards for a few things to eat, which also went into his bag. Again, the few cleaners he saw paid him no attention.

Back outside, he took one last look out at the bay, swallowed down the urge to cry, then turned for the path heading back up the way they had come.

He would walk if he had to.

∼

Wilhelm was woken from a doze by a sound like hundreds

of wicker baskets creaking in the wind. He frowned and, climbing stiffly to his feet, shook out the aches in his back and legs from where the tree roots had pressed into his skin. The small hollow had been the only shelter he could find, and while he wasn't exactly dry, at least he didn't feel like a soaked mouse.

The sound came from just behind the hill, approaching quickly. Wilhelm climbed up out of the stand of scrubby trees and jogged up the slope.

'Stop!'

He dived to the side as a huge circular shape rolled right past where he had been standing, crushing flat the grass. He rolled over and sat up as it came to a stop, rocking back and forth, balancing on the slope.

'Well, I never.'

It looked like a giant wicker ball—a ten-foot-high sphere made of woven-together twigs. It turned as if recognising his voice, and a section popped out of the main ball to swing down and form three woven steps leading inside.

'Fallenwood, you made it,' Wilhelm said. He reached into his pocket to touch the little twig he had found, which now pulsed with warmth. Patting the ball on the side, he climbed up the steps into what felt like a giant hamster wheel. A thicker pole hung from one side to the other, supporting a crude wooden seat that swayed back and forth. Wilhelm climbed up onto it, and it adjusted for his weight to stay balanced. Twin armrests were his only support as the seat rocked, so he held them firm and then shouted, 'Onward!'

The ball rolled forward and Wilhelm marveled at the way the central pole revolved with the motion, allowing the seat to stay balanced. It was a wonder of mechanics that deserved to win a design award.

'Fallenwood, you're a genius.' He patted one of the armrests, then poked the little twig into a gap on the other, as though it were a lucky mascot. The woven mesh ball gave a sudden crispy crackle, as if in acknowledgement.

'To the Bay of Paper Dragons!' Wilhelm shouted, and the sphere picked up speed, bumping over the uneven ground like a giant ball of twine with a mind of its own. The faster it spun, the easier he could see through the mesh, and the world outside soon revealed itself behind a flickering sepia like an old movie reel.

The ball didn't appear to be too sure of the best route, however, occasionally barreling down a hill so fast, Wilhelm was sure it would break apart, before coming to a halt at some obstacle like a stream or an outcrop, then turning back and creaking its way slowly back up the hill. As the hours passed, though, and after the feeling in his back and thighs had long been battered out by the relentless buffeting of the hard wooden seat, they inched further and further north, creeping ever closer to the Bay of Paper Dragons and the danger that hung over Miranda and Benjamin like a big dark cloud.

~

'You can see here'—Jim Green pointed at the ground —'where the rock appears a little lighter in colour than the rest of the cliff. You can also notice that slant, as though it's not natural?' He began to laugh. 'As if anything here is, of course. But look, this is where Jeremiah Flowers blasted the cliff to close up the entrance to the bay. There's still a small span, of course, to allow water in and out, but it's mostly filled with rocks to make it impossible for any dragons larger than a couple of feet long to get through. Even then there used to be a net to stop them from escaping, but after the net was damaged in a storm, Jeremiah had no means to replace it, so he established the breeding pool. Since then, the curators of the Bay of Paper Dragons have routinely captured expectant females and monitored the births.'

'Wouldn't there be thousands of dragons, then?' Cherise asked.

Jim Green flashed a sadistic grin. 'Oh, they eat each other. They have a pretty good way of maintaining their optimum population. Like all frying species, though, if the conditions were right, they would populate the whole ocean, given the opportunity.'

'What happened to the ones who got out?' Snout asked.

'Destroyed by the strong water currents,' Jim Green said, then his eyes turned storyteller again. 'Although there are rumours ... and there have been sightings—'

'Of what? Of what?' shouted Tommy Cale, jumping up and down.

'There have long been tales of a great dragon, one many times larger than the rest, that long ago escaped the bay before the others were sealed in, and since that time has been trying to find a way back in to be with its friends.'

'Do reanimated objects have friends?' Snout asked. 'My science book says—'

'Yes, well, don't worry about all of that theory stuff,' Jim Green said. 'Even in the writings of Jeremiah Flowers, there are mentions of a great dragon, the lord of all of them. In the summer, this headland is a popular place for travelers to come and watch for him.'

'How do you know it's a boy?'

Jim Green smiled. 'Because the stories talk of a great black dragon, colourless, so dark that only the glory of the red sun allowed him to be seen at all. You see, only the female paper dragons have colour. Rather the opposite of life as you might have known it. The males are dark and mostly black or grey, easy to mistake as rocks or seaweed floating in the water. They're also generally much smaller, and don't live so long.'

'Why not?' Cherise asked.

'Because the females eat them.'

Miranda snorted. 'Dragons are awesome.'

'Doesn't the water make them fall part?' Snout asked.

'As the legend goes,' Jim Green said, 'they've developed a way to protect themselves. What that way is, no one's quite sure, but if you come up here at night and look carefully at the water, you might just spot it.'

'Can we? Can we?' Tommy Cale shouted at Professor Eaves, who waved away his request with a flap of his hand. 'Tonight is diary writing in the dining hall,' he said. 'The cliffs aren't safe after dark.'

'Not when there are dragons about, no,' Jim Green said. 'Now, shall we move on a little bit, down into that hollow, and stop for a snack?'

As the group started off again, Miranda hung back. Cuttlefur started to walk after the others, until he realised she wasn't coming and turned to look at her.

'What's the matter?'

'When are we leaving?' she asked.

'I told you, soon.'

'But you keep saying that. I'm tired of all this waiting around. I just want to leave.'

'Be patient. In a couple of days. Maybe tomorrow, actually.'

'Really?'

'Yes. Just ... wait. Come on, let's catch up with the others.'

As he started off down the path, Miranda scowled and,

unable to help herself, reached inside for her magic. But there was nothing there. As before, she felt cold and empty. What if it never came back?

She started to follow Cuttlefur, then stopped to glance over her shoulder. Back the way they had come, Edgar stood looking out to sea, one hand shading his eyes from the sunlight.

Maybe he could help? Secret lessons with Edgar had revealed her magic to her in the first place. She was ashamed to tell him it had disappeared, but it might be just a simple thing, easily explained. She started to go to him, only for Edgar to step down out of sight, so she hurried to the cliff edge and saw him clambering down a steep path to a strip of beach far below.

Edgar had always been a collector, perhaps much like the famous Jeremiah Flowers had once been. Perhaps he had seen something interesting lying in the flotsam at the top of the shore.

She was just about to shout to him, when a voice behind her called, 'Miranda! Hurry up!'

Professor Eaves stood, hands on hips, a scowl on his face. With a sigh, she turned and headed back to the group.

Hopefully, she would get a chance to talk to Edgar later. With a bit of luck, her magic might have returned by then, anyway.

She crossed her fingers behind her back and hurried after the others.

31

DARK HAPPENINGS

'Just stop struggling, or I'll throw you down a well or something. If he finds out you're not dead, we might both end up that way. Remember, this isn't personal. Not between me and you.'

Tied to an old leather easy chair with a gag in his mouth, the real Alan Barnacle glowered at Godfrey, then he chomped down on the gag again and said something Godfrey couldn't understand. The fat innkeeper's shock at being abducted by an uglier, fatter version of himself had given way to outright anger.

'Look, do you want to eat or not?'

Barnacle gave a single, sharp nod.

'Right, then stop struggling so I can remove your gag.'

Barnacle relaxed and gave another nod. Godfrey, circling him like a man approaching a bear that may or may not be asleep, went behind the chair and untied the handkerchief.

'Look,' Barnacle said, 'I don't know who or what you are, but if you let me out of here, we can strike a deal. We can make a profit off of this. Start a circus or something?

How many twins do you know that could ever look like us?'

'I'm not your brother.'

Barnacle guffawed, a shower of spit spraying over his chest. 'No, you're not. You're me. At least you're close. You're like my ugly older brother. You vile heathen, who or what are you?'

'Once I've done what I came here to do, I'll be gone and you'll be free to go back to what you were doing,' Godfrey said. 'Look, hold still.' He lifted a spoonful of mashed carrot.

'No sugar!' Barnacle spat, coughing the mash all over the floor. Godfrey shook a bit off of his shirt and glared at the innkeeper.

'It's carrot, you fool!'

'You expect me to eat that without any kind of seasoning? What do you take me for?'

'Are you hungry or not?'

'No.'

'Fine.'

Godfrey turned and marched to the door.

'Wait, wait …' Barnacle said, 'let's not be hasty now. I'll eat it. Bring it back.'

Godfrey glared for a moment, then relented, trying not to cringe at the pig-like noises Alan Barnacle made as he chewed down the spoonfuls of mash.

'Finished?'

Barnacle nodded. 'Toilet. I need the toilet.'

'No!'

'Come on, you know what it's like. You're me, after all. Just prop me forward out of the chair. Lean me on a table or something.'

Godfrey scowled. The Dark Man's instructions had been to dispose of the innkeeper by whatever means necessary, but Godfrey hadn't been able to murder in cold blood such a pathetic specimen of a man. Now, he was beginning to regret being so jelly-bellied.

'Get that table over there,' Barnacle said. 'It's easy. I'll tell you what to do. You'll need a bucket, too.'

When it was over, Godfrey scrubbed his hands at the water faucet in the corridor, closed his eyes against the horror he had just witnessed, then locked up the old guest room and went back downstairs, trying not to think about what he had just done. Had he just used his magic, it would have been so simple ... but then the Dark Man would have sensed him.

The pupils weren't back yet. Only Ms. Ito, the crazy-haired art teacher with the permanent plaster cast on her leg, was still there, though she was relaxing in a sun lounge on the second floor, reading some recently deanimated magazines.

Godfrey went into another back room, locked the door, then pulled out a glass bottle from his pocket and, setting it down onto an upturned box, closed his eyes.

The warmth of the reanimation magic was so strong, like a blast of hot air on his face. He'd felt no such power ever before; not from another pupil, nor any of the teachers. The tiny circle of liquid in the bottle was enough to create an entire world, he knew.

Pure, liquid dark reanimate.

'Hear me, Master.'

Is it done?

Godfrey nearly fell over. The voice had come from everywhere at once, and he peered up at the dark room's corners as if expecting a shadowy figure levitating against the ceiling, hooked fingers stretching for him.

Godfrey's voice shook as he said, 'Tomorrow.'

When I have the girl, Forrest will come of his own free will. He will not be able to leave her to her destruction.

'Cuttlefur and I are ready, if the, um … transportation is.'

It will be. Where is Forrest now? He must not be allowed to interfere. It would be convenient if he was out of the way while we deal with the girl. A little addition to his food, perhaps? Something that will keep him sick in bed until it is too late. He has proved himself … powerful.

Godfrey shivered. Benjamin's power had nearly cost him his life. The kid barely knew how to control it, but if he ever learned, he would be difficult to capture.

'I'll find out,' he said.

The heat from the dark reanimate cooled, the room warmed, and when Godfrey opened his eyes again, he knew he was alone.

He hid the liquid away and went upstairs to the guest rooms. Soon, the pupils would be back from the excursion. The cleaners were busily preparing dinner in the kitchens. He would have to tread carefully when he asked them to find him something that might turn Benjamin's stomach enough to sit him out of tomorrow's trip. He had no idea how much they would communicate to each other or to the guests. The Dark Man had put him in a difficult situation, but if he failed, his own life might be at stake.

Benjamin shared a room with Cuttlefur and Adam. Godfrey leaned in through the door and looked around.

He frowned. Something wasn't right.

It took him a moment to realise what it was, something that, as a kid himself, he had nearly overlooked.

Cuttlefur and Adam had acted like typical kids—bedclothes in a crumpled mess, bags coughing up all manner of belongings onto the floor. The third bed, though, had been neatly made, the duvet tucked under the pillow.

Like someone was checking out.

Benjamin Forrest.

Where was he?

Disturbed, Godfrey lumbered over to Benjamin's bed and squatted down, peering underneath for some clue left behind.

'Barnacle! What on earth are you doing, man?'

As always, it took Godfrey a moment to adjust to the name people were calling him now, and when he realised someone was addressing him, he jerked back, bumping his head against the bottom of Benjamin's bed, then turned around, his newly created cheeks already reddening.

Professor Eaves stood in the doorway, wearing a frown so deep, it had fused both of his eyebrows together. Godfrey resisted making some quip about cobwebs caught in the professor's hair. After all, he had gotten his nickname 'Dusty' for a reason.

'Um, you're back early, Professor. I was just doing a little, um, dusting. In a guesthouse as old as this, even the dirt starts to reanimate. And the cleaning staff, well … they have minds of their own….'

'Quite. Have you seen Master Forrest?'

'Um, who?'

'The boy whose bed you're cleaning beneath. He left the hiking party in a bit of a sulk.'

'Well, his bed was made.'

'And his things?'

'I haven't seen anything. Is there a problem, Professor?'

Professor Eaves swore. 'It looks like the fool might have run off. We'll have to send a search party. Much as few of us would mind troublesome Master Forrest conveniently wandering off, he's something of a favorite of the Grand Lord.'

'Oh, is he now?'

Professor Eaves frowned. 'You know something, Barnacle? You're barely the man I remember from last year's trip. Have you been sick as of late?'

Godfrey shrugged. 'I suppose it must be the sea air,' he said.

'Well, if you see Forrest, let me know.'

As Professor Eaves went out, Godfrey breathed a sigh of relief. The professor, it seemed, suspected nothing.

Didn't clear up the mystery of where Benjamin might have gone, though, and it was imperative Godfrey located him at once. If the Dark Man were to find out Forrest had gone missing right as the jaws of his trap were about to snap tight, he would be most displeased….

32

SEARCH PARTIES

Benjamin had found nothing in the sheds around the back of the guesthouse that could take him to Source Mountain quickly, so in the end, he turned back to the only form of transport he could wholly trust: his own feet.

The road leading up the cliff headed too far south, so instead, he headed back down to the breeding pond and found, through the trees, where the river entered the small lake.

During his mission with Lawrence, he had seen several small tributaries, and this one had to eventually join with the Great Junk River not far from Source Mountain. There was not much of a path, so he clambered up the rocks over which crisp, clear water gushed—noticeably trash-free—until the bay was far back down the valley behind him.

He had quit on the hiking trip just before lunch, so he still had several hours of daylight, followed by the red sun's eternal twilight. As long as he wasn't in thick undergrowth, he would be able to see, though his main concern was slipping on the slick rocks and turning his ankle, or worse.

The river valley continued to rise steeply, and after an

hour of climbing, the valley began to flatten out, the trees on either side no longer as tight as curtains hanging over him. Slowly, the vegetation relinquished its hold, and the river itself became no longer a treacherous ascent of slimy rocks and invisible pools, but a wider, flat stream with an easy-to-traverse gravel bed. He had long given up hope of keeping dry boots.

When the hill to his right had flattened out and dropped away, Benjamin approached the confluence with a much larger tributary of the Great Junk River, one that flowed south, to a headland they had passed on the way to the Bay of Paper Dragons. Here, he again found trash, but also an ancient metal grate blocking the head of the smaller tributary, gummed up and rusted. Perhaps a remnant of Jeremiah Flowers's legacy? Benjamin gave it a pat on the top for luck, then climbed out of the river, onto a thin, partly overgrown path to follow the larger river north.

When he guessed it was about teatime, Benjamin sat down beside the river and took some food out of his bag. He was close to solving the mystery; he knew it. He had climbed right up out of the valley now, and here, the land was a lot flatter. There was nothing to stop him getting to Source Mountain and finding out, once and for all, if Jeremiah Flowers had been right, that it was a way out of Endinfinium.

After some cold vegetables and a piece of leftover fish from yesterday's dinner, he packed up his things, shouldered his bag, and got moving again. The yellow sun had started to set, though the sky was clear, so the red sun would remain his companion until he decided to rest for the night. He hoped he could make it all the way to the foot of Source Mountain before he had to sleep.

An hour later, though, he was on the verge of giving

up. His feet were dragging, his shoes felt full of rocks, and carrying his bag was like carrying a dead horse. Each step was like pulling himself up a chain. There was no way could he go on.

He stopped to catch his breath, wondering why he sounded so hoarse, until he realised most of the sound wasn't his breathing at all, but something else.

A short distance ahead, the river bent around a natural curve, and Benjamin steeled himself to walk that far, gritting his teeth at the ache in his legs and back. Then, as he reached it, all of his aches and pains melted away.

The view had opened out to the west, and there, standing high above the surrounding hills, he saw it.

Source Mountain.

It rose high into the air, the beginnings of the Great Junk River a vast cobalt grey snake wrapped around it.

He was so, so tired, but he was nearly there. Gaining an extra spring in his step, Benjamin broke into a kind of stumbling jog, something like a magnetic pull drawing him relentlessly toward his destiny.

~

'Where is he?'

Cuttlefur shook his head. 'I don't know. He ran off in a sulk and didn't come back.'

Godfrey scowled. 'He must not be allowed to disrupt the Dark Man's plans.'

'Wherever he's gone, it doesn't matter. He'll be out of the way tomorrow.'

'I hope you're right, but I have a bad feeling about this.'

'Look, just get back to being an innkeeper and let me

worry about tomorrow. Make sure they go on the cruise without any trouble.'

'The creature … is it ready?'

'I—'

A bell rang from somewhere further up the corridor, cutting off Cuttlefur's words.

'What's that?'

Godfrey scowled. 'The dining bell. But it doubles as an alarm. Besides Barnacle, only that fool Jim Green knows how to activate it. One of the professors must have wanted an assembly.'

'Why?'

'Only one way to find out.'

They split up. Cuttlefur headed back to the guest rooms to make his appearance look less suspicious, while Godfrey took a circuitous route through the kitchens that would bring him to the dining hall. When he arrived, Ms. Ito was standing up on the small stage at one end of the dining hall, with Professor Eaves on one side and Professor Caspian on the other. While Cuttlefur came in through a side door to slip in among the pupils near the back, Godfrey made a point of not looking at him.

'I'm afraid we have a small problem,' Professor Eaves said, stepping forward. 'One of our number has gone missing.'

A murmur passed through the crowd. Godfrey noticed the red-haired girl, Miranda, looking around desperately as though searching for someone.

Ms. Ito stepped forward. 'Anyone seen Benjamin Forrest since this afternoon?' she barked. 'Fool boy has run off. Although, I couldn't give a hoot and believe he deserves to get eaten if that should prove his fate, Professors Eaves and Caspian have convinced me otherwise. Anyone seen him?'

No one answered.

'Thought as much,' Ms. Ito said. 'In that case, we'll be going out to scout around the grounds in an attempt to find him.'

Godfrey lifted a hand. 'Um, wouldn't it be better to wait for the morning?'

Ms. Ito glowered. 'Quiet, fool. You can see well enough with that red sun up there, and if he's near, now's the best chance to grab him. Jim Green has located some torches to aid us under the trees, however.' Turning back to look at the pupils, she said, 'Make pairs. No less, no more. If you don't have any friends, your job will be to search the guesthouse itself. I'd like to point out that this could be a grisly matter. If you are to find Forrest, or even just a piece of what might have once been Forrest, then by all means, call it in.' She gave a grim smile, which Godfrey thought had more humour in it than was appropriate. 'We'll do our best to piece together what happened to him.'

A couple of sniggers came from the back, but most of the pupils didn't know whether or not to laugh. Miranda stuck up a hand. 'What if we can't find him?' she asked in a frightened voice. 'What if he's run away?'

'Jeremiah Flowers made the Bay of Paper Dragons as safe as anywhere could be in Endinfinium,' Ms. Ito said. 'However, if he's gone outside the boundaries, then his fate is his own. We might come across him again, or we might not.'

More murmurs rose up from the pupils as they began to bunch together into groups, and then, with a series of mini-discussions and rock-scissors-paper games, into pairs. Miranda snapped at some girl for trying to pair up with Cuttlefur. Fat Adam noticed Godfrey's old buddy, Snout, standing awkwardly off to one side and barreled forward to claim Tommy Cale for his partner. Three second-year girls affirmed their resolution to fight to stay as three by linking arms and huddling together like penguins.

Ms. Ito sighed and waved everyone to the door. 'Be back in one hour,' she said. 'If we haven't found him by then, we'll figure out what to do. Of course, "nothing" gets my vote, but we'll see.' She paused. 'Oh, and don't get lost. Anyone not back here in one hour officially no longer exists. We haven't got time for any more search parties.'

As the room emptied, leaving only Ms. Ito sitting at a table at one end, drinking the tea that Jim Green had brought for her, Godfrey backed away into the shadows. This wasn't good. None of this disruption would please the Dark Man. But he didn't know what else he could do.

∽

'I've changed my mind,' Miranda said, as soon as they were out of earshot. 'I don't want to leave Endinfinium anymore; I want to stay.'

Cuttlefur stared. 'What do you mean? You can't ... Things have been arranged.'

'Have they? Tell me how we're going to leave, then. Because you haven't told me anything.'

'I've been waiting for the right time.'

'Now is the right time.' She glowered. 'Spit it out.'

'Tomorrow afternoon,' he said. 'Someone I know is coming to pick us up.'

'Who?'

'I don't know his name.'

'Well, where is he?'

'On the other side.'

'The other side of what?'

'The world. He's not here, in Endinfinium. He's

coming through tomorrow at approximately five o'clock. He's going to pick us up and take us back with him.'

'How?'

Cuttlefur shrugged. 'I don't know for sure. He didn't say.'

Unable to stop herself, Miranda slapped him hard across the cheek. His head snapped back, her hand smarted with the impact, and immediately a wave of shame washed over her, almost choking her.

'I'm sorry.'

Cuttlefur rubbed his cheek. 'What was that for?'

'I don't know. I'm sorry. I think I'm just worried about Benjamin.'

Cuttlefur smiled. 'Don't be. He's a Summoner, isn't he? He can look after himself. He'll be back soon.'

Miranda sighed. Would he? Cuttlefur had the kind of face that made it easy to forgive, but she was quickly losing her feelings for him. All he did was talk, talk, talk …

'Look, I can't tell you everything, but I can show you something that will help you make your decision.'

'What?'

Cuttlefur pulled out a photograph from his pocket and held it out for Miranda to see.

A smiling, middle-aged man stood with one arm around a woman who had a kindly face. Just to his side stood a boy of about ten, holding a dog on a leash. Behind them was a stone farmhouse set against a clear, blue sky.

'Who are these people?' she asked.

'That's them. That's your family. I was given this to show you if you began to doubt me.'

Miranda snatched it out of his hands. All three people were looking right at the camera, and everything about them seemed peaceful, welcoming.

It was perfect. Everything she had ever dreamed of.

'The lady, her name's Nicola,' Cuttlefur said. 'She runs a dressmaking shop. Her husband, George, is a fireman. And the boy, Stanley, he's your foster brother.'

Miranda tried to pass the photograph back, but her hands began to shake and instead, it fell to the ground between them. As Cuttlefur bent to pick it up, Miranda bolted off into the forest, climbing off the path and pushing through the trees until Cuttlefur's shouts had grown faint in the undergrowth behind.

Then, when she was sure he wouldn't be able to find her, she began to cry.

33

SOURCE MOUNTAIN

When Benjamin woke up, the yellow sun had set, but the red sun still hung low over the hills to the east. Clouds like wisps of smoke left behind by some passing airplane drifted across the evening sky. He shook out the stiffness of his legs as he stood, estimating he had only slept for about three hours.

Source Mountain rose high above him, a black cone that buzzed with the sound of rushing water. The river beside which he had camped grew rapidly more violent as its path steepened toward the mountainside, while the Great Junk River swept away to the south. Up this close, the climb looked nightmarish—steep, jagged patches of open rock face broken by torrents of water. Benjamin followed the tributary up the slope until the noise of the water was so great, he could barely hear himself think. Source Mountain was solid rock out of which the Great Junk River and its tributaries had carved their channels. Trying to cross one was a death wish, so he had no choice but to follow the gradual upward spiral of the riverbank, freezing water sloshing over his feet.

The difficultly of the ascent meant he could think of little else but the next hand- and footholds. By the time he had found a ledge wide enough to sit and pause for a breath, Benjamin was surprised to see he was already halfway up. From so high, the world looked strange—great clouds of swirling mist to the north, and above the sea hung curtains of churning white-and-grey that kept secret what lay behind.

The ledge faced north, so the south was hidden, but forested hills to the west rose and fell, dipping into valleys fertilised by the great river's tributaries, opening up into wide lakes, and finally reaching the foothills of the High Mountains themselves. Benjamin shivered as he stared at the peaks poking up through the clouds. Was the Dark Man out there somewhere, watching him? They had sent him running back to his lair with his power depleted once, but in time, he would regain it, and he would return. How long would that take?

Pangs of guilt filled him again. His fledgling power had helped to save the school and everyone in it, so if he left … what would happen? The Dark Man had captured Grand Lord Bastien, supposedly the strongest magic user in Endinfinium. If he had caught him once, surely he could catch him again?

Benjamin pushed himself up onto stiff legs, forcing himself to begin climbing again. Nothing could be gained by thinking about it. He had made his choice: to follow Jeremiah Flowers into the unknown. Endinfinium and its struggles no longer belonged to him.

Hours passed, and each step blurred into the next, while his senses numbed to the roaring of the water, his skin to the spray that soaked him continuously like a broken showerhead. Source Mountain took him higher and higher over the land, so by the next circuit, he was afforded a panoramic view of the Bay of Paper Dragons, a dark green 'V' of forest connected to an oval of deep blue encircled by twin headlands as tight as crab pincers. From high up, it looked like a giant stag beetle pointing out to sea.

Finally, the mountain, which had for so long seemed to rise straight up, had flattened out. He was near the peak and whatever he would find there. He remembered what Basil had said about Jeremiah weighing himself down to get into the source water, but he had made no such plan.

He had just one other, and he had no idea if it would work or not.

Soon, he would have no choice but to find out.

When he rounded a final bend, he was there, at the top of Source Mountain. Benjamin let out a long gasp and sank to his knees in a mixture of exhaustion and relief.

From the ground, Source Mountain had looked flat-topped, but now he realised it was an inverse cone. He had arrived at the rim of a crater, down which he looked onto a wide lake. The surface seemed calm and serene, but at the southern end, a single gushing river led away through a channel gorged into the rock.

Except for a few shrubs, very little vegetation grew among the rocks, and it was cold enough Benjamin was glad he had remembered to pack an extra sweater and pair of socks, even if both, like the rest of his gear, were damp from the constant spray.

A path led down through outcrops to the lakeside. With his legs feeling odd to be descending after so much time climbing up, he started down with a spring in his step and a feeling that, at long last, he was about to find some answers.

The lake's edge was as calm as it had looked from a distance, but out in the centre, the water churned and bubbled as if rising up from a spring below the surface. Benjamin dipped a finger into the water, then drew back, shivering. Freezing, like from snowmelt.

Everything held an air of lifelessness. When he picked up a plastic toy robot from the water near the shore, it flopped lifelessly in his hands, casing broken, chilled by the water. As he held it, though, a strange sense of warmth began to seep through it, and after he put it back into the water, his palms felt warm when he touched them together. For a few minutes, he watched it drift toward the head of the river, wondering if he would one day see it again, bouncing around, filled with the joy of reanimation.

Benjamin took a deep breath. It was time. He closed his eyes, feeling for the power like the Grand Lord had shown him. Always before, with no knowledge of what he was doing, he had drawn the power from himself, using his own life-force to give power to something else and hurting his body in the process. But now he understood. His mind searched out to the ground and to the air around him, gently pulling, taking just a little from hundreds of tiny sources and bringing it all together in a way he could use it.

In his mind, it felt like a ball of energy. But reanimation magic wasn't like storybook magic; he couldn't create something from nothing. All he could do was push and pull, influence one shape to become another. When he felt like he had enough power, he pushed it forward, using it to influence the air to create a wedge within the water, parting it to reveal a path down into the lake and to the very source of the water itself.

And when the path was wide enough, he began to walk.

34

CONSPIRACY

It didn't really bother Snout that nobody wanted to work with him. It was always easy enough to amuse himself. After lights out last night, for example, when everyone else sat in their rooms, chitchatting about the day's events and recalling the thrilling horror stories Jim Green had told them around the campfire, he had excused himself for a toilet break and gone off wandering into the guesthouse's unused corridors, finally coming across a small amusement arcade that had been ignored and forgotten beneath sheets that had collected so much dust as to become grey. A couple of machines still worked, and a bucket of metal tokens he had found in a corner had kept him entertained until the small hours, when he had finally crept back to his bed and lain in the dark, listening to the soft snoring of his two roommates.

Now, with the rest of the kids out looking for Benjamin, Snout saw a perfect opportunity to see if any of the other machines worked. He had spent his time before playing a couple of fruit machines, but hiding underneath another sheet was an ancient space invaders game, the kind that sat in the corner of pub family rooms and hardly ever got played. Unfortunately, he had been pretty tired when he left the arcade last night. Now, he struggled to find the room again.

Left here, surely? He took a left, but ended up at a dead end. He retraced his steps and tried again, but came to a staircase this time. Was he even on the right floor? He went down, and because he didn't recognise the floor he was on, he went down again. It looked more promising, but surely he was now in the basements? He shrugged. No matter. Perhaps he would find something even more interesting down here.

He was just about to turn a corner, when he heard someone coming the other way. He ducked into an alcove and cowered down behind a fitted bookshelf that had begun to detach itself from the wall. A moment later, a fat shadow stumped past, huffing and puffing.

'Stupid fools … not long now … I'll be out of this dump by tomorrow.'

Snout lifted an eyebrow. Alan Barnacle, the oversized innkeeper? But his voice sounded different now that he was talking to himself. Almost familiar. Snout frowned, trying to recall where he had heard it before, but it was like listening to someone you know speak with their head inside a box of tissues.

Where had he heard that voice before?

He peered from his hiding place to see Barnacle stop at a door at the end of the corridor and poke a key into a lock. The door swung open, and Barnacle muttered a greeting to someone inside, then went in and closed the door.

The lock clicked.

Snout thought about the arcade machines, wishing he knew where they were so he could quickly forget about all of this and hurry off. However, whether he liked it or not, his curiosity had bloomed like a giant sunflower until it was so big, it crowded out all other thoughts, leaving him only one option. With his heart pounding in his mouth, he crept up to the door and pressed his ear against it.

'Look, I'll do you a deal. I'll do your toilet for you, if you tell me where you keep your, um, laxatives. No, I don't want them for you. I need to keep a couple of people back at the guesthouse tomorrow while the others go out on the cruise with Jim. One kid in particular, although he's actually gone missing. I reckon he'll show up, though. They always do when you wish they wouldn't.'

'Third cupboard from the left in the second pantry,' a gruff voice answered, and Snout froze. It was like Barnacle was talking to himself, only he was answering in his proper voice.

'They in a packet?'

'No, powder. Don't ask me the dose. Stuff's ancient. Probably comes from Flowers's time. No doubt ground up out of some herbal junk he came up with. I only know it works because I put it in a soup once, thinking it was cornflower.'

'Well, I won't be making that mistake with your breakfast tomorrow.'

'You'd better not. Now, I've told you what you wanted, so it's your turn to keep your end of the bargain.'

'All right. Hang on.'

Snout began to slowly back away up the corridor. He needed to speak to the teachers right now. It had taken him a while to figure out where he had heard that first voice before, and now that he remembered, he couldn't believe he hadn't figured it out sooner. After all, it had once been a constant source of inane comments not far from his ear.

Godfrey.

What was he doing here? And what was he doing impersonating Alan Barnacle?

He was almost back to the staircase, when he tripped over a loose roll in the threadbare carpet and crashed into the wall. As he recovered himself, he heard the door opening back down the corridor, and the air filled with a sudden warmth. He knew it was that magic thing some of the other kids talked about.

He didn't want to think about that, or who might be using it, so he gritted his teeth and ran up the stairs as quickly as he could.

~

'Caspian, I need a word.'

Edgar turned, surprised by Ms. Ito stumping toward him across the car park. Ten pupils had returned so far; thirteen more were still down in the forest. Professor Eaves was with one group, with most of the rest on their way back. Aside from the missing Benjamin Forrest, only two pupils were unaccounted for: Cuttlefur and Miranda.

Edgar frowned, shaking off his unease. Eaves had set him up on watch because of his sensitivity, the simplicity with which he could feel the gentle glow of the pupils' magic—even of those who had no idea of its existence yet —but two worried him.

Cuttlefur held some kind of power he hadn't felt before, though he had no way to investigate it because the boy—whether intentionally or not—had erected a magical wall to prevent his feeling it, by reanimating the surrounding air to push away other magic users sensing it. He was trying to make himself invisible, yet had made it glaringly obvious he was hiding something.

Miranda's problem was different. For nearly a year he

had secretly taught her about her magic, and of all of the power in Endinfinium, he could have picked hers out of a crowd. Now, when he felt for her … nothing. Even when she stood in front of him, magically she didn't exist, and he could see in her eyes she knew something was wrong. He had been waiting patiently for her to approach him about it. He was worried he had missed his chance.

'We have a problem, Caspian. Where's Eaves?'

'Down in the forest. He's on his way back. What's happened?'

Ms. Ito, her wild hair like a giant seeded dandelion framing her face in black, white, and grey, glared up at him through eyes much younger than they looked.

'Kid came to me. What's his name? Simon Patterson? The dimwit? The one they call Snout?' She rolled her eyes as if frustrated he couldn't reel off answers as quickly as she asked her questions. 'Alan Barnacle. He's an impostor. We have to get the kids out of here right now.'

Edgar stared. This was the worst possible moment for a crisis, with all of the pupils scattered across the forest, searching for Benjamin.

'Are you sure?'

'Kid said he heard Barnacle talking to Barnacle. Voice wasn't Barnacle's.' She leaned closer as Edgar shook his head, trying to make sense of her words. 'Godfrey. Kid who went missing back when we had that trouble? Said Barnacle spoke with his voice.'

Edgar turned to the guesthouse. 'The returning kids … we told them to assemble in the dining hall. He'll be there with them.'

'What's all this?' came a voice from out of the gloom. Professor Eaves was striding across the car park.

Ms. Ito repeated for him what she had said, then Eaves

turned to Edgar. 'Let's see what he has to say for himself. We'll be safe enough if all three of us are there.'

Edgar wanted to stay to wait for Miranda, but Godfrey was a Summoner, known to have helped the Dark Man in the past, so his presence might have something to do with Benjamin's disappearance.

Ms. Ito was already stumping away to the dining hall, with Professor Eaves in pursuit. Edgar gave the dark edge of the forest one more pained glance, then turned to follow.

35

WILHELM'S SURPRISE

Wilhelm was shaken awake by the great wooden ball coming to an abrupt stop. He wiped at his eyes, then rubbed his chest where a makeshift seat guard made from woven twigs had stopped him from falling out.

'Where are we?' he muttered, peering out into the gloom. The afterglow of warmth suggested it was evening but, surrounded by dark forest, it could have equally been early morning. Only the dark orange glow in the sky gave him enough light to see by. They had come to rest on a dirt track that angled downhill, and from somewhere not far away came the gurgle of a stream.

With a crackle, a section of the ball untangled itself as twigs and strands of dry straw weaved into a series of curves and lines. Wilhelm frowned, then as the distinct shape of a 'W' appeared, he realised they were writing something.

The spelling was poor, and at first, the interconnected letters were hard to read in the gloom, but when he pulled his computer out of his bag and turned the little screen light on, they began to make sense.

Welcom. We hav arivd.

Wilhelm grinned. 'Economising, are you?'

The twigs twisted again. *Ys.*

'Thanks for the ride. Where's here?'

Bay of P.D. is jst ahed.

'Can you wait for me?'

Hde undr trees.

'Thanks.' He started to get up, then added, 'I can't thank you enough, Fallenwood. You're a true friend.'

Dn't forgt promis.

Wilhelm laughed, already wondering how he could talk himself out of cleaning up the old botanical garden building. 'I won't.'

With a rustle like burning paper, Fallenwood's wheel unfolded itself and disappeared into the undergrowth. Wilhelm stood alone on the path, with only the glow of the red sun outlining shadowy things.

Only a few paces in, he saw lights glimmering through the trees, weaving back and forth. He crept a little closer, then climbed off the path into the undergrowth, moving slowly so as not to announce his presence.

He hadn't gone far when he heard an unmistakable voice:

'We should go back now. It's time.'

Cuttlefur. Wilhelm scowled. He wanted to jump out to confront the bigger boy, but someone of his size needed an advantage. He edged a little closer, trying to find out what Cuttlefur was doing.

'No, just a little longer.'

Miranda's voice. Wilhelm slapped a hand over his mouth to stop himself from crying out for her.

'Look, I told you, he's long gone. But don't worry, he can look after himself. He'll be fine.'

'He was upset.'

'He'll get over it.'

'Benjamin!'

'Forget him. If he was your friend, he wouldn't have run off, would he?'

'*Benjamin!*'

Wilhelm flinched. Miranda's shout was so close, it hurt his ears. He dropped down behind a tree, then felt around for something he could use as a weapon. A rock or a long twig. If he was quick, he could catch Cuttlefur by surprise before he could use his magic.

A sudden icy chill crept across his back. He touched his skin, though it felt normal—same skin, same heat.

Which meant the feeling was in his mind.

Wilhelm closed his eyes. From through the trees came an intense chill. Edgar had shown them how to feel for the magic of each other, but it had always been warm. This was different, and could only mean one thing.

Cuttlefur was channeling dark reanimation magic.

He knows I'm here.

Wilhelm backed away, but tripped as something pushed up out of the ground by his feet.

'Come on,' Cuttlefur said from through the trees. 'We promised Professor Caspian. We can look again when it's lighter.'

Miranda sniffed. 'If we have to.'

Again Wilhelm slapped a hand over his mouth, this time to suppress a gasp of terror as the ground below his feet glowed orange. Ghouls. He scrambled out of range as a half-human, half-machine arm poked up out of the ground reached for him. Through the trees, he was dimly aware of Miranda and Cuttlefur leaving.

He wanted to call out to Miranda, but that would only put her in danger, and not for the first time he wished he were more than a lowly Weaver. Allied with others, he could bring forth great power; alone, he was powerless, with just his wits, and his legs.

He turned too sharply and crashed face-first into a crusty tree trunk. Something wiry wrapped around his ankle, but he twisted and kicked out, striking something fat and orange that looked like a microwave with a face and arms. The mouth where a door would once have been snapped at him, though the force of his blow had broken off the ensnaring wire from its casing and it fell away, wriggling like an orange snake.

Then he was on his feet again, dancing through the undergrowth, while a dozen or more orange-tinted monstrosities ran, wriggled, and bounced after him.

Stumbling among the trees, he barely kept ahead of them. The slower ones had dropped back, but one creature, a cross between a crocodile and a coffee table, ran close behind on wooden-peg legs while savage jaws snapped. He glanced back to see how close it was, then turned away, almost smacking into another tree before dodging left at the last moment. Crashing through a stand of brush, he rolled out across a cobblestone road.

Though the ghoul was right behind him, the road angled downhill, and it became a straight sprint. Wilhelm summoned his last strength and bolted, trusting his footing, trusting the road, trusting his luck. The creature gave chase, but its wooden legs slipped and slid over the polished stones, and by the time the road had angled around a corner and leveled out alongside a wide pond, it had given up. Wilhelm scrambled off the road into the undergrowth and lay down to wait, but the creature never appeared, perhaps choosing instead to wander back into the forest. As soon as he was sure it was safe to continue, he climbed back down onto the road and hurried in the direction of a building he could see through the trees.

He recognised the Paper Dragon Bay Guesthouse from a faded sign over the door. The parking area was dark and empty of vehicles, while a grassy area overlooking the bay showed signs of having hosted a bonfire within the last couple of days. Wilhelm paused by the door, closing his eyes and feeling for the heat of reanimation magic. Spots of it were not far off, indicating the other pupils were nearby, though a worrying wall of cold surrounded everything.

He had to be careful. He crept around the back of the guesthouse, looking for an unlocked door, and on his third attempt he found one that led into a pantry. The clanging of pots and pans came from an adjacent room, and when he opened the door a crack, he saw a group of cleaners preparing something in a large silver vat. The smell was intoxicating, and Wilhelm wanted to run inside.

Chocolate.

How long has it been?

Something in the trees outside let out a long, lonely howl, and he snapped back to his mission. Voices came from up ahead. At the end of a corridor stood a set of wide doors, which swung open and admitted a cleaner carrying an empty tray. Wilhelm ducked back out of sight into a connecting corridor until the cleaner had passed. He had found the others, though. All of the pupils were gathered in the room beyond the double doors, lined up on trestle tables.

With his heart in his mouth, Wilhelm sneaked up to the doors to see what was going on.

A huge, ugly man was just climbing up onto a stage at the far end. He coughed, then tapped the old microphone in front of him. The pupils, lined up in rows, paid him little attention, chatting while taking snacks from bowls the cleaners had placed along the tables.

'Um, order please.'

A gradual hush came over the pupils and, one by one, they turned to look at him.

'I'm afraid I have some good news and some bad news.' He flapped a hand to order as catcalls and jokes rang out. 'The bad news is: all three of your teachers have taken sick.' He sighed. 'We think they were picking wild vegetables. We did warn them not to touch anything.'

'How's that bad news?' someone shouted.

'Some of the plants in the surrounding area work as a strong laxative,' the fat man said, to sniggers of delight. 'It is believed that Jeremiah Flowers grew them. His notebooks mention feeding them to the dragons in order to relieve the pain of childbirth.'

'What's the good news?'

'The good news is that on tomorrow's cruise around the Outer Bay, you'll be accompanied only by Jim Green and myself.' He smiled. 'We'll be able to take you a lot closer to the rocks than if we had … supervision. And who knows?' he added, spreading his hands. 'We might even see the fabled great dragon.'

'Is that all?'

The fat man laughed. 'No, of course not. To ease your frustration, we have cooked you up something you might not have had in a while. Hot chocolate.'

As the pupils cheered, two cleaners stumbled forward with the vat of hot chocolate held between them, and Wilhelm ducked backwards out of the way as they pushed through the doors to more cheers.

He shivered. Something was wrong. The chill of the dark magic was everywhere now, as if Cuttlefur and whomever he was working with had set up a barrier.

He had hoped to be right. Throughout the bumping journey inside his wooden transport, he had looked forward to telling Miranda she was wrong. He wasn't a fool; he wasn't stupid; he wasn't lying to her, and he could prove it.

Now that he was here, though, such thoughts had been tossed from his mind like sailors from a storm-stricken ship. It didn't matter who was right or wrong, only that people would get hurt unless he did something. But being a Weaver, he was useless on his own.

He had to find Benjamin.

As quietly as a cat, Wilhelm crept back down the corridor and slipped through the kitchens. The door was still open and, with a huge sense of relief, he stepped back out into the perpetual twilight. The encompassing chill of dark reanimation was still apparent, but out here in the open, he felt like he could breathe, like he could run.

Then he glanced up at the forest and his heart sank.

Between the trees glowed orange light, the collective glow so bright it was like thousands of flickering candles had caught alight all at once. He took a few steps forward, until shadowy forms began to appear, creatures that walked like men or crawled like snakes, bounced like broken chairs or rolled like old wheels. None moved. Whoever had called forth the army of ghouls hadn't intended for them to attack; they were to contain, to keep the pupils and the teachers trapped inside the guesthouse.

Staying close to the wall, Wilhelm crept around the front of the building, looking for an escape route. He squatted behind a row of smelly septic tanks, then cautiously peered out. The car park was as empty as before, but out from the bushes on the other side came the same familiar orange glow as from the forest behind the guesthouse. Ghouls were everywhere, waiting back in the undergrowth for further orders.

Wilhelm grimaced. Back in the orphanage, he'd been

pretty good in a sprint, and some of the care staff had even said he'd make a decent rugby player if he filled out in his teens. What they hadn't known was that outrunning and dodging some of the bigger boys had been the only way to keep sticky boogers from dripping into his ears. They'd caught him once behind the storage sheds, and he'd promised it would never happen again.

'Catch me if you can,' he muttered, then he bolted from his hiding place, racing across the car park to the path that led to the pond, then up to where he had left the Fallenwoodsmen. Low moans came from the bushes, and the orange line lurched forward, with dozens of monstrous creatures lumbering in pursuit. Up ahead, others stepped out of the undergrowth to cut him off, but Wilhelm dodged right, then left, then executed a swift roll that made his shoulder ache, and suddenly he was through them, racing on down the path while the host shrieked and wailed in his wake.

He had to lose them quickly. Ghouls were like cars with an endless fuel supply; until they broke down, got lost, or were switched off, they would keep coming. As he reached the pond and raced across the causeway cutting it in two, he glanced back, and immediately wished he hadn't. At least twenty still followed him, and some ran low to the ground, heads keened forward, rapid feet quickly closing the gap.

As the hill rose up, Wilhelm came to a stop. Downhill, he had an advantage, but the steepening path had sapped his last strength. Here, on this thin, cobblestone causeway, he had to stand and fight.

With tears in his eyes, he pulled an old branch out of the weeds beside the path. It felt brittle and damp, easily broken, but it would have to be enough.

'Come on!' he shouted as the host started across the

causeway. The nearest was a lumbering thing with wheels and snapping jaws that had once been a cupboard door. It blocked the way forward for the rest, so as it approached, Wilhelm darted forward and jammed the stick into the hard plastic above its jaws, pushing it backwards.

Two ghouls at its rear fell into the water. Something long and snakelike glided across the surface and dragged one of them away, while the other floundered, ignored by its companions, unable to get out.

The first ghoul sneaked forward, ducked low, and snapped at Wilhelm's legs. He knocked it back with the stick, but lost his footing, one leg slipping off the causeway edge. Warm, sticky water soaked him up to the knee, but he shrugged it off and struggled back out.

'No....'

Something dark rose above him, a beating orange heart on the outside of its body casting enough light to reveal black wings. Wilhelm stabbed the stick upwards, but it jarred and then snapped. The ghoul squawked as if in pain, then spindly arms made of lime-crusted plastic frames stretched out for his neck.

Wilhelm didn't get a chance to jump aside. Something heavy landed on the causeway at his back and a sudden wave sloshed over him. He rolled over, coughing. He turned, looking for the ghoul that loomed behind, until a massive claw swept it away.

'Lawrence!'

'Where, Master Wilhelm?' the snake-train boomed.

'Anywhere!' he shouted, and Lawrence scooped him up in a huge paw, then rolled him gently across his back until Wilhelm fell through an open skylight into the first train carriage. He hung on to a ceiling safety strap as Lawrence swatted the nearest ghouls out of their path, then turned and bounded away.

When they were safely out of the forest, Lawrence let Wilhelm climb out, then he curled around into a coil to peer down at him.

'What happened?' Wilhelm asked.

'Master Edgar, no recent speak,' Lawrence said. 'Lawrence feel nothing but cold, like long winter come.'

'They've been captured,' Wilhelm said. 'All of them, even the ones who don't know it. The place was full of dark magic. It was like taking a cold shower but not being able to get dry.'

'Master Edgar...?'

'He was with them, I think.'

Lawrence's head lowered and he let out a low, slow cooing sound.

'We'll save them,' Wilhelm said, patting the snake-train's giant head. 'But I can't do it alone. I can't control reanimation magic. We need to find Benjamin.'

'Master Benjamin?'

'They were looking for him. He wasn't there when I snuck inside. Back at the school, he was talking about finding this place where the river begins. Do you know it?'

Lawrence's head lifted and fell, creating a wind that made Wilhelm shiver. 'Master Benjamin ... yesterday. Climb the mountain, he wanted. Lawrence brought him back.'

'Source Mountain? Is it near?'

Lawrence gave the best awkward look a snake with the head of a train could give. He lifted his great headlight eyes and, swinging them toward the northwest, gave one massive blink and then a low groan expressing his displeasure.

'Too near,' Lawrence said. 'Always too near.'

'I need to go there.'

'Noooo …. Source Mountain is death for Endinfinium.'

'What do you mean?'

'We come, we live. We go back, we die.'

Wilhelm nodded. 'Like real life in reverse. You fear your birthplace, because that's the only place you can't be what you are now. Is that right?'

Lawrence gave a long nod.

'Can you at least take me close?'

Lawrence growled, and his body shook as though afraid. Then, when Wilhelm was about to give up and set himself for a long walk, the snake-train nodded again. 'Close,' he said. 'Close enough to see where death becomes life.'

36

THE BEGINNING

The pathway between the two walls of water grew steeper and steeper. At first, Benjamin walked normally, then scrambled with his hands out behind him, then finally tumbled forward into a free fall, rolling and bouncing over the rocks until he thought it might batter him to pieces before he even got to where everything began.

All around, the roar of the water was deafening. He tried to scream, but the thundering sound swallowed his voice, as though he was trapped in the centre of a circle of waterfalls all falling upwards. As he crashed into the ground, his first thought was relief that he wasn't dead. His second was that the world had become so loud, he couldn't be sure he wasn't. As he climbed to his feet and brushed himself down, he looked up at the wall of water surrounding him, and gasped.

Hundreds of people floated there, arms outstretched, faces turned upwards, mouths open and eyes squeezed shut as if they had found divine enlightenment. Some were adults, old men and women, and some were children. The nearest were close enough to touch, hands trailing in the edges of the water walls, fingertips as white as bone.

Let go, Benjamin. Release your hold on the magic and join us.

He looked around, searching for the voice, though there was no single voice; it had come from all of them—the sound of a thousand people at once.

It's wonderful where we are. If you want to go home, join us.

Panic rose, and for a moment, the towers of water shifted and shook as his magical hold faltered, the air he had instructed to push them back losing its strength.

Join us, Benjamin. All paths lead here. We are the end, and we are for infinity. We are Endinfinium. Look.

Cold fingers closed over his, but instead of a rising horror, he felt only a loving warmth. He smiled and let the hand draw him toward the edge of the water—

∼

David is playing with a wooden train set on the floor of his bedroom. Over in the corner, a video game console sits untouched. Benjamin can never understand why his brother prefers these older, physical toys that came from a dirty cardboard box in the attic, labeled 'Grandpa's Stuff,' but now as he watches, his five-year-old brother touches a finger to the back of one toy train and it jerks forward, as if by magic. David giggles and claps his hands, then reaches for another wooden locomotive. As he lifts it up, the top bends toward him, and a score line in the wood meant to represent a radiator grill bends up at the corners.

It looks like a smile.

Benjamin lifts a hand to attract his brother's attention, when he realises he is sitting on the edge of a bed. There seems to be only one in the room, when he is sure there used to be two. In fact, as he stares at the shadows on the other side of the room, details knit together, and he sees a bookcase filled with all of his books. His desk and bed are gone, though.

David?

His voice isn't his own. It comes from somewhere outside, as though he is drawing it from the air. Still, his brother frowns and starts to turn back.

A door opens, and a tall woman with her hair tied back in a ponytail marches into the room. *Mum!* Benjamin shouts, and this time David does turn, eyes briefly lighting up, mouth falling open. His mother, Jennifer Forrest, shows no acknowledgement as she marches through the room like an organised wind, scooping up wooden blocks and pieces of train line in hands that work like the buckets of some great machine, to pour them into a toy box that sits against the wall.

'Dinnertime, David,' she says in a voice that makes Benjamin's heart creak with longing. Then her scooping hands shovel David up and usher him from the room.

David! Mum! Wait! Benjamin cries out. He tries to get up off the bed, but suddenly there is nothing underneath him, and he crashes forward. To avoid the inevitable impact, he closes his eyes—

∼

The young man is sitting hunched in an armchair, a book open on his lap. Benjamin doesn't recognise him at first because David is much older, and the bob of hair his five-year-old brother couldn't help sporting is gone, cut short, neat and trim, slightly curled up at the front; the kind of haircut you would walk right past in a crowd.

The book is a picture book of wild birds. David runs his fingers over the photographs, a relaxed smile on his face, when a door opens somewhere behind and in walks a man, grey-haired, white-coated. He leans over David, who looks up and smiles. The man pats his shoulder and, lifting a clipboard off his chest to make a quick note in pencil, leaves again.

As soon as the door closes, David smiles once more, and this time, the picture lifts up off the page. The bird, before static and inanimate, takes on dimensions and shape, its feathers blurring as it ruffles them. Then it looks up at David and tweets. David grins and pats it on the head, then watches as it sinks back into the page moments before the door bursts open and three men rush in.

Two of them grab David under the shoulders, and the third grabs the book. Benjamin jumps up, realizing for the first time he's been sitting on a chair a little off to the side.

David!

Again the scream comes from all around. David looks up, and his eyes widen with surprise. He starts to say something, but is instead dragged out through the door. Benjamin takes a few steps forward and stops as the white-coated man from before comes in. He stands still, clipboard held protectively against his chest, and looks from left to right, eyes passing through where Benjamin stands.

Where are you taking him? Benjamin screams, but the man pays no attention. He goes out, slamming the door. Benjamin tries to follow, but when he gets to the door, nothing happens. He tries to reach out a hand, but when he looks down, nothing is there. The space in front of the door handle holds nothing but empty air.

Panicking, he turns. The room is sparse. A bed, a dressing table, a chest of drawers. A bookcase filled with picture books and children's stories. He starts to go to it, then stops and turns back.

Toward the mirror.

He needs to see who or what he is. The men looked right through him, but there was recognition in David's eyes. Benjamin gulps as he steps in front of it.

The mirror is empty. Benjamin's heart thunders, and he takes a step forward to make sure.

And he sees that, no, it isn't quite empty. A shadow is there, a vague difference in the light, something that suggests a person. He grits his teeth and concentrates, and for the briefest of moments, an outline appears. Then it is gone. Frustrated, he squeezes his eyes shut and howls with anger.

When he opens them again—

∼

A woman sits in an easy chair set on a porch overlooking a garden that is lovingly untended. Wild roses and hydrangeas fight for space amongst lower-sitting shrubs and scraggy patches of azalea. Her hair is almost entirely grey, the hands that hold the coffee cup in her lap wizened like old tree branches.

Benjamin is standing behind her. He has a compulsion that is impossible to resist to see her from the front. He takes a step forward just as she gets up and turns to him.

Mum! he screams, and for an instant, she lifts a hand and puts it over her chest, then she shrugs and walks toward him, bent with the shackles of age. He waits for her to look up at him, but her eyes lower. She lets out a long sigh.

'Benjamin ... where did you go? Why did you leave us?' she mutters to herself, so quietly that he wouldn't have heard from any further away. He wants to cry out and tell her that he's here, right here, right here in front of her, but his eyes fill with tears and he blinks to clear his vision—

∽

A hand grabbed him, pulling him backwards, and Benjamin gasped, looking up as the walls of water shuddered above him, threatening to bludgeon him with their load.

'You going to haunt them forever? What use is that?'

The voice sounded brittle, scratched, like two pieces of rusty metal rubbed together. Benjamin started to look down, but was instead swept off his feet, pulled into the earth, a sudden rush of compression washing past him. He closed his eyes, trying not to scream.

When he opened them this time, he was sitting in a dim, underground rock chamber. The surrounding air had a thermal warmth that banished the memory of the chilling towers of water. Benjamin stood and turned around, wondering where the light was coming from, but there was no one source—the walls themselves lit the tunnel with a soft, comforting glow.

'You like the décor? It was the best I could do.'

He turned. The man sitting on a rock-hewn throne was ancient beyond words. Clearly he was a man from the grey stubble that poked out from his chin, but his body appeared shrunken and shriveled, sucked dry of moisture to leave only a mummified remnant that had found the ability to talk.

'Jeremiah Flowers,' said Benjamin.

The creases where the man's mouth should have been widened into a smile. 'It's rare that I'm recognised. And you are?'

'My name is Benjamin.'

'Welcome, Benjamin.'

'Where am I?'

Jeremiah smiled again, holding the gesture as though enjoying a long-forgotten feeling. 'You are at a place that many seek yet few find. The beginning of everything.'

37

SHIVERS

'I'm not sure I want to go,' Miranda said. 'It doesn't feel right without the teachers being there. That man, Barnacle, gives me the creeps.'

Cherise grinned. 'No, I think you're right. You should stay here. It might be dangerous.'

'No it won't!' Amy shouted from the other bed. 'It won't be dangerous at all. She just wants you out of the way so she can talk to Cuttlefur.'

'Shut up!'

'Admit it.'

'I'm not some silly little girl like you, Amy. I'm just thinking of her. It's not like he likes her anyway. He told Sally—'

'What?' Miranda said, turning on her. 'What did he tell Sally?'

'Oh, nothing. Just that he was getting tired of hanging around with a first-year.'

Miranda's cheeks burned. Obviously a lie. Listening to Cherise and Amy backstabbing each other to their faces was almost theatrical, but doubts had crept in. Cuttlefur had said they were leaving together today, so it didn't matter what these two airheads said. And it also wouldn't matter if she gave them something to remember her by.

She reached for her magic, aware that using it on another pupil would get her enough cleans to see the end of infinity.

Nothing.

In the upheaval, she had almost forgotten. Now, frustration from the previous day returned with a vengeance, like an angry dog snapping at her heels. She pulled her knees up in front of her and lowered her head.

'Oh, what's the matter?' Cherise said. 'Don't worry, I'm sure Sally was just telling tales. I mean, she also said she saw him around the back of the guesthouse with some girl, and that's got to be a fib, hasn't it? There aren't any other girls here.'

Miranda wanted to scream. Instead, she rolled over on her bed and, grabbing hold of one of her shoes, lifted it over her shoulder, ready to fling it at Cherise.

'You'd better not try that—'

'I can prove he likes me.' Miranda's eyes narrowed. 'He gave me something.'

'What?'

She had caught their interest. Both Amy and Cherise crawled over to the ends of their beds to sit and wait patiently for the revealing of some great secret.

Miranda put down the shoe, reached into her top, and pulled out the ruby, holding it up so the glow caught the light through the window.

'This. He said it matched my hair.'

'Ooh ... pretty.'

'Can I look?'

In seconds, they had gone from savage bullies to gawking fangirls, and Miranda couldn't resist the gnawing craving for acceptance. 'Sure. Just don't get fingermarks on it.'

Amy and Cherise came closer. Amy's head swayed from side to side as if hypnotised, while Cherise pouted, cooing quietly, when she suddenly lunged forward and pushed Miranda back, pinning her shoulders to the bed with her knees.

'Quick, grab it!'

Miranda struggled, but Cherise had pressed all of her weight down onto her shoulders. Amy's fingers closed over the ruby and started to pull, then she screamed and jumped back.

'It's freezing!'

'What are you talking about? Grab it!'

'No!'

Cherise twisted around. One knee slipped off of Miranda's shoulder and Miranda immediately pushed her, swinging her free hand as hard as she could into Cherise's midriff. Cherise ignored the blow and grabbed the ruby, when she, too, screamed and leapt back in shock.

Miranda stood up as the girls backed away across the room.

'That's freaky,' she said. 'What's he given you there, a red piece of ice?'

'What are you talking about?'

Cherise ignored her. 'Come on, Amy, let's get out of here. I'm getting bored of the company.'

They grabbed their day packs and left, Amy slamming the door behind her. Miranda stared after them for a moment, then looked down at the ruby still hanging outside of her shirt. She reached out to touch it, but it wasn't cold, not really. A kind of cold had permeated the room, though, all around. She looked up to see if they had left the window open, but it was closed.

Miranda shrugged. Perhaps cold water pipes ran under their floor? Didn't matter. The ruby showed how much Cuttlefur liked her, no matter what they said. As she closed her fingers over it, though, she wondered why she kept doubting him. He had always supported her. No one else could be trusted. Perhaps the girl Sally had seen him with was his contact, to take them back to England and her new family.

Didn't matter that Benjamin had disappeared. Shame she wouldn't get to say goodbye to either him or Wilhelm, but no matter. Perhaps she would write them a note after breakfast and find someone to give it to them after she had gone.

Yes, that was a good idea. She would write them a letter, thanking them for their friendship.

Miranda smiled and put the ruby back under her shirt. As she turned to get her bag, she shivered, but she wasn't sure why.

All of a sudden, she felt warm again.

38

SECRET DOORWAY

'You can't go back,' Jeremiah said. 'Not through the Source. The best you can do is glimpse aspects of their lives ... and in some cases, haunt them.'

'My brother saw me.'

Jeremiah nodded. 'Some can. My sister was able to see me. My brother and my parents ... nothing. Some are more susceptible than others to what we have become.'

'I was a ghost?'

The old man sighed. 'That would be too simple a way to put it. Time has no meaning here. The Source has both no time and all time. When you step into that water, you return to where you came from, but you are nowhere and everywhere at once.'

'I don't understand.'

'You can't be in any single place or time. That is why you appear as you appear to them—like a shadow, an outline, sometimes a translucent figure. Like a ghost.'

'But I went back?'

'To everywhere and nowhere, to all time and no time. Our primitive human minds are unable to comprehend the enormity of it, which is why we see just short visions. You cannot choose.'

Benjamin rubbed his temples. 'Is this all there is? If there is no way through the Source, how can I go home?'

'You can't. Yet many try. Many refuse to give up. You saw them out there. Did they call to you? They no longer control their own minds, but they so hate to be alone. I have made it my life's work to turn them away, but I am so old now. It becomes harder to discourage them with each passing day.' The old man stood up and stumped a few steps across the cave, then he stopped and turned back. 'Did you see my dragons?' he asked. 'For a while I found peace with them. Are they still beautiful?' A light had come into his eyes, a glimmer of ancient longing.

'They are magnificent,' Benjamin said. 'You did well.'

The old man sighed once more. 'Good, good. How I dream of seeing them again … I was so foolish. If only I had known. Now, it is too late.' He shrugged and sat down, this time on the floor. 'But you don't need to make my choice. You still have time.'

'What happened to you? You disappeared hundreds of years ago. How can you still be here?'

Jeremiah shook his head. 'Like you, I wanted to leave. I wandered to the ends of the world and found only an impenetrable wall of gas and wind. Source Mountain was my best chance. I stood in the water, as you did, and I gave myself over to the visions. I watched for years and years, and saw the lives of my old family. I watched their births and deaths. I saw everything, and the misery of it became too great. I turned away from it, and when I did, I saw the foolishness of my ways. I saw I still had time to help others, to stop them from losing their souls to the Source, as I almost had. I used my last magic to create this place, and from here, I have waited and watched ever since, giving counsel to those, like yourself, who come seeking their old lives, turning them away when I can.'

'Why can't you leave?'

Jeremiah laughed. 'What you see around you, dear Benjamin, is the result of pure magic. What you think of as rock is just life with the life taken away. I draw from it, and it keeps me alive, but if I leave, it will no longer protect me.'

'And you'll die?'

Jeremiah spread his hands and smiled, the look in his eyes almost romantic. 'I'll vanish quicker than a gust of wind.'

'Am I stuck here now, too?'

'No, my dear boy, you are not. The magic is protecting you, but youth is protecting you, as well. You can leave any time you want.'

Benjamin clenched his fists, holding back the urge to cry. 'I've come so far ... I've tried so hard ... I just want to go home.'

Jeremiah's eyes became watery, and he cocked his head, giving Benjamin a long, regretful stare. 'Imagine how much that feeling will have grown five hundred human years from now. Sometimes, there aren't answers, Benjamin, just the quest, and each of us has to find our own way to move forward, our own reason to carry on. Mine is to protect people like you from becoming people like them.' He flapped a hand at the cave roof, and although Benjamin doubted Jeremiah's cave was quite where geology suggested it should be, he understood the gesture. 'Maybe there is a way back. I failed to find it, but that doesn't mean you won't, in time. You're still young. You are a Summoner; you have great power. And you have a whole world building itself in front of you.' He smiled again. 'Endinfinium belongs to you. There's nothing you can't achieve.'

'But I just want to go back to England. I don't want to stay here. Everyone I've met, they all had a past they didn't miss. But my family … I love them so much.'

'Perhaps that's a mystery yet to be solved. Stay strong, Benjamin. You have far more resolve than I ever had.'

Benjamin fell silent as a great weight pressed down on his chest. He had come so far, yet he was no closer to getting any answers. Some questions still nagged at him, though, like a dog tugging on the leg of his trousers, refusing to let go.

'Those people I saw, are they still alive?'

'Some, maybe. Wanderers still appear from time to time. A few every year. Others are long dead.'

'Are they in pain?'

Jeremiah laughed. 'Depends what you call pain. Did you take joy or sadness from seeing your old life?'

'Both.'

'Then that is your answer. Few whose lives were hard come here. They accept their new lives in Endinfinium, building small frontier villages far from here, living in quiet peace. There are always those who crave knowing, though, like you or me.'

'Can we free them?'

Jeremiah shook his head. 'Only by stopping the water, but there is no power in Endinfinium great enough to do that. Do you think they want to be freed? Maybe they have found contentment.'

'It's so sad.'

'Only from your point of view, or mine. Living in an eternal dreamlike state, forever watching those you loved … for some, that is rapture.'

'I want to look again.'

'Are you sure?'

Benjamin took a deep breath. 'You talked about finding a quest, Jeremiah. I need to find mine.'

The ancient man nodded. 'That is your choice.'

'Can you pull me back?'

Jeremiah shook his head. 'I don't have the strength to bring you here twice. The water affects you in a way I can't explain. If I let you go now, the best I can do is try to expel you safely, before the water claims you, not as a prisoner, but as a victim.'

'Then this is goodbye.'

Jeremiah smiled. 'Say hello to the two suns, and to my dragons.'

'And your old friend, Basil.'

Jeremiah's eyes lit up. 'That old fool still lives?'

'In a sense, I suppose.'

Jeremiah's head rocked backwards in a silent laugh. 'Does he really? Those folk of Underfloor really had things figured out. Cajole him into a final flight, if you can, dear Benjamin. Tell him … tell him I found my quest.'

'I will.'

Jeremiah closed his eyes. 'Goodbye, Benjamin Forrest, it was a pleasure to meet you.'

Benjamin looked up. 'How did you know my—'

~

Mum doesn't know where David is. He's supposed to be napping upstairs while she's watching her afternoon TV shows. After waiting for her to settle down with a cup of tea, though, he has sneaked out the back door and has taken his bike from the shed.

He hasn't been out alone since Benjamin disappeared, and since he woke up from the coma after the accident.

Over his shoulder, he has a little backpack with a picture of Spiderman on it. It's too small to be of any great use, but it's big enough for a banana and a small packet of digestive biscuits. He's forgotten to bring any drink, but he doesn't expect to be gone for too long.

He pushes the bike around to the front of the house, ducks down as he wheels it past Mum's parked car, then jumps onto the pedals to get it moving down the driveway's slope to the road. The living room window faces out onto the street, so if Mum stands up at the wrong moment, she'll see him, and while David might think he's moving fast, even Mum could probably outrun his little pedal bike. The other kids at school think he's stupid, but he isn't. He knows how to get away, and he knows which roads to take to get to the forest where the accident happened.

He's so pleased, he talks to himself as he rides, telling himself how happy Benjamin will be when he finds out what he is planning to do.

But Benjamin already knows, because Benjamin is along for the ride with him. If it were all of Benjamin, the bike would surely topple over; however, Benjamin is present in part only. Perhaps soon David will realise. Perhaps not.

He heads for that section of road where the accident happened. He remembers nothing, other than being on his bike one moment, then waking up in hospital an indefinite time later.

The road, curving downhill through the trees and arcing out of sight a short distance further on, looks the same, and David parks his bike up by the side of the road to walk out into the middle.

He sits down. His fingers trace lines in the tarmac. Yes, this is the place.

This is where he found the door.

Over in the trees, something glows orange. It could be the eyes of a cat or a fox, except that it's morning and nothing could reflect back the light. It's one of them, he knows, one of those things that appear to him but not to other people. Mum thinks he's crazy, and the kids at school laugh at him if he says anything about it, but he knows the truth. The orange things aren't from Basingstoke or even from England; they come from somewhere else, though sometimes they find themselves pulled here.

He didn't realise it at first, but it's he, David, who is doing the pulling.

The tarmac begins to fold backwards, neatly rolling up like a carpet being packed away and the roar of gushing water immediately fills the stillness of the forest. Looking over David's shoulder, Benjamin has the sudden urge to push the road back into place.

David leans over, peering into a hole that appears to reveal an underground water culvert that gushes whitewater rushing past so quickly, he can't clearly make out the objects it carries.

'Are you in there, Bennie?' David calls. 'Here. This is for you.' He pulls out a little object from his pocket. It's a toy robot with a silver head and a black body. One arm has broken off and been fixed again with a piece of black duct tape. David leans over toward the river flowing under the rolled-back section of road, then pulls the robot back at the last minute.

'Almost forgot!' His fingers fumble with a catch on the front of the body cavity and it flips open to reveal a little space inside. From out of his pocket David pulls a piece of coloured paper. Benjamin gets a brief glance of the words "I miss you, Bennie" scrawled in blue fluorescent pen before David's chubby fingers fold it down to the size of a thumbnail. He then puts it inside the cavity, and clicks shut the little door.

'Wherever you are, Bennie, keep a watch out for this little guy,' David says, patting the robot on the head. Then, holding the robot up with one hand and waving it goodbye with the other, as if it was a friend leaving a birthday party, he leans forward and drops it into the water.

In a second it is gone, caught in a roll of whitewater and dragged away. David lets out a contented sigh, then leans forward to touch the rolled-up section of road, which folds neatly back into place, leaving neither creak nor bump to suggest it was ever displaced.

The sound of an engine makes David start. He climbs to his feet and drags his bike to the side of the road, just as a vehicle comes roaring around the corner. Benjamin gasps as a large white truck comes rushing past. It roars past, the backdraft around its rear sending a flurry of leaves up into the air. One comes to rest on David's head, and he plucks it off, holds it between his fingers.

Benjamin, still a shadow at his little brother's shoulder, stares as the leaf bends and folds itself into a rough man-shape. It dances a little jig on David's palm before David flicks it away into the air, where it spins and comes to land on the road as just an ordinary little leaf once again.

David climbs back onto his bike and turns it toward home. Benjamin sighs, and finally allows himself to blink—

~

Benjamin knew he was screaming, but water covered every part of his body, so no sound came. While he spun over and over, caught in a tempest of churning violence, arms and legs flailing like the branches of a tree caught in a wild storm, there was no breath in his lungs and no chance for any, as the water battered him from all sides.

This is it, he thought. *This is the end.*

Then, as quickly as it had begun, the ordeal was over. The suffocating press of water gave way to air as he broke through the surface at the top of a gushing fountain.

The euphoria of flying had lasted only a moment before he struck the water's surface, side on. The impact knocked the wind out of him, then the water claimed him again, and he flailed to keep his head above the surface as it cascaded down all around. But as he desperately kicked and flapped his arms, the thundering rain began to subside.

His strength was almost gone. But then, as he briefly slipped under the water and came up coughing, he remembered his magic. Using his remaining strength, Benjamin pulled at the water, urging it to push him forward.

A small wave lifted behind him, and dense patches of water felt like hands holding him up. His mind heaved and his temples throbbed, and cuts opened up on his arms and legs, just as they had done before he had learned how to control it.

He had failed—the magic was out of his control, his strength was gone, and he could swim no longer.

Then, something brushed his shoe. He stretched down and felt solid ground beneath his feet. He released the magic and struggled the last few steps toward the shore, his knees dragging in the shore break.

Benjamin pulled himself up onto a grey, shingle beach and lay gasping with the water lapping at his feet. All around, cliffs of grey stone rose up to form the crater's rim, while the yellow sun hung high above him to the east, signaling morning. Benjamin gazed up at it for a few seconds before exhaustion overtook him.

He closed his eyes, head slumping down into the smooth, grey shingle, which felt more comfortable than any pillow he had ever known.

39

SHENLONG

'Jeremiah Flowers called the Great Dragon Shenlong,' Jim Green was saying as the little skiff chugged out from beneath the shadow of the cliffs. 'It's a name that comes from Chinese mythology. Shenlong was the dragon master of storms and rain. Farmers would do well not to displease him, or he would blast away their crops, but not with fire as dragons usually do in stories, with great floods and torrential rain. It makes sense, don't you think, that the Great Dragon should be a master of water?'

Miranda glanced up at Cuttlefur, who gave her a little wink. Most of the other pupils leaned precariously over the boat's railings, peering down into the water in the hope of catching a glimpse of something huge and majestic.

'Won't he breathe fire, too?' asked Tommy Cale, as the boat topped a little swell then dropped into a short plunge, making several pupils squeal with excitement. 'If he's the master of storms?'

'Yes, but this isn't the real Shenlong,' Jim Green said. 'It's just the name that Jeremiah Flowers gave to the Great Dragon. He might not be able to do any of those things.'

'Then he wouldn't be very great, would he?'

Several pupils laughed. Miranda moved a bit further down the boat, closer to Cuttlefur. The boat had a lower deck, with stairs leading up to a smaller, upper viewing platform, where Cherise and Amy both stood. As Miranda approached, Cuttlefur glanced up and gave a little smile, making her tingle with jealousy, but when she came out from under the shadow of the upper deck and looked to see who he had acknowledged, she saw only Alan Barnacle leaning on a rail above her, his huge body looking capable of breaking right through it, his clothes damp from the spray.

She didn't feel right being out on the water without the teachers. No one had seen Edgar, Ms. Ito, or Professor Eaves since yesterday. Barnacle claimed they were sick, and Jim Green usually agreed with whatever Barnacle said. Cuttlefur told her not to worry, that they would be gone soon anyway. He still refused to tell her how, insisting that secrecy was of great importance. The further they got from the shore, though, and out into the open waters from where the very edge of the world was almost visible, the more she felt like a mouse out in an open field, trying to hide from a circling hawk.

'Has anyone ever seen Shenlong?' Snout asked. 'Like, ever?'

'Many have claimed sightings,' Jim Green said, at which a half-dozen heads leaned over the railing again to peer down into the water. 'But perhaps you're looking in the wrong place. Consider this: if Shenlong is related to the paper dragons of the bay, wouldn't he be at risk from the seawater, the same as them? How might he have countered that threat?'

'Got a swimsuit,' someone said.

'Grew wings!' shouted someone else.

'Ping-pong,' Jim Green said, lifting a hand. 'All supposed sightings of Shenlong have claimed he could fly; that he wasn't like the paper dragons at all, but some giant flying beast.' He paused for emphasis as the pupils gasped and muttered shocked exclamations. Then, with a wide grin, he walked to the railing and pointed at the horizon. 'And there, in the lee of the winds that buffet the edge of the world, is his lair. Behold, Dragon Rock.'

Miranda couldn't stop herself from looking. At first she saw nothing, but then as whoops from the other pupils began, she spotted it.

On the horizon, so close to the edge of the world it gave her knots in her stomach, stood a little black dot.

'Are we going there? Are we going there?' chorused several boys crowding around Jim Green as though waiting for him to start handing out cakes.

Miranda looked at Cuttlefur, but he was staring up at the second level again. She glanced up and saw Barnacle meeting his gaze.

'I'm afraid we can't go all the way there,' Jim Green said. 'It's too close to the edge. The currents are strong, and discovering what's over the edge of the world isn't on today's itinerary.' He grinned again. 'We'll go close enough to get a good look, though.'

More whoops and cheers rose up, and Jim Green led them in a fist pump, then climbed down from the stage and headed back to a refreshments cabinet to get something to drink while several other kids headed for the upper level to get a better look as they approached Dragon Rock. Miranda turned to look for Cuttlefur, who was marching toward the upper deck.

'Hey, wait for me.'

He turned to her, but the look in his eyes was so horrifying, she stopped dead in her tracks. At first it was difficult to pinpoint exactly what had changed, until she realised it was an absence of everything. Instead of looking at her with interest and compassion, he stared right through her as if she didn't exist at all.

Then he shook his head a little, as if waking up. 'What?'

'Wait for me,' she said.

'Oh. Don't worry. I'll be back.'

'Cuttlefur—'

She stared as his feet disappeared onto the top deck. Then she looked around. She was nearly alone on the bottom deck, with only Jim Green sitting on a chair at one end, and Snout sitting on a bench with his hands over his stomach, for company.

'Are we going back soon?' Snout asked Jim Green. 'I think I'm going to be sick.'

Jim Green smiled. 'Hang in there. Let them get their thrill, and we'll be back before you know it.'

'There's no real dragon, is there?'

Jim Green continued to smile. 'Oh, I couldn't tell you something like that. Let's just say that no one's ever seen it. Sometimes, the most exciting things are those in your imagination, aren't they?'

'I don't have an imagination,' Snout mumbled.

'Hey,' Jim Green said, turning to Miranda, 'why don't you go up and join your friends? You might not see any dragons, but there are some cool sea birds, and the edge of the world looks pretty spectacular from here.'

'I'm cold,' Snout said.

'We're on a boat,' Jim Green answered.

'No, I'm really cold. I think I'm getting sick.'

Miranda frowned. Snout was right. It was cold—really cold. And it had become cold really quickly, as though, in the last few minutes, a switch had flicked to turn spring into winter. She closed her eyes, and there it was, like a bank of fog rushing in from the sea.

Dark reanimate.

Miranda stood up. 'We have to turn back. Something bad's about to happen—'

The boat lurched, throwing all three of them sideways. Jim Green dropped his bottle of drink, and it smashed on the floor. From above came the excited screams of the other pupils, as if this were the beginning of a theme park thrill ride.

'Turn the boat around!' Miranda yelled.

As if it had heard her, the boat began to bank sharply to the right, its back end swinging out, and a groan came from the motor below her feet, followed by a sharp snap. The engine gave one last wheeze, then went still.

The calm left by the suddenly absent engine noise was quickly filled by the pupils' screaming as several came running down the steps. Then, realising that the boat's lower deck was no closer to an escape than the top, they ran back up again.

'It would be a good idea for all of you to sit down,' a voice boomed over a loud speaker. 'You wanted to see Dragon Rock, didn't you? Now's your chance.'

Still unsure that this wasn't part of the ride, several pupils cheered. Only when the boat listed sharply and a wave broke over the side did they fall quiet.

'Everyone downstairs.'

Pupils crowded back down the steps to fill the lower deck, and Miranda pushed her way forward, looking for Cuttlefur, but found the way blocked by Alan Barnacle.

'I told you to sit down.'

With a loud *thwack*, twenty bums hit seats, and Miranda scowled at Barnacle. The chill of his magic emanated from him like the cold water from an old well.

Miranda tried to call on her own, but just as before, nothing happened.

'What on earth's going on here?' Jim Green said, standing up. 'Alan, what's gotten into you?'

'Oh, be quiet, you garrulous fool,' Barnacle said, and he flapped a hand at Jim Green, who fell against the railings alongside the boat. A couple of pupils grabbed for his hands, but it was too late as he toppled over the side, into the water.

A couple of girls screamed. Miranda twisted her head, caught a glimpse of Jim Green lifting up on the rise of a swell off the port side, then he dipped over the top and was lost from sight. A long, mournful cry was the last she heard from him.

'Barnacle!'

'Take us back to shore!' demanded Cherise, trying to stand but finding herself stuck. 'I'll see that Ms. Ito chops off your head for this!'

'Oh, be quiet, you idiot. Ms. Ito won't be finding out anything, because you'll all be going over the edge in a couple of hours. Not much coming back from that, is there?'

A couple of the smaller kids began to cry.

'Where's Cuttlefur?' Amy said. 'He's not here.'

Several kids began to shout for him, and despite what Miranda had seen in his eyes, she began to wonder if it wasn't all part of his plan to get them out of this. She'd caught him looking at Alan Barnacle, after all. Perhaps he had picked up on the fat innkeeper's plan before the rest of them and was working on some form of escape.

Then, steps on the metal stairway made everyone fell silent. Cuttlefur appeared, face lit with an evil grin. The boat had spun around again so that the back end now faced Dragon Rock and was caught in the sunlight.

Cuttlefur strolled to the end of the boat and propped one foot up onto the inside railing, like an ancient seafarer finally about to come home. He chuckled, then turned back to them, the sun glinting through his hair.

Miranda gasped. The vibrant aquamarine blue was gone, replaced by chestnut brown. He brushed it out of his face and cocked his head.

'Oh, sorry, didn't you know?'

'You lied to me.'

'Did I really? Sorry.'

'You're a pig! You're not from England. You can't take me back, and there's no family waiting for me. You lied!'

Cuttlefur shook his head. 'Oh, dear. Two out of three isn't bad. No, there's no family; I made that up, got hold of some photographs in the library. Found some old picture album that had washed down that stupid river. Fooled you, though.' He flashed a smile. 'However, I am from England—at least, I was once, before I found a much better place to be—and I am taking you home, but not to the home you were expecting.'

He raised his arms above his head, and the boat heaved beneath a great gust of wind, lurching sideways and knocking several pupils off their feet. Miranda grabbed hold of a railing to steady herself, again hunting inside herself for her magic. Nothing. She glanced at the others. A slight warmth rose up from some of them, though none had learned enough about the magic to be able to use it.

She alone had the means to protect them, and she could do nothing.

'Let us go!' someone screamed.

'Oh, you'll be let go, all right,' Barnacle said. 'You'll be let go right over the edge of the world. Once *he* gets what he wants of, course.' The fat innkeeper turned to Cuttlefur. 'Hurry up! I don't want to go over with them!'

Cuttlefur grinned, and Miranda saw hate and madness in his eyes. 'Goodbye, Miranda,' he said. 'It's time to make good on my promise.'

At first she didn't know what he meant, until a scream rose up from some of the pupils nearest the side of the boat. She looked across the water at the black lump of Dragon Rock, close enough now she could make out the jagged cliffs rising out of the water, and a swamping terror like a thick, black cape filled her heart.

The whole top of the island was lifting up—a great, black sheet rising into the sky. Miranda had the bizarre feeling that the world was turning upside down, when wings and a head separated from the black mess, and she saw the massive creature for what it was.

'Shenlong,' whispered Snout from beside her.

Miranda stared at the gigantic black dragon as he flapped his great wings powerfully enough to cause a wind to buffet their faces, then she did what many of the other pupils had already begun to do.

She screamed.

40

REUNION

Wilhelm cried out as the jagged rock edge cut through his trousers and into skin, deep enough to draw blood. Weariness had made him clumsy, and his forearms and palms were spotted with blood from several other cuts and scrapes. With a sigh, he peered up at the summit of Source Mountain, wondering how much further he had to go.

Lawrence had left him at the foot of the mountain, and Wilhelm didn't want to look back down at the valley, but he couldn't resist. As the yellow sun rose over the forests to the west, he tried not to trace Lawrence's path of retreat, leaving Wilhelm to make the climb alone.

After another half an hour, he sat down for a rest, picking a flat stone with a view of the cliffs that marked the Bay of Paper Dragons. He couldn't see the guesthouse from here, but the encircling twin headlands protruded into the sea like the pincers on a crab hiding under the earth. Behind it, the red sun made its circumnavigation of the horizon, and the edge of the world was a smudged pencil line unnaturally close to the shore.

His natural curiosity made him wonder what was over

there. If you went right to the edge, did you just look down into space, or was something else down there, like a secret world? The teachers, as usual, wouldn't talk about it, which only made it worse. For a long time he had thought they were hiding something. Now, he knew better. They didn't know. They had just gotten old and had lost their desire to care.

As he watched, a fog bank that had covered the yellow sun broke apart. Light spread out across the water, yet something lumpy not far from the edge glinted black.

Wilhelm frowned. It looked like an island, though he didn't remember seeing it before. It was definitely there now—a black lump sitting in the water about three-quarters of the way out to the horizon.

He shivered. Resting too long had made the sweat on his back go cold. He pushed himself to his feet, but before he turned back to the rocky slope, he took one last look at the black island out on the sea.

Something definitely wasn't right about it.

∾

By midmorning, Wilhelm had finally crawled, battered and bruised, over the edge of the crater and found himself looking at a grey moonscape with a lake in the middle. No vegetation grew here, except for a few wind-battered bushes, but at least the huge waterfall gushing over the edge just a few paces to his right offered something to drink.

He crawled to the edge and scooped up cold handfuls of the water. It hurt as he gulped it down, but once it was nestled in his belly, he began to feel better.

Then he stood up and looked around. The waterfall was fed by a river flowing out of the crater lake, where in its centre bubbled a whitewater fountain. Random objects floated around, bouncing on its swell. As he watched, a fridge-freezer, followed by a handful of books, drifted past to the waterfall on the crater's rim, where they paused for a moment, then dropped out of sight, beginning their journey down the spiral of Source Mountain to the flatlands far below.

There was no sign of Benjamin, so Wilhelm started walking in the direction of the river gully and the lake beyond, wishing he had more of a plan.

A man named Jeremiah Flowers had come here looking for a way back to England, yet all Wilhelm saw was a grey landscape of volcanic rock. Besides the lake and the river, nothing moved, nothing was alive, nothing was—

Far across the lake, a tiny figure appeared from between two large rocks of the bland moonscape, following a path, climbing over one boulder, then going around the outside of the next. He was heading for the crater rim on the far side of the lake, the side that faced the coast.

'Benjamin!' Wilhelm screamed. 'Wait!'

At first, Wilhelm was sure Benjamin hadn't heard him. After all, he had the continual splashing of the bubbling fountain to contend with. He screamed Benjamin's name again, and this time Benjamin half turned, though he didn't look back.

Wilhelm's voice was already hoarse from the arduous climb, and Benjamin was getting further and further away. Wilhelm had two options. Swim across the lake, or run around the side.

Neither was particularly appealing. Wilhelm swore under his breath and headed for the shore.

∽

There was not a lot to do other than to head back to the Bay of Paper Dragons and do his best to enjoy himself. Benjamin knew he could stay and wander around, picking up rocks like some self-chastising monk, but it wouldn't solve anything. If he had found out about Source Mountain from it, perhaps more information could be had in the library. When he got back to the school, he would head straight there to see what he could find.

He sighed. He felt like a failure, and he worried both about getting in trouble with the teachers and with having to face his friends. Miranda liked to hold a grudge anyway, but she also seemed to have given up on everyone else in favour of Cuttlefur. And how would Wilhelm react, when he found out what had happened? Benjamin had tried to abandon them all. Wouldn't they feel like second best? He would end up shunned by everyone. Perhaps even Snout would refuse to hang out with him.

He picked up a rock, turning in one motion to heave it into the lake.

'*No!*'

Benjamin stared, arm raised, poised to throw. Someone was swimming across the lake, flapping their arms wildly as the current tugged them toward the mouth of the river. As the arms flailed and the person briefly bobbed up out of the water and waved, Benjamin's eyes widened.

'You've got to be joking….'

'Benjamin!'

'Wilhelm!'

He broke for the shoreline as fast as he could, heedless of the shifting rocks underfoot threatening to trip or injure him. He reached the water's edge and dived in before he could even think about using his magic, wading out as deep as he could, then swimming the last few feet to grab hold of Wilhelm's arms.

'Didn't you hear me shout?' Wilhelm gasped. 'You ignoring me or something?'

Benjamin laughed. Water splashed into his throat, and he started to cough. Wilhelm clapped him on the back as they helped each other onto the shore, and before Wilhelm could even find his feet, Benjamin grabbed him in a fierce hug.

'I'll never ignore you again,' he said. 'What on earth are you doing here?'

'Collecting rocks for Dusty. Not. Came to find you, didn't I? What do you think?'

'Why?'

'To stop you from being an idiot. And because you're in trouble. You and Miranda both.'

'What kind of trouble?'

'That shifty so-and-so, Cuttlefur. He's plotting to kidnap her in order to set a trap for you.'

'Cuttlefur? That blue-haired punk?'

'Yeah, not working on his own, is he? I'd put money on that he's working for the Dark Man.'

'The Dark Man?'

'Yeah. Come on, we don't have much time. Today's the day.'

As they hurried up the slope to the crater's edge on the seaward side, Benjamin kept glancing at Wilhelm as if refusing to believe he was really here.

'How did you get up here?'

'Same way you did. I walked. I tried to get Lawrence to help me, but he won't come near the place.'

Benjamin looked down. 'I don't blame him. I wish I'd never come here, either.'

'What did you find?'

Benjamin sighed. 'A graveyard of dreams.'

'So no sign of Jeremiah Flowers or where he went?'

Benjamin opened his mouth to tell Wilhelm what he had seen ... then closed it again. Didn't matter. Jeremiah had chosen his quest, and now Benjamin had to choose his.

'Tell me what you know about Cuttlefur.'

Wilhelm scowled. 'I don't even want to think about him, only about what I'm going to do to him when I catch him, if no one else gets there first.'

They reached the crater's edge and paused. Below, the grey rock sloped down to the first twist in the river's spiral. Benjamin was still staring down the slope, wondering if the journey down would be easier than coming up, when Wilhelm grabbed hold of his arm.

'Benjamin, look!'

This high up, the views stretched right to the edge of the world, and there, on the horizon, something black and terrible had risen up into the sky.

41

ATTACK

The pupils screamed. With a screeching roar, Shenlong flapped his massive wings and rose high over the boat. Miranda gripped the railings behind her, so terrified she could barely breathe. Beside her, Snout repeated a desperate mantra: 'Close your eyes, don't let it in … close your eyes, don't let it in…'

The great dragon was the length of a swimming pool, and he was shaped like the dragons from fairy tales: pointed, fang-filled jaws in a triangular head at the top of a long, curved neck, with an elongated, almost snakelike body. Two wings the size of a yacht's sails rose from his back, and four powerful legs ended in vicious claws.

'Who's first?' screamed Barnacle. 'Shenlong's hungry!'

A hail of screams rose up from the boat. Only Cuttlefur and Alan Barnacle were laughing now, with the others in various stages of distress, from casual, are-you-sure-this-isn't-part-of-the-trip disbelief, to outright hysterical terror. Despite everything, part of Miranda was secretly happy to see Cherise retching over the railing while Amy, practically hyperventilating, picked pieces of vomit out of her friend's hair.

'You fat pig!' Miranda glared at Barnacle. 'The only one who could fill him up is you.'

'I always admired your mouth,' Barnacle spat back. 'Luckily we don't have to put up with it much longer.'

With a scream, Tommy Cale darted forward to pummel Barnacle's stomach with his little fists. The fat man wobbled, then scowled, and Tommy bounced back against the side of the boat, held fast. Miranda closed her eyes, sensing the ebb and flow of the magic. Barnacle was a powerful Summoner, though inexperienced—while attacking one pupil, he would lose his grip on another. Cuttlefur, on the other hand, was a Channeller like her, able to use the magic, but only in small amounts. Between them, it didn't seem likely they could have created a dragon out of nothing.

Which meant they had to be working for someone else.

The Dark Man.

Miranda started to get up, determined to at least slap Barnacle before Shenlong ate her, but a hand closed over her wrist. As the boat lurched, throwing them all off balance, she looked up to see Snout staring at her.

'That's Godfrey,' he hissed. 'I don't know how it is, but it is.'

'What?'

'I think he's working for the Dark Man.'

Miranda rolled her eyes. 'You *think*? Why didn't you tell anyone?'

'I did. I told the teachers. They went to have a word with him, but they never came back.'

'And you said nothing to anyone else?'

'Who was I supposed to tell?'

Miranda held her breath until her anger subsided. 'I don't know … someone!'

Before Snout could answer, Shenlong roared and dived at the boat. His huge jaws closed over the gunwale of the upper deck, and he dragged the boat back and forth. A couple of pupils fell over the side. As they screamed and flailed in the water, others took off their shirts to create makeshift ropes to pull them back.

Barnacle had been thrown into the bowl of the lower deck, and Miranda dived at him, only for his arms to encircle her, holding her tight. A chill ran through her body as his magic trapped her.

'Well, what happened to you?' he whispered.

She snarled and kicked out hard, catching his ankle. He howled, his magic hold releasing. She darted away as the boat shook again, and she turned to the upper stairs, only to see Cuttlefur blocking her way.

'Hold still,' he said.

Chilling magic reached out, and the stairs' railings became as flexible as snakes, wrapping around her wrists. She tried to pull away, but the magic abruptly died and the railings went cold, changing into hard, immovable metal handcuffs. As Shenlong roared and shook the boat again, Miranda screamed as they bumped against her wrists.

'Tell him to get off the boat,' Barnacle shouted. 'He'll tear it apart.'

Cuttlefur headed up the stairs. Miranda felt another chill of magic, then the dragon roared and flew up again into the sky.

'We need to leave here,' Cuttlefur said, coming back down. 'He'll take the whole boat. The Master wants her alive, but Shenlong will eat her if he gets half a chance. Get the rest of them into the dinghy.'

With pupils in various stages of hysteria, Cuttlefur and

Barnacle pulled an inflatable boat from a compartment in the stern and, with a rope, secured it to the gunwale railing. Then Barnacle pulled a cord, and it inflated alongside.

'If you don't want to end up as dragon food, get in the boat,' Barnacle shouted.

Pupils immediately hurried to clamber over the side. As Snout passed her, Miranda hissed at him. 'Snout! You know what you can do, don't you?'

Snout shrugged, rolling his eyes. 'I don't know what you're talking about.'

'Yes, you do. Wilhelm told you, remember! Call one! Call a ghoul to fight it! Hurry!'

'Ms. Ito told me to forget about all that rubbish,' Snout said. 'There's no such thing as magic—'

The boat lurched again as Shenlong made another attack, this time, using his huge hind legs, and the metal railings screeched as they buckled under the weight. The boat rose out of the water, only for a blast of air as cold as an Arctic wind to cut through Miranda's clothes right to her bones.

'Get back!' Cuttlefur shouted from the upper deck. 'We're not ready!'

As the last of the pupils jumped into the dinghy, Miranda looked up at the dragon through a rent in the deck above, studying Shenlong closely for the first time. Luckily, he hadn't decided to incinerate them with fire, and now she understood why.

Shenlong wasn't a true dragon at all. He had been created and shaped from hundreds of thousands of brown paper bags all bound together by reanimation magic, like a giant model kit, moulded and shaped into something fearsome. He wasn't even black, but more of a wet-earth brown, like peat or compost. He really was the king of the

Paper Dragons, and Miranda knew what would destroy him far quicker than water.

Fire.

As she struggled against her bonds, soaked to the skin by sloshing waves, she only wished she knew where to find some fire in the middle of a churning sea.

42

WATER RIDE

'Benjamin, we have to help them!'

Only one glass worked in the broken pair of binoculars Wilhelm had plucked from the water, but it was enough. With the binoculars, they could just make out the little boat toiling in the water not far from the island close to the edge of the world.

They didn't need any help to see the dragon as it rose and fell in great swoops, first its teeth and then its claws taking hold of the little boat. And while they couldn't make out any people, they didn't need to know who was on the vessel.

The rest of the pupils.

Benjamin stared helplessly. They were miles away from the coast. It would take hours to get down the mountain and back to the bay. But even if they did, how would they ever get out to the boat? It was useless. All they could do was watch.

'Think of something!' Wilhelm shouted. 'Can't you use your magic?'

'To do what?'

'Like, fly or something?'

'We can't just fly! I don't have that kind of magic. I can only push and pull things.'

'Well, can you give us a push if we can find a boat?'

'Where from?'

Wilhelm grabbed Benjamin's hand and spun him around. 'There's our ride,' he said, grinning, lifting a finger to point back down from the crater rim to the lake below.

Benjamin gasped. 'You can't be serious….'

A battered wooden table floated across the lake, its three remaining legs poking up like periscopes. One corner was under water as it turned in a slow circle, drifting toward the waterfall at the edge of the crater.

'Come on,' Wilhelm said. 'That tributary goes right down to the bay, doesn't it? It's worth a try.'

Benjamin's heart pounded at the very thought of it. 'Yes, I think it does,' he said, his throat dry.

Wilhelm was already running down the slope, skipping over the uneven ground as agile as a mountain goat. 'You can control it with your magic, right?' he shouted back as Benjamin gave chase. Benjamin wasn't sure if he even could; the trip into the source had left him empty and exhausted, and though he could feel his magic slowly returning, it would take time to recover.

Benjamin reached the water's edge just as Wilhelm waded back to the shore, with the old table dragging through the water behind him. Not only was one leg missing, but there was also a massive crack down the middle that could split it into two at any time.

Too late. Wilhelm was climbing on, gripping one of the legs, his lower body still in the water. 'You coming?' He grinned at Benjamin as he pushed it back away from the shore.

Benjamin took a deep breath. Was death the quickest

way out of Endinfinium? If so, he might be about to find out.

'Let's go,' he said, his voice sounding strangely high-pitched as he climbed on beside Wilhelm.

Together they kicked off the bottom, pushing the old table toward the mouth of the river. Within a couple of minutes, the current caught it, and they found it drifting of its own accord, slowly picking up speed.

'Right,' Wilhelm said, as the roar of the waterfall over the crater rim grew louder and louder, 'let's get this sorted out. I think we might be about to die, and if we are, I want to die as brothers. You got that?'

'Brothers?'

'Okay, not actual brothers, but you're my best mate. Here, there, everywhere. If we're going to die, I want you to know that. I'm sorry for being a dick, even if you sometimes deserved it. We're in this together.'

Benjamin let go of the table leg and draped his arm around Wilhelm's shoulders. 'I'm so sorry,' he said, struggling to keep the tears out of his eyes. 'I got blinded. I just wanted to go home so bad. I was such a rubbish mate, wasn't I?'

'Mates are allowed to make mistakes,' Wilhelm said. 'We've both made them, which makes us even. Now we have to save Miranda so we can say sorry to her.'

'It's a deal,' Benjamin said. 'Once we sort out that Cuttlefur twit first.'

Wilhelm grimaced. 'I knew he was trouble. I just knew it.'

'And I just wish I'd believed you.'

'Mates?'

Benjamin grinned. 'Forever.'

'Hopefully that's longer than the next couple of minutes. Here we go!'

In front of them, the waterfall roared, and Benjamin gritted his teeth, holding on as the old table began to buck and twist, bumping over rocks beneath them. He wasn't sure if he wanted to see them go over, but right as the lip of the falls approached, the table twisted around, facing them forward, and for a moment, all that was below them was empty sky.

'Hold my hand, Benjamin.'

'I can't, I'm trying not to slip off!'

'Just take it!'

'I can't.'

'Yes, you can.'

'Okay, now what?'

'Kick!'

'No!'

'Yes!'

'Oh … my … *ahhhh!*'

The old table tipped forward, dropping into a roaring maelstrom of whitewater. Both boys were screaming, but Benjamin could barely hear Wilhelm over the din. He waited for the impact with the ground, but it never came. Instead, they hit a slope, paused for a couple of seconds, then burst out into fast-moving rapids.

Wilhelm screamed with delight, and Benjamin wished he shared the wild excitement in Wilhelm's voice. The water churned and frothed as it threw them at a rock wall on the first corner of the spiral, only to drag them around into the next straight like an overweight bobsleigh car fighting not to fly off the track. For a couple of seconds, they crested the outer lip, rock scraping along the table's bottom, then the water threw them forward and down the next slope.

This one was even sharper than the last. As they hit it, Wilhelm screamed to lean left, and Benjamin, on that side, threw himself sideways into the churning water to stop them from overbalancing. As they came out of the turn and bumped past an old car floating end-down in the water, the only thing louder than the wild river was Wilhelm's hysterical laughter.

'I knew it!' he shrieked. 'The ride to end all rides!'

At the next turn, Benjamin lost the lunch he didn't remember eating, but the water washed his clothes clean. His stomach felt upside down, his head inside out. Then, at long last, after what felt like days, but was probably only a few seconds, they spun around the widest corner yet onto a straight cascade of frothing white water bulging with random objects emptying into a wide river channel to begin its languid flow south.

'Sharp left!' Wilhelm shouted. 'Man the oars!'

Benjamin had no idea what oars Wilhelm referred to, but suddenly the smaller boy dived sideways. Benjamin had no choice but to roll with him, upside down in the water, hanging on to a single table leg. For a moment his mouth filled with water, then he broke the surface to find Wilhelm bobbing next to him.

'Easier to steer this way up,' Wilhelm gasped, wiping a wet piece of newspaper off of his face. 'Quick, kick left.'

The tributary that led to the Bay of Paper Dragons began as a soggy marshland on the flats alongside the main river with its own outlet as the land sloped away to the east. The main river channel, angling into a valley heading south, quickly narrowed, the water picking up speed. Benjamin kicked out as hard as he could, but the current was too strong.

'Kick harder, Benjamin,' Wilhelm gasped. 'It's a long walk if we overshoot that tributary.'

Exhausted, Benjamin tried again to kick, but he had no strength left.

'I can't.'

'Use your magic, then.'

Benjamin frowned, closed his eyes, and pulled, concentrating as Grand Lord Bastien had taught him, trying to draw power out of the objects around him. He felt a slight ache in the back of his hand from the old scar, but none of the sharp sensations of his skin breaking. He gritted his teeth, trying to jerk on the magic, a sensation like a balloon expanding in his hands.

Wilhelm let out a scream as the table cut a sharp left through the water as though dragged by a shark. Water barreled up and over them, then the riverbed was under their feet, and hard sand scratched at their arms and legs as they came out of the water. The table rolled over a grassy hillock, only to plummet down a short slope and splash into a marshy puddle of water. Grass whipped at their legs before they picked up speed toward the tributary channel. As they climbed, gasping, up onto the underside of the table again, Wilhelm glared at Benjamin.

'What happened there?'

'I used my magic. I only touched it, though. It just went crazy.'

Wilhelm held up a hand. 'I was holding your shoulder. I suppose Weavers don't have to be asked. Useful for future reference.'

'Put your hand back on my shoulder,' Benjamin said. 'Let's see if we can speed up this journey a little.'

'Got it.'

Wilhelm grabbed hold of Benjamin's sleeve, and Benjamin ignored the growing ache in his hand as he pulled on the magic, and they bounced across water like a skimming stone leaping back and forth from the top of ripples. Not quite the thrill of the descent from Source Mountain, but it had a certain peaceful charm. With the ability to steer around objects floating in their way, Benjamin preferred it much more.

Soon, drained by dozens of little streams, the tributary lost its forward motion and began to stagnate, until they were steering through thick, swampy water filled with vegetation.

Finally, with Benjamin's strength at its end, the table split in two with a large crack, and they stood in waist-deep water, surrounded by multi-coloured reeds and a few shrubs that looked half natural, half plastic.

Wilhelm gave the table a pat of thanks, then helped Benjamin out of the water and onto the bank. A path ran alongside, one Benjamin recognised from his trek to the mountain.

'What do we do now?' Wilhelm asked.

Benjamin leaned on his knees and took a deep breath, then he looked up at Wilhelm and smiled. 'We run,' he said.

43

OVERBOARD

Godfrey, masquerading as Alan Barnacle, had found a rope in a life-rescue box, and the pupils now sat bound together at the bottom of the dinghy, with Cuttlefur sitting at a little outboard motor as it buzzed toward Dragon Rock. Behind them, Shenlong wheeled and dived at the boat they had just abandoned, knocking it sideways, then picking it up out of the water a short distance before letting it drop back down. It was playing with it, Snout realised, like a cat toying with a mouse. Sooner or later, it would tire of its game and eat it, sink it, or carry it off. But all the while, poor Miranda was stuck on the lower deck like a maiden put out for sacrifice.

Snout liked Miranda. Among the boys, he was sure all of them liked her, despite her personality having a certain … spikiness. Even if he hadn't liked her, he still wouldn't have wanted to see her end up as dragon food, and when she asked him to do something, he was a lot more inclined to do it than when he was asked by someone else.

Didn't make any sense, though. Sure, one time, a creature had appeared after he had thought about it for too long, but that was a once-off. He'd not been able to make it happen again. Blind luck. Things weren't quite the same here in Endinfinium as they were back home, but you still couldn't command monsters like some devilish Dr. Doolittle. It just wasn't possible. Might look like magic, but the teachers insisted it was all a special kind of science, despite what some others whispered about Benjamin Forrest. But since Miranda had asked, and he couldn't exactly run to help her, it wouldn't hurt to imagine something awesomely brilliant coming up out of the sea to fight that dragon. Some kind of sea monster, perhaps, like a kraken or a giant squid or a … or a…

A submarine?

The water's surface was changing colour from a deep aquamarine blue to green and then finally to orange. Snout wanted to close his eyes, but he was too terrified. What if the creature he had unleashed ate their dinghy before he even got a chance to see it? The surface bulged, then exploded with spray as something huge and cylindrical burst out of the water. It revolved for a few seconds as though getting its bearings, then rushed off towards the boat, where it's massive tooth-filled jaws began snapping at Shenlong's feet. The pupils screamed both in terror and excitement as the dragon shrieked and wheeled up into the air, its wings going wide to steady it. Then, with its neck straining as it snarled in response, it dived in to attack.

Claws met teeth, and for a few seconds, the giant orange submarine monster was hauled up out of the water. Tentacles where its stern would have been spread wide, raking at the ocean's surface, while fins the size of buses flapped in response to Shenlong's wings.

The dragon, rattled by the attack, spun out of the submarine's jaws, and the sea beast crashed back into the water, dived under, then blasted back out for another attack.

This time, Shenlong was waiting, and as the submarine beast opened its jaws, the great dragon ducked sideways. Teeth snapped closed over thin air, and the submarine beast crashed back into the water. Again it dived, but when it reappeared this time, it just nosed above the surface, watching the circling dragon. The pupils in the dinghy hollered at it, urging it to continue its attack, but the battle appeared to have reached a stalemate.

Then, like a missile emplacement swinging round to find a fresh target, the submarine beast turned to the dinghy racing away across the surface of the water.

Snout gulped. 'Down, down,' he whispered, 'go back down. Please go back down.'

If it heard him, the submarine paid no attention, and a wake of whitewater spread out around its nose as it motored in pursuit.

∽

'Cuttlefur! Stop that thing!'

The formerly blue-haired boy turned to glare at Barnacle. 'You think I had anything to do with that?'

'Where'd it come from? Did you see what it did? If Shenlong doesn't take the girl, we're done for.'

'Yeah, I saw. This boat's going as fast as it can go, though. See if you can speed it up a bit. Use the stuff if you have to.'

'He'll know if I do.'

'Well, maybe he'll be able to help us.'

Cuttlefur turned to the pupils tied up in the bottom of the dinghy. They weren't supposed to know about their magic, but one of them had used it, and his inner senses searched for the tingles of heat as the Dark Man had taught him.

There. That boy. The rather plain one everyone called Snout. Cuttlefur could see why—with that bit of an upturned nose and an appetite like a pig.

The Dark Man commanded the ghouls, but the Dark Man was currently hundreds of miles away. Perhaps the pig boy would make a decent snack for this new threat.

He wasn't subtle. Whatever lies the teachers had told the pupils about the nonexistence of reanimation magic, it was up to them to answer this one. He glared at the group of boys trussed up with Snout and commanded their rope to reanimate.

They gasped as it became a shifting, twisting snake, and Cuttlefur commanded it to unwrap itself, allow Snout to go free, then tie up the others again. When Snout was standing aside in the bottom of the dinghy, looking as awkward as a kid who had pooped himself in class, Cuttlefur deanimated the rope.

'Walk the plank, fool,' he snapped at Snout, who stared at him blankly. 'Oh, you need some help?'

Cuttlefur called on the air to push and pull, and Snout jerked toward the side of the dinghy with eyes filled with horror. Cuttlefur glanced back at the rising prow of the ghoul sliding through the water toward them, an orange glow just under the surface. They couldn't stay ahead of it for long.

'Over you go.'

'Godfrey!'

'Huh?' Cuttlefur turned back. Snout was looking at Barnacle, crouched near the front as though to balance the weight.

'Godfrey! I know that's you. I heard your voice. We're

mates, don't you remember? I never let you down, Godfrey.'

'Shut up!' Barnacle shouted, though the tone of his voice was different, as if he'd let a guise unwittingly slip. Several other pupils turned to him, murmurs of suspicion on their lips.

'Don't let him hurt me, Godfrey!'

Cuttlefur scowled. 'Enough of this.' And Snout pitched forward into the water. Barnacle/Godfrey started to stand up, but Cuttlefur glared at him. 'Stay right there,' he said.

Barnacle looked about to say something, but he instead closed his eyes. Cuttlefur wondered what the fat fool was doing, until he felt it: a wave of cold like a sudden chill wind.

Godfrey was summoning.

'What are you *doing*?'

Godfrey looked up as though he hadn't realised Cuttlefur could know, the sign of an inexperienced user.

Dragon Rock was coming up on their left, and Cuttlefur glanced at the nearest bay, scanning for the speedboat they had hidden the day before, one that would whisk them up the coast to where the Dark Man's people would pick them up.

Seemed he would have to complete the last leg of the journey alone.

Looking down at the outboard motor, Cuttlefur drew on the water to work like a turbine around the engine, speeding it up. Then he fixed the direction for the edge of world. As a final act of destruction, he cast a wall of protection around the boat so no more magic could escape.

Then, with a smile, he jumped over the side.

The little boat sped on, taking Godfrey and the rest of the pupils with it, straight for the edge of the world. He closed his eyes, feeling Godfrey trying to use his magic to turn the boat around. But it was too late. He was trapped.

'Enjoy the view from the edge,' Cuttlefur muttered darkly, then he began swimming as fast as he could for Dragon Rock.

44

BATTLE CHARGE

'Fallenwood!' Wilhelm screamed. 'Fallenwood! Where are you?'

Benjamin joined in, but no sound came from the undergrowth.

'I left them right here,' Wilhelm said. 'If they could make us a boat or something, perhaps we might have a chance.'

Benjamin laid a hand onto Wilhelm's shoulder. 'We have to go,' he said. 'Come on. We'll think of something.'

Wilhelm shook his head. 'You saw it, didn't you? There's no way we can stop something like that.'

Benjamin's first instinct was to agree, but he refused. He had seen the dragon, too, though admitting defeat was like saying goodbye to Miranda. He wouldn't do it until he'd tried everything to rescue her.

'Come on,' he said. 'This isn't over yet.'

Her luck wouldn't hold for long. As Shenlong prepared for

another pass, his huge wings beating at the sky as if trying to tear through it, he looked angrier than ever that she had found a way to defy him. Only the narrowness of the staircase had kept his jaws from tearing her apart.

The anchor. The old boat had a manual anchor crank set into the port side of the boat, not far from the stern. Stretching out to a point where she was sure her shoulder would pop out of its socket, Miranda could just reach to kick out the lever, releasing it.

Shenlong, briefly distracted by the giant ghoul submarine, hadn't heard the chain reeling out, so now, whenever he tried to lift the boat out of the water, it jerked him back down, incensing him even more. Eventually it would slip loose of whatever rock or ledge it had caught on, but at least it had bought her some time.

The air above her had gone quiet, and Miranda peeked out from the railing. No sign of Shenlong. To the right floated the dinghy in the distance, a black speck moving to the right of Dragon Rock. She could no longer make out the people inside, but it was now angling away from the island and toward the edge of the world.

What would happen if they went over the edge?

She growled in frustration, butting her shoulder against the railing, wishing there was some way she could free herself and help them.

∽

Benjamin was breathing too hard to speak, so he flapped a hand toward the beach, at the paper dragons swimming languidly around in the water.

'You're not serious?' Wilhelm said.

'Yes,' Benjamin gasped. 'Come on.'

They ran down to the shore. Benjamin wrapped an

arm around Wilhelm's shoulders and told him to concentrate. Together they closed their eyes, and Benjamin pulled on the surrounding ground, feeling the life collect inside him. Then he projected it outwards into the water.

When he opened his eyes, two of the largest paper dragons were lying in the shallows in front of them, their colourful heads bobbing up and down in anticipation.

'They remind me of dogs,' Wilhelm said.

'And they're going to be our horses,' Benjamin answered. 'Come on.'

He didn't wait. He waded out into the water, right up to the nearest of the dragons, one far larger than that which had almost eaten Fat Adam for breakfast.

'Can you take me out there?' he asked. 'Can you take me out to the island?'

The huge head continued to bob.

'Don't eat me.'

Bob, bob.

'Okay, I'm getting on now.'

Bob.

He swung a leg up over its neck and climbed up, leaning forward so that his chest pressed against the back of its head. Then he patted it on the side.

'Ready to go—!'

The paper dragon ducked into the water and swam in a fast circle, its long tail beating back and forth. Benjamin grabbed hold of its soft, papier-mâché skin, then turned to look back at Wilhelm, who had just climbed up onto the other dragon.

'Hang on!' he shouted. 'I get the feeling that the river wasn't the only ride we're going to endure today.'

A squeal of delight was Wilhelm's reply, his paper dragon taking a scenic route round a few outcrops that made a rough racing course. Benjamin grimaced as his own headed for the thin gap between the headlands, wishing the dragons weren't so playful.

'Do you have a name?' Benjamin whispered, patting the creature on the back of the neck.

Tianlong, replied a voice that he took a moment to place as in his head. *Celestial dragon.*

Benjamin nodded. 'Jeremiah would be happy to know how much you've grown,' he said. 'My name is Benjamin. I'm an, um, friend of Jeremiah's.'

I hope he's well.

Benjamin smiled. 'I think he is. He misses you.'

Good.

Benjamin smiled at the dragon's attempt at humour. Then, perhaps in case he'd missed the creature's natural playfulness, Tianlong did a sudden twisting roll, dunking Benjamin into the water. As he came up coughing, he felt a shiver from beneath as though Tianlong were laughing.

They approached the rock pile blocking the channel out of the bay between the two headlands, and Benjamin took a deep breath, closing his eyes, trying to think of a way to get the rocks to move. Perhaps if he animated one rock to move another … but rocks were the hardest thing to reanimate, or so Grand Lord Bastien said. Of all things in existence, rocks were the only ones that were truly dead.

No.

'What?' He realised Tianlong was talking to him again. 'We have to get through the channel entrance.'

There's a way. Benjamin sensed Tianlong's playfulness again, as if the dragon was smiling. *How do you think we got out to meet him? Didn't you know? All of the dragons are female. Except one.*

'But Jim Green said—'

'You humans are so easy to fool. We can change our colour at will. We light to look beautiful when we meet him.'

'Who?'

His name is Shenlong. He is the father of all paper dragons.

'How?' He glanced across at Wilhelm, whose dragon had come up alongside. 'She said there's a way through the channel.'

'She?'

'Isn't yours talking to you, too?'

'You're the Summoner, remember? I can't hear anything.'

Benjamin nodded. 'I can hear her thoughts.'

Tell your friend to hold on.

'Hold—'

Tianlong ducked and dived, drowning out Benjamin's second word. Benjamin hung on for his life as the dragon powered down through the water, into the depths below the shadows of the headlands. Benjamin opened his eyes but he could see only vague shapes and forms, so he closed them again as the chilly water buffeted his face.

It's not far. I forgot you humans can't breathe under water. How unfortunate that must be.

Benjamin wondered whether Tianlong's humour extended to his discomfort. He clamped his mouth shut, hoping Wilhelm would do the same. The water had gone full dark and freezing, and he sensed they were passing beneath the headlands. Then, when he was sure he would have to gasp for air and fill his lungs with water, he felt the pressure lessen and the chill ease.

In a sudden rush, they burst through the surface, and Benjamin gasped in a desperate lungful of air. He glanced back at the choppy surface of the open sea, but saw no sign of Wilhelm or his dragon. He was about to ask Tianlong, when the other dragon exploded out of the sea right in front of them, leaping up into the air with Wilhelm hanging on to its neck. Wilhelm's look made Benjamin laugh. From his pale cheeks, it was clear he'd taken one thrill ride too many.

Shenlong lives at Dragon Rock, Tianlong told him. *We will find your friends there.*

The two dragons moved swiftly through the water, although now Benjamin sensed Tianlong's playfulness was gone, replaced by a gradually building apprehensiveness. Beneath his fingers, the papier-mâché of her body had begun to soften and flake away, and he wondered how long she had before the rougher waters pulled her apart.

We can rest at the rock, she said, as though reading his innermost thoughts. *We can rest there until we are able to make the journey back again.*

'Where are they?' Wilhelm shouted across to Benjamin. 'We're too low in the water to see far.'

'They were near the rock, weren't they?' Benjamin said. 'Tianlong, how far is it?'

Another couple of miles. But something's wrong, Benjamin. I can feel it. Something is wrong with Shenlong.

'What?'

I don't know.

A bank of clouds had begun to move in from over the edge of the world, and Benjamin grimaced as he peered down into the dark waters, sensing what else might live down there, knowing that if Tianlong fell apart, he'd be stuck in the middle of the ocean. His magic could buoy him for a while, but it would eventually run out and he would either drown or drift over the world's edge.

Beneath him Tianlong shuddered.

'Are you all right?'

Shenlong. But that's not him.

A huge, dark shadow rose up off the surface of the sea. Massive wings beat at the air, and the Great Dragon roared loud enough to make Benjamin's ears sting. As they rose up on a swell, the small boat they had seen from Source Mountain came into view, bobbing in the water, its bow skewed to one side as though caught in the middle of a tug of war.

What's happened to him?

'What do you mean?'

Shenlong ... I can feel him, but he's changed.

'He's the Great Dragon, right? He looks pretty great to me.'

You don't understand. Shenlong can't fly. We're all water dragons. And he would never hurt anyone.

Benjamin closed his eyes. Though his body ached with the chill of the water, an even darker chill came from all around him.

Dark reanimate.

'He's under someone's control.'

He didn't have to wonder whose. Only one source of power was great enough to create and control a dragon, and that had come from the Dark Man.

Benjamin, I need to go the island. I need to rest.

'Benjamin, look!'

He turned to Wilhelm, who pointed at something floating in the water. It looked like a water barrel with a rope attached, only now, a man was clinging on for dear life.

'Jim!'

The tour guide and part-time chef looked up at Benjamin through dazed eyes. 'There was something of a mutiny,' he muttered as Tianlong swam alongside and Benjamin helped Jim onto the dragon's back. 'Barnacle and that kid, Cuttlefur. I should have trusted you. That boy's a real bad seed.'

'I think he's working for the Dark Man,' Benjamin said.

Shenlong had turned for another attack on the boat,

but at the sight of Tianlong peering up out of the water, he paused.

Husband! Benjamin felt the dragon cry. *What's happened to you?*

A wave of cold struck Benjamin in the face, so strong, it nearly knocked him off the dragon's back. He could sense Shenlong trying to answer, but his voice had been blocked by the magic controlling him. Behind, Jim Green screamed as Shenlong dived to the attack.

I have to dive, Tianlong said. *I have to get to the island. Hold on.*

They were near the boat. As the dragon lifted out of the water to begin her dive, Benjamin saw a flash of red hair on the lower deck of the skiff.

Miranda.

As Tianlong dived under the water, Benjamin leapt clear. Beside them, Wilhelm's dragon had also dived, taking Wilhelm with her. Benjamin looked up as Shenlong bore down, then ducked his head and closed his eyes. If he was about to be crushed to death by a giant paper dragon, he didn't want to see it.

45

FIRESTARTER

'We have to go back!' Wilhelm shouted to the man who had appeared on the back of Benjamin's dragon as if taking his friend's place. 'We have to go back to that boat!'

'Well, if you can control them, be my guest,' the man said, patting the dragon's neck. 'Not going to listen to me, are you, old girl?'

The dragon's colourful head swung back and forth. Benjamin had claimed they were speaking to him, but all Wilhelm saw were two gigantic hand puppets swimming through the water, seeming no more alive than anything else out here. But they did seem intent on heading for the lump of black rock sticking out of the water.

'Where are they taking us?'

The man pointed. 'Dragon Rock,' he said. 'It's an uninhabited island so close to the edge of the world it gets endlessly battered by storms, making it a particularly unpleasant place to reside. No one likes a view of just fog, do they?'

Wilhelm leaned over the side. They were in the shallows now, rocks passing beneath them, and pieces were beginning to fall off of his dragon, like shedding scales; small, colourful circles that dropped into the water and floated away. The great beast was starting to dissolve.

As his dragon followed the other up onto the shore, sliding through the shingle like a giant snake, Wilhelm jumped off. The other man was already waiting for him, reaching out a hand to help him up out of the shore break.

'Jim Green,' he said. 'I was leading a tour that ran into a few difficulties. And you?'

'Wilhelm Jacobs. I got left behind at the school for causing trouble. What on earth is going on?'

'I don't know what we can do from here,' Jim said, 'but the other kids escaped that boat in a dinghy. It went east, toward the edge. I don't like to think what might have happened to them.'

Wilhelm turned back to the dragons, who had gone halfway up the shore to curl up on the dry shingle. Unmoving, they looked like two shabby carnival floats about to be shipped off to the dump.

'Can they help us?'

Jim Green shook his head. 'They have to dry out or they'll fall apart. Hence the paper part of the Bay of Paper Dragons. I'm amazed they made it this far.'

'That other one, what is it?'

'The Great Dragon? Shenlong?' Jim Green sighed. 'A myth. Until today. How did you get out of the bay?'

'An underwater tunnel.' Wilhelm shivered. 'Scariest thing that's happened to me today. And if you knew the day I've had, you'd understand how scary that was.'

Jim Green smiled. 'Those cheeky beasts. Barnacle and I wondered where the fry kept coming from. Jeremiah's notes claimed they were all female, but there was plenty of seasonal evidence to the contrary. We always just assumed the black ones were males. Come on, this way.'

Jim Green led Wilhelm to a path that led up the side of the rocky cliff. From where they had landed, the boat and its circling dragon were both out of sight, and as they started up a line of natural steps eroded into the rock, Wilhelm could understand why it was called Dragon Rock: everything was black, with no sign of vegetation anywhere, looking for all the world to have been scorched by a dragon's fire.

'This is the closest landmass to the edge,' Jim Green said as they climbed, seemingly unable to slip out of tour guide mode. 'We used to offer tours out here because of how good the views were, but the sea currents can be a bit unpredictable. We had a boat go over once, and we called time on it after that.'

'You had a boat go over?'

Jim Green nodded.

'Over the edge?'

'Yes.'

'What happened to it?'

'It fell.'

'Where?'

'No idea. We hardly went to look, did we?'

Wilhelm stared. 'Were there people on it?'

'We managed to escape on a dinghy. There are rocks near the edge—jagged teeth sticking up out of the sea. It doesn't just fall off, you know. The water. Some does, but only that which sloshes over the teeth. It's more like a sink overflow, otherwise there would be none left. Plus, there's the tides. The red sun and all that.' Jim Green sighed again. 'The teeth, though. Gotta watch out for them. Lethal. The boat got caught on them, and while we managed to escape, it eventually broke up and fell.'

They crested the clifftop, where black volcanic rock was slippery under their feet. Wilhelm followed Jim Green as he skipped nimbly over outcrops and bowls until the ocean beyond the island opened up below.

'Oh, wow. I've never been this close.'

So close Wilhelm felt like he could reach out and touch it, the edge of the world looked like the line of a single, immense waterfall. Blue-grey water suddenly became white and frothy as it poured over into … nothing. Rising up along the edge were great clouds of mist and steam, and in the air beyond it, clouds toiled and rolled, creating an impenetrable white wall masking whatever might lie beyond.

'There!'

Jim Green pointed. So close to the edge of the world they had to be able to feel it over their shoulders, the rest of the pupils clung to jagged rocks poking up out of the water, with the remains of a dinghy floating in the shallows between them.

'They must have gotten smashed up on the reef,' Jim Green said. 'We have to find a way to get to them.'

Floating in the water at the base of the cliff, something shiny caught Wilhelm's eye. 'There's a boat,' he said. 'Is that one of yours?'

'Where?'

'Down there.'

Jim Green stared at him. 'It's one from the guesthouse,' he said. 'I don't know how it got down there. Unless … someone was hiding it.'

Wilhelm crept closer to the edge and peered down while someone clambered over the rocks at the foot of the cliff, making their way toward the boat. At first, he didn't recognise the brown-haired boy until, thanks to slipping on a rock, the boy happened to look up.

The old hair colour had washed out, but even from this distance, the sour face was unmistakable.

'Cuttlefur,' he said. 'I knew it.'

~

'Miranda!'

'Benjamin! What are you doing here?'

He tried to grin, but the dragon's jaws had closed over the battered upper deck and pulled, knocking him down. As he sat up, he said, 'Rescue mission. Wilhelm was with me, too, but we got separated.'

'Wilhelm?'

'It was all his idea. No time to explain right now.'

'The dragon!'

The boat shuddered again, knocking Benjamin against the side rails. As he rubbed where his back had struck the metal, he said, 'Yeah, I noticed it.'

'Cuttlefur trapped me.'

'Miranda, your magic—'

'It's gone! I've been trying to get it back, but I can't!'

Benjamin closed his eyes, and as before, nothing was there. Nothing to suggest she had ever had magic to control, or ever would.

Along the rails wrapped around her wrists, though, he felt a terrible, chilling cold. He probed at them, but his own magic shrank back as though a frightened child were peering into a dark, dark room.

'Dark reanimate,' he said. 'Cuttlefur … I think he's working for the Dark Man. He's controlling the dragon, too.'

The boat shuddered again as Shenlong made another attack, and this time, the stern rose up out of the water.

'The anchor!' Miranda screamed. 'He's pulled it free!'

The boat began to rise up out of the water, and Benjamin grabbed on to a railing as they lurched sideways.

'Let go of it!' Miranda shouted at the dragon, kicking out at the side of the boat in the only way she could express her anger. 'Let go of this boat right now!'

Shenlong paid no attention. Satisfied the anchor had broken, he swung his body around to grip the bow of the boat in his massive hind claws, and a huge draft nearly pulled Benjamin's hands free as the boat turned up on end. The few remaining objects not already shaken loose began a rapid migration into the water below. Miranda, trapped by her wrists, screamed as her body swung back and forth. Benjamin tried to concentrate enough to pull on his magic, but when one slip of his hand could send him plummeting into the water, he couldn't draw more than a little bit at a time. The rails went soft and warm under his fingers, but reanimating a metal pole wouldn't stop a dragon the size of a small ferry.

'Fire!' Miranda screamed. 'It's made out of paper! You have to burn it!'

Benjamin looked around. Everywhere was just water, and wood, and a little bit of metal. What could he possibly cause to burn?

Now, they were moving through the air with the black mass of Dragon Rock approaching on their right. But Shenlong was heading further east, right to the edge of the world.

'Do something, Benjamin!' Miranda screamed.

'I'm thinking, I'm thinking!'

'Stop thinking!'

'It's easy for you to say! You don't have to worry about it!'

Miranda glared, and for a moment her lips curled up in the briefest of smiles. 'If you let me die, I'm going to come back and haunt you forever!' she shouted. 'I'm going to come back as a cleaner and follow you and

Wilhelm around like a bad smell! You got that? Do something!'

A clank of metal made Benjamin turn. Of course.

The engines.

He hooked his feet over the rail and began to haul himself up the side of the boat as though it were a jungle gym in a school playground. There were plenty of ropes and metal rails to hold on to, but in a few seconds, his arms and shoulders were aching.

A little further....

The thing he wanted was just up ahead: a metal screw cap on the side of the boat. The fuel tank. If enough was still inside, he could use his magic to ignite it.

Benjamin closed his eyes, concentrating on the liquid sloshing around inside the tank. Not much left, but there was some. It would have to be enough.

He hooked his arms around the nearest rail so he wouldn't need to worry about falling off, then he began to work the air to push the remaining fuel up out of the tank. It emerged from the fuel chute like a snake, then formed into a silver bubble the size of a beach ball. There was so, so little left.

'Benjamin! The edge of the world!'

Shenlong had flown over Dragon Rock and was now approaching the last horizon, where whitewater tumbled down into mist as clouds swirled up around him.

'Where's he going?'

'I don't know, and I don't want to find out!'

Benjamin closed his eyes. Three, two, one....

'Now!'

He put all the heat he could muster into igniting the ball of fuel, and for a moment, it glowed slightly orange ... then died. With this failure, his hand started to ache. He closed his eyes once more, gritted his teeth, and tried again. Nothing. The fuel simply didn't want to burn.

'It's organic!' he shouted. 'It won't catch fire!'

'You have to make a real fire!' Miranda screamed. 'Hurry, Benjamin!'

As Shenlong roared in triumph, Benjamin hung his head. Down in the water below was a cluster of small figures hanging on to the jagged rocks of the last reef before the edge of the world. Those were his classmates down there, and he could no more help them than he could help anyone else.

He had failed at everything—Source Mountain, saving Miranda, even protecting Wilhelm. He had no plan, no idea, and nothing left to give. It was over. Miranda would die, he would die, and all of his classmates would die, too.

And there was nothing he could do.

He closed his eyes a third time, trying not to let his anger overcome him, when he felt a slight warmth he hadn't noticed before. It didn't appear to come from outside of him; rather, it came more from deep in his chest. As he let the anger fill him, it began to grow stronger.

My heart.

The fire has to come from my heart.

He opened his eyes, steeling himself.

I can do this.

'This isn't over!' he shouted at Shenlong, pushing himself up and clambering higher. The dragon's huge claws were just above him, yet he carried on climbing until he felt strange paper scales under his feet. Shenlong shifted as though touched by a bug or a mouse, but Benjamin looped his hands around the great dragon's ankle and held tight.

'Leave me and my friends alone!' he screamed, then

gave himself over entirely to the rush of heat rising up from inside.

At first, it was just like putting his hand into hot water, then it seemed to sear him from the inside out. A yellow mist filled his mind, and he finally blacked out as the surrounding air filled with the roar of fire.

46

RESCUE MISSION

'Jim, you're a Channeller. You realise that, don't you?'

'What are you talking about?'

'You can channel the magic. You can control things.'

'Don't be ridiculous. I can't do anything.'

Wilhelm slapped a hand against his thigh. 'They only told you that to protect you. You can! I can feel it!'

'You're crazy.'

'Look, that kid down there, he's super dangerous. He doesn't know we're here, though, and if you can just distract him, I'll sort him out the old-fashioned way.'

'What do you mean?'

Wilhelm grinned. 'Playground style.'

'What do you want me to do?'

'Just glare at that kid and imagine him getting slapped down or something.'

'That's all? How's that supposed to help?'

'I don't know! Just try it!'

As they clambered down the rocks to the shingle shore where Cuttlefur made for his boat, Wilhelm realised he was probably committing himself to enough cleans to last for all eternity, by giving a wizard who didn't know he was a wizard a sudden crash course in powers he had no idea he had. What might happen if Jim Green concentrated too much, he was nervous to find out, but if there was someone to test out one's powers on without fear of reprisal, it was Cuttlefur.

'Okay, we haven't got much time. Do it.'

'Do what?'

'Slap him down!'

Jim Green looked terrified. Wilhelm gave him a shove from behind, pointing him at Cuttlefur. 'Okay, I'm trying!'

'I don't see you trying very hard! Try harder! Slap!'

Further along the shore, Cuttlefur cried out and crashed to the ground.

'Nice!'

'What did I do?'

'I don't know, but it worked! Quick, do it again, and I'll grab him!'

As he reached the top of the shingle beach, Wilhelm started into a run. Dragon Rock had really gotten the 'end of the world' theme going on well—the air itself was chilly and thick with spray from the ocean pouring away to nothing just a stone's throw from the shore, while clouds of mist dipped and rose like shower curtains. One moment, Cuttlefur was there; the next, he was gone. And then he was back again, climbing up from a hollow in the beach, making for the speedboat waiting in the shallows.

'It's payback time,' Wilhelm muttered as he closed within a few feet. Cuttlefur waded out into the water, eyes fixed on the dinghy broken up on the rocks offshore and the cluster of frightened pupils hanging on at the world's edge as a giant snappy ghoul tried to eat them.

'Face slam, punk!' Wilhelm shouted, and he leapt onto Cuttlefur's back. He caught the other boy flush, knocking him into the water, and the resounding clunk as Cuttlefur's forehead struck the wooden edge of the speedboat sounded like the ringing of a victory bell.

As Jim Green came up behind him, Wilhelm hauled Cuttlefur up out of the water. The other boy's eyes were closed, and his mouth hung open.

'Is he dead?'

Wilhelm slapped Cuttlefur's cheek, and the other boy groaned. 'Nope, unfortunately not. Just stunned. Get him in the boat. We'll pick up the others, then swing back to help Benjamin and Miranda.'

'Will they all fit?'

'You tell me. It's your boat.'

Jim Green climbed up into the boat and pulled open a box in the stern, revealing a coil of rope. 'We can use this to tow what's left of that dinghy,' he said.

'Now we're talking. Quite a team, aren't we?'

They pulled Cuttlefur into the boat and sat him up near the back, where he groaned and reached up to rub his head.

'Tie him up. Then imagine the ropes are snakes, and if he moves, they'll bite him.'

'You're mad.'

'I'm a kid. I have a good imagination.'

'Okay, I'll try, but I think this is all crazy.'

'We're in a speedboat at the edge of the world, about to try to save a group of kids from a giant orange submarine that's come back to life and looks like it really wants its first meal. Tell me something that isn't crazy.'

'You have a point.'

Wilhelm grinned. 'Let's go.'

Snout didn't really need to swim. With the currents speeding him rapidly to his doom, he only had to keep his head above the water.

The sea near the edge was freezing. At his school back in England, he'd never liked swimming, and he now felt justified for all those times he'd pretended to forget his swimming costume to get out of it. Watching the other pupils floundering in the reef only confirmed his belief that the sea was a terrible, evil thing that should be filled in and turned into something much more pleasant, like farmland or concrete.

Behind him, the dragon carried the boat through the sky. To his left rose Dragon Rock, dark and imposing, a jagged, volcanic outcrop that couldn't have been less welcoming if it'd had a barbed wire fence around the outside. As he turned around in the current, he was afforded a panoramic view of the whole spectacle, as though a 3D disaster movie was taking place around him.

'Help!' someone screamed. It sounded like Fat Adam. Snout had liked Fat Adam; they'd had interesting conversations about dinner each evening, even though it never changed much. The huge ghoul that had come to fight the dragon had trapped the pupils on the reef by the edge of the world, which Snout presumed had been created from all of the junk that had failed to reanimate, brought down the Great Junk River.

Snout sighed. Nothing he could do, of course. Best to just give up and drown.

Then, in the sky high above, came a sudden burst of fire.

It had originated from the dragon's claws, and it was slowly working its way up the dragon's legs toward its body.

With a boom, the dragon ignited. It had been climbing

into the sky over Dragon Rock, but now it veered east again, dropping toward the edge of the world.

The boat still hung by one claw. Snout gasped. Miranda was still on that boat. If the dragon didn't stop, it would drop the boat into the abyss beyond the reef, and Miranda would be lost forever.

Snout wished he could do something, but unfortunately, not everyone could be a hero. That was for other boys, not a dorky nobody like him.

∽

With Jim Green at the wheel, the speedboat skimmed across the water's surface to the trapped pupils. Wilhelm sat in the back, next to Cuttlefur, who was slowly waking up.

'Snakes, Jim!' he shouted, as Cuttlefur groaned. 'Think of snakes!'

The ropes around Cuttlefur's waist shimmered. To Wilhelm, they still looked like ropes, but when Cuttlefur opened his eyes and looked down, he gasped.

'No! Don't make them bite me!'

'Shut your punk mouth,' Wilhelm said. 'There's worse than snakes waiting for you in prison.'

'What prison?'

'*The* prison!'

Wilhelm couldn't think of what else to do, so he scooped up some water from the bottom of the boat and splashed it into Cuttlefur's face.

The boat slowed as it came up against the nearest pupils. 'Get in!' Wilhelm shouted, clambering over to help them into the boat. Patting Jim Green on the shoulder, he repeated, 'Snakes! Keep thinking of snakes!'

The water's roar was almost deafening, and the air was

so thick with spray, it was impossible to see more than a few paces in front of them.

Wilhelm climbed over the boat's edge, trying to remember how many kids he was looking for. Cuttlefur, their not-so-honourary first year, was already on the boat, so that left fifteen, minus Benjamin, Miranda, and himself. Thirteen second years, minus Godfrey, was twelve.

Twenty-four kids, struggling among the rocks.

He stumbled across the jagged rocks just beneath the surface as water rushed for oblivion and pulled at his knees. As shapes appeared out of the mist, he pushed them back in the direction of the speedboat. Some looked scared but unhurt, others had blood on their faces from where the rocks had cut them. Wilhelm counted them off on his fingers, unable to believe none had fallen over the edge.

'Fifteen … sixteen—that way, Kate, be careful! Get in the boat and hold on. You're safe now. Twenty-two, twenty-three …. Who's missing?'

He turned around, but no other shapes appeared out of the mist, and he was so close to the edge now, he could see nothing but spray and rocks. He only knew the way to the boat, because there were only two directions—forward and back.

'Who's missing?'

A hand fell on his shoulder. It was Fat Adam. His hair was soaked to his scalp, and the front of his T-shirt was flecked with blood. 'Snout. Cuttlefur threw him off the dinghy.'

Wilhelm sighed. 'We can't help him now. Get back to the boat. Come on, let's go.'

He followed Adam back to where the speedboat waited and helped the fat boy over the side. Then he climbed in next to Jim Green.

'Let's go,' he said. 'Back to Dragon Rock. We can drop them off there, then come back and look for Snout.'

Jim started to turn the boat around.

'Look!'

Several pupils pointed at the sky. At first, Wilhelm thought he was witnessing the dynamic birth of a third sun, until he realised—

'It's the dragon!'

A grey lump hung from one claw. The boat. Miranda and Benjamin were supposed to be on it.

'Back to Dragon Rock,' he shouted, jumping over the side and into the water. 'Go, Jim!'

The speedboat started to turn. Wilhelm stared at the group of shivering pupils crouched inside, wondering what seemed wrong, when a massive crash came from behind. As the fireball that was the dragon had smashed into the water and the boat it held now leaned precariously over the edge of the world, he realised what he hadn't noticed before.

Cuttlefur was no longer in the boat.

47

BATTLE

Benjamin opened his eyes to find himself lying in shallow water. Hard rocks at his back prevented him from moving in a strong current that rushed past his chest.

He coughed and sat up. From somewhere to his right came the heat of flames, and he turned his head toward a roaring inferno caught among jagged rocks sticking up out of the water.

Shenlong. The great paper dragon was gone, consumed by flames.

He turned away. Where was Miranda?

To his left, on the rocks, lay the crushed and battered remains of the skiff, its top deck folded inwards, its hull broken apart. He stared at it as memories of what had happened flooded back, then he climbed to his feet and staggered through the flowing water, calling out Miranda's name.

He reached the skiff and leaned over the side, the railings where she had been trapped bent and broken. Only a single lock of hair caught on a crack in the wood showed she had been there.

'No!' he screamed, turning toward the edge of the world. The swirling mists ignored him, the thunderous fall of the water his only answer. He fell to his knees, his head in his hands.

He had stopped the dragon but had failed Miranda. She was gone, and only now did he realise how foolish he had been to try to leave Endinfinium.

'I'm sorry,' he whispered as water rushed past his knees.

'Benjamin!'

The voice had called out as though in a dream. Benjamin lifted his head as it came again, movements sluggish and lethargic. His whole body ached. Perhaps he had died in the fire, too, and he only needed to close his eyes and let his body slip over the edge of the world into oblivion.

'Benjamin, over here!'

It was real. She was real. Miranda was alive.

She stepped out from behind a needle of rock, hair slicked to her head like blood. 'Come and see this!'

He stumbled to his feet. 'Is that really you?'

'Of course it's me!'

As he reached her, she pulled him into a tight hug. 'Quick, come see what I found over here.'

He waded after her while Miranda pointed at something bloated and bulky caught in another crag. At first he thought it was one of the paper dragons, because it was disintegrating. The colours, though, were too dull and bland, and as a sudden surge of water turned it sideways, he saw a pale human face.

'It's Barnacle,' he gasped. 'What's happening to him?'

'It's not Barnacle.' Miranda nudged the lump with her foot so that a large piece broke off and flowed over the edge of the world. 'It's Godfrey.'

Benjamin stared. From out of the dissolving ruins of Alan Barnacle's face stared Benjamin's arch-nemesis. He looked in parts exhausted, angry, and defeated.

'Surprise,' he said. 'Push me over and be done with it.'

Benjamin shook his head. 'No chance. You think you're getting off so easily? Was this a setup from the beginning?'

Godfrey glared. 'You have no idea what's coming for you, do you, Forrest?'

'What do you mean?'

'There's someone who really wants to see you. But if he can't see you, I think he'd be happy enough to know you were dead.' He shifted. The two halves of his false body broke open, and he lifted a bottle out of a pocket in the jacket underneath.

'What's that?'

Godfrey smiled. 'It's what made Endinfinium. Pure, distilled.' His grin turned sadistic. 'Deadly.'

He pulled the bottle cap free and made to fling it forward. With a scream, Miranda leapt in front of him. A blinding flash of light burst between them, then Miranda fell back.

Benjamin caught her in his arms before she plunged into the water. Godfrey had fallen against the rocks, eyes closed.

'Miranda! Wake up!'

Her eyes opened to slits. 'Friends?' she whispered. 'You saved me … so I….' Her eyes closed again, and her head lolled to the side. Benjamin shook her, but she had gone limp in his arms.

'No!'

Her skin felt cold, and when he pressed his fingers against her wrist, there was no pulse. He slapped the side of her face, but she didn't respond.

Rage filled him. He lifted her in his arms and walked toward Godfrey. His enemy's eyelids fluttered.

'You did this,' he whispered, his heart filling with the heat of his magic. 'I'll ... I'll ... kill you.'

Godfrey's arm lifted and he pointed at the edge of the world. Benjamin frowned, wondering what it meant. Then he realised. He glanced down. The water was rising up his legs.

'Huh?'

'Benjamin!'

The voice had come out of the fog to his right, and he turned. Something huge and orange loomed out of the gloom.

'Benjamin! It's me, um, Snout! Are you all right?'

Benjamin waded a few steps away from the edge, and the reanimated submarine appeared out of the mist. Snout sat on its back, hanging on to a couple of protruding tentacles.

'The water level's rising!' Snout said. 'The red sun's drawing the tide!'

'What are you doing?'

Snout shrugged. 'It does what I say.'

He climbed down into the water and waded over to Benjamin, where he looked down at Miranda and wiped away what could have been sea spray, but equally a tear.

'We have to take her back,' Benjamin said. 'She deserves better than to stay here.'

'What about Godfrey?'

Benjamin nodded. 'I'd happily see him go over the edge, but that's not what she would have wanted. We take him back, too. It's up to the teachers to punish him.'

They hauled Miranda up onto the back of the submarine then returned for Godfrey. By the time both were secured, they were gasping for air, and the water had risen to their waists.

'Benjamin! Where are you?'

He spun around. The cry had come out of the mists back at the world's edge. Benjamin exchanged a glance with Snout.

'It's Wilhelm,' he said.

'It certainly sounded like him,' Snout answered.

'This way!' Benjamin shouted. 'We're over here!'

The water was getting deeper. Soon the current would be too strong.

'Go and get him,' Snout said. 'The ghoul can't get through the rocks. Hurry!'

Benjamin waded through the rocky spines to the world's edge, shouting Wilhelm's name, while eddies of water tugged at his ankles, pulling him into deeper pools and crevasses. By the time he heard Wilhelm's voice again, his knees and shins were bruised and bloodied.

'I'm over here! I saw the fire!'

Wilhelm appeared as a shadow out of the mist. Benjamin waved, then dropped his hand as Wilhelm's shadow appeared to split in two.

Cuttlefur stepped out from behind him.

'Wilhelm!'

Cuttlefur grinned, then clubbed Wilhelm in the side of the face. With a grunt, Wilhelm collapsed into the water. His body rolled like a log, turning in the current, before he dropped over the edge of the world.

'No!'

'It's come to this,' Cuttlefur said, eyes narrowed, lips drawn back in a snarl. 'Fight me, Forrest, you little runt!'

With a screaming hiss, the water rose up to wrap around Benjamin's waist, throwing him against the nearest rocks. He gasped as a jagged edge cut into his skin, feeling the back of his hand ache at the same time. Scowling, he summoned his magic and drew the water out from under Cuttlefur's feet, leaving hard, reef rock for the other boy to fall onto. Cuttlefur gasped as he cut his hands, then Benjamin sent the water rushing forward to smash Cuttlefur back. When he stood up again, his face was streaked with blood.

'How easily they turned from you,' Cuttlefur spat. 'You call them friends? You've got none, Forrest. You never did and you never will.'

A club of water rose up from nowhere and smashed into Benjamin's chest. For a moment, he went under, then he came spluttering back to his feet just inches from where the ocean poured away into mists and steam. He drew on his magic again, mustering the strength to fight. Cuttlefur waited, a grin spreading over his face, hands poised like a fighter making a ring comeback. Benjamin shook his head.

'What's the matter, Forrest? Did you use all of your magic setting Shenlong alight?'

'I've got plenty left for you,' Benjamin shouted, but as he reached for it, he felt only a few brief tingles, like the residue of petrol in an empty tank.

Cuttlefur shook his head. 'Oh, Forrest. I hoped this would be more of a challenge.'

You saved me.

Benjamin started. At first, he thought the voice had come from Miranda. Then he realised it was in his head as Tianlong's had been.

A favour deserves a favour, Benjamin Forrest.

Something huge, black, and snakelike rose out of the water behind Cuttlefur's back. A square head filled with clacking teeth opened and closed, and Benjamin tried not to look at it as it swooped down.

'Say good—'

Cuttlefur's words were cut off as Shenlong—the real Shenlong, once trapped inside the body of the giant paper dragon—picked up the boy in his mouth. Thick, wooden teeth held Cuttlefur firm, then, in one fluid motion, Shenlong's head snapped sideways and flung Cuttlefur out into the abyss.

Benjamin steadied himself against an outcrop. He waited, but Cuttlefur was gone. As soon as relief had flooded in, so did misery. He gritted his teeth, refusing to cry. Both his best friends, dead. As Shenlong swam through the water and lifted him up onto the dragon's huge square head, Benjamin wanted to scream out in anger, but he had nothing left to give.

'Benjamin!'

He didn't even have the energy to shout back to Snout. He lifted a hand to wave, but the mists were too thick. 'Thank you,' he whispered to Shenlong, half wishing the Great Dragon had left him to his fate. He tried to wave Shenlong back to Snout's ghoul-submarine, but instead, the dragon turned back to the edge of the world.

'No, the other way....'

Shenlong stretched out until his head was far over the edge, his tail wrapping around an outcrop to support him. Benjamin peered down into swirling mists. Would the dragon put him out of his misery after all? Shenlong leaned over the edge, and Benjamin saw black, shiny rock through curtains of falling water.

And there—a face.

Wilhelm stuck out a hand out from the ledge. 'Grab me!'

Benjamin stared in disbelief. The ledge below the edge of the world barely protruded more than a few inches. Wilhelm looked terrified, but as he leapt out onto

Shenlong's head and climbed up beside Benjamin, he flashed a wild grin.

'Now that, my friend, was one too many thrill rides.'

Benjamin grabbed Wilhelm in a bear hug, overcome with relief. Wilhelm was alive. And for now, that was all that mattered. He would worry later about how to tell Wilhelm about Miranda.

'Shenlong,' he whispered. 'Let's go home.'

48

REVIVAL

The teachers were all waiting in a line on the beach. Ms. Ito looked ready to kill Jim Green, who was trying to explain that the boat had gotten into a little trouble. Behind him, Alan Barnacle—the real Alan Barnacle—watched the proceedings with something like disbelief.

Edgar had taken Miranda's body up into a hut at the top of the beach, and he allowed no visitors. Godfrey had been led away by Professor Eaves, while the rest of the pupils were loaded into Lawrence and taken up to the guesthouse. Benjamin and Wilhelm stood apart as Ms. Ito stumped over.

'We'll discuss this in more detail at a later date,' she said, then she lowered her voice. 'I'm happy that both of you are all right, but you have to remember the Oath.'

Wilhelm glanced at Benjamin, who was too tired to even roll his eyes. 'There is no magic,' they muttered together.

'Good, good.'

Behind her, Edgar ran out of the hut, waving to them.

'May we be excused?' Wilhelm said.

Ms. Ito nodded. 'It looks like he wants you to hurry,' she said, turning her head in the possibility of a smile.

'Quickly,' Edgar said, waving them inside.

Miranda lay on a chalet bed with her head propped up on a dirty pillow. She gave them a weak smile, then closed her eyes again.

'You're alive!' Benjamin cried, pulling Wilhelm into another hug, and the two of them beamed at her, disbelieving.

'I'm fine,' Miranda muttered without opening her eyes.

'What happened?' Benjamin said.

Edgar lifted up a piece of stone on a string, which had broken in two. 'This was a dark reanimate charm,' he said.

'That's what Cuttlefur gave her!' Wilhelm shouted.

'It blocked her magic and it preyed on her feelings and emotions,' Edgar said, 'but when she took the blast from the pure dark reanimate, this charm blocked that too. Cuttlefur's evil saved her life.'

Benjamin and Wilhelm exchanged glances.

'Will she be all right?'

Edgar nodded. 'I think she'll be back to normal in no time. Now, you two look exhausted. I'd suggest you go up to the guesthouse and try to get a bit of sleep. I've heard there will be a great feast tonight to celebrate.'

'To celebrate what?'

'The return of the Great Dragon.' Edgar pointed out into the bay. They both looked at the sleek, black shape of Shenlong circling in the water, with other, more colourful dragons circling around him.

'He was captured and encased in a body formed of dark reanimate,' Edgar said. 'The same that happened to Godfrey.'

'Who was behind it?' Benjamin asked.

Edgar lowered his voice. 'The Dark Man,' he said. 'I

don't know why he's after you, Benjamin, but it seems he'll do what he must to get to you. It would be a good idea to take great care from now on.'

Benjamin glanced at Wilhelm. 'I'll try,' he said. 'What's going to happen to Godfrey?'

'I think that's up to the Grand Lord to decide. Ms. Ito and Professor Eaves are keeping a close eye—as well as a magical restraint—on him, but it's out of our hands now. I'm sure the Grand Lord will want to know what was going on up in the High Mountains, although whether Godfrey will tell him or not is another matter.'

The bed behind them creaked, and all three looked around to see Miranda pushing herself up onto her elbows.

'Where am I?' she asked, her voice barely more than a croak.

Edgar patted Benjamin and Wilhelm on their backs. 'I'll give you three a few moments alone,' he said, then headed for the door.

They crowded around her bed in an awkward silence while all of them thought about the best thing to say.

'Sorry!' 'I'm sorry, too!' 'Yeah, and me!' all three blurted out, then they started to laugh.

'That was quite something, eh?' Wilhelm said. 'Look, I'm sorry I spied on you. It's just, you know, he got my back up from the start, waltzing in here with his blue hair and smug smile.'

Miranda shrugged. 'I should have trusted you. We've been friends a long time. It's just that you're a bit of a sneak sometimes.'

'And can't you see why?'

Miranda smiled. 'Yeah, I kind of can. Have you caught out Professor Eaves yet?'

Wilhelm shook his head. 'Operations resume on our return to the school.'

'I'll help you.'

Wilhelm lifted a tentative hand, then patted her on the shoulder.

Benjamin looked from one to the other. 'And I'm sorry I tried to leave,' he said. 'I got obsessed with finding a way home. You know, everyone here seems to like being here, except me.'

Miranda watched him. 'No one can blame you for wanting to leave, Benjamin. What did you find?'

Benjamin sighed. 'I'm not sure I could explain it in a way it would make any sense. I've given up on the idea for the time being, though.' But even as he said it, he wasn't really sure he believed it. 'It would be nice just to have a quiet life for a while, wouldn't it?'

'You can say that again,' Wilhelm said. 'Not likely, though, is it?'

Benjamin grinned. 'Probably not.'

A knock came at the door. Edgar peered inside. 'We're going to try to move Miranda up to the guesthouse. Do you guys want to help?'

Miranda glared at them. 'I can manage,' she said, and both boys stepped out of range as the familiar fire appeared in her eyes.

'She can manage,' Wilhelm said to Edgar, a grin on his face.

∽

'I think he's up there. That's about where she said, isn't it?'

Benjamin nodded, placing a hand on the rickety wooden ladder. 'A little to the left, please.'

With a crackling of twigs, the wooden ladder that was Fallenwood shifted across the front of the building.

'Right, up you go,' Benjamin said. 'I'll hold it.'

Fallenwood crackled in a way that suggested holding the ladder wasn't necessary.

'Well, after you ran off and hid,' Wilhelm said, 'I wouldn't put anything past you.' At the sound of another angry crinkle, he lifted a hand. 'But I haven't forgotten my promise. I'll leave that botanical society building as clean as my own dorm room.'

'Which is spotless,' Benjamin said with a sarcastic grin.

Over in the car park, a large, coal barbecue spat sparks up into the air while children danced around it. Edgar moved among them, at times entertaining, at others supervising. Ms. Ito and Professor Eaves were absent, off somewhere, most likely keeping an eye on Godfrey, who, according to Edgar, had so far refused to cooperate.

Benjamin peered up into the dark. The light from the barbecue flickered off the soles of Wilhelm's shoes, but otherwise he couldn't see anything.

'Any luck?'

The wooden ladder creaked. 'Got him!' Wilhelm shouted jubilantly, then he shimmied down the ladder with something shiny in his hands.

'Nice to see you made it, Rick,' Benjamin said with a smile, patting the little Scatlock on the part he presumed was its head.

∼

The next morning, they left for the school, with all of the pupils loaded up into Lawrence's front two carriages, Godfrey and the teachers in the rearmost one. Jim Green and Alan Barnacle came to wave them goodbye, the former with a lot more luster than the latter, who was part embarrassed, part disappointed with what had ensued in his enforced absence.

Lawrence took an alternate route this time, heading up the hill behind the guesthouse toward the clifftops. As they reached the peak, Benjamin, Wilhelm, and Miranda pressed their faces to the window. Far below, two shapes moved through the water—one black and shiny, the other coloured like a rainbow. While Benjamin couldn't be sure, if he let his eyes relax enough for the colours to blur, it appeared they were marking out letters which went together into a message:

THANKS FOR THE MEMORIES. WE LOOK FORWARD TO SEEING YOU AGAIN.

Wilhelm, who didn't quite catch it, just shrugged, while Miranda, who did, stared unblinking at the bay until it was out of sight, a misty look in her eyes.

The journey south to the school took a lot longer than the arrival journey, with Lawrence, upon the teachers' insistence, taking a more relaxed, scenic route. Most of the pupils fell asleep, and when Benjamin woke, they were already back outside the main entrance.

Captain Roche and Professor Loane greeted them, as did Gubbledon, looking even more worried than usual. Without much fuss, Godfrey was led away into the school, while the other pupils watched through Lawrence's windows. Then, in no uncertain terms, Ms. Ito made it quite clear they should immediately return to their dorm rooms and prepare for dinner, over which a list of punishments would be read.

Benjamin was happy to receive just five hundred cleans —for 'various misdemeanours unbecoming of a pupil of Endinfinium High'—while Wilhelm received three thousand, payable in installments, for 'direct disobedience of teachers' instructions.' Rather unknown for a punishment of such scale, the cleans were 'transferable' to any pupil wishing to lighten the load, so Benjamin and Miranda offered to take five hundred each, and even Snout chipped in with a round one hundred.

After dinner, Benjamin made his way down into Underfloor and had Moto take him to meet Basil again. When they arrived, the ancient biplane looked asleep, but he perked up when he realised who was paying him a visit.

'He's still there,' Benjamin said. 'He's trying to stop people like me from making the same mistake.'

Basil gave a tired snort. 'He always was a fool. But I hope he's found some level of peace,' he said.

Benjamin nodded. 'I think he has,' he replied. 'He had one request of you, though.'

'Oh? What's that?'

'He wants you to fly again.'

Basil snorted again. 'Impossible. Even if I still could, I'm not sure I'd want to.'

Benjamin smiled. 'I think it would make a very, very old man, very, very happy,' he said.

Basil gave a grave nod. 'In that case,' he said, 'I'll try.' Then, as Benjamin turned to leave, he added, 'I'll need a good pilot, though. My wits aren't what they used to be.'

Again Benjamin smiled. 'I think that can be arranged,' he said.

49

RECOGNITION

It was some weeks, and time for Endinfinium to pass through a lazy, quiet summer and slip into an autumn of sorts, before Benjamin would scratch the itch that had really been bugging him since the episode at the Bay of Paper Dragons.

Godfrey was being held in a basement cell room with a view overlooking the ocean, right to the edge of the world. So far, he had refused all attempts to reintegrate him into the school, deciding instead to remain a prisoner.

'Try not to rattle him up,' Edgar said. 'He's safely secured, but I don't want him making a fuss. And the less you anger him, the less likely he'll shop you to the other teachers. Are you sure you want to go through with this?'

Benjamin nodded. 'There's something I need to know,' he said.

'All right, but remember, you stole the key. This comes back on you. I can't afford another exile.'

'Don't worry.'

Benjamin took the key and headed for the cell door at the end of the corridor, leaving Edgar standing back in the shadows. As he reached it, he took a deep breath, then slipped the key into the lock and gave it a single, sharp turn.

He opened the door and felt a sudden sense of shock. Godfrey stood by the window, his back to Benjamin, with plastic chains that looked no stronger than a piece of string stung around his body. Of course, they had been reanimated and then enchanted with special magic that would prevent Godfrey from escaping or using his powers, but they looked so terribly weak.

'Godfrey.'

The other boy turned. 'Oh, well look who it is.'

'Hello, Godfrey.'

'What do you want?'

'Look, I'm not going to pretend this is a social call. You can either be straight with me or not. I just wanted to know what you meant when you said I had no idea about what was coming for me. What does he want from me?'

Godfrey glared. 'Why should I tell you?'

'Why shouldn't you? What difference does it make? It's not like you need a bargaining tool, is it? You're free to return to the school, if you'll only follow a few rules.'

'I don't care about this school's rules. I make my own.'

Benjamin sighed. Apparently, Godfrey wouldn't play easily. He turned to go.

'Wait.'

Benjamin turned back.

'What?'

'I saw his face,' Godfrey said quietly. 'He lifted his hood and I saw his face.'

A shiver ran down Benjamin's spine. 'And?'

'He was a little older, perhaps, but not so much as you'd think. More aged, but not in the way people age. More like ... a vintage.'

'What are you talking about?'

'You ought to know, Forrest. This is all down to you, after all.'

'What do you mean?'

'It was you, Forrest. When the Dark Man lifted his hood to show me his face … it was you.'

END

For more information about forthcoming titles
please visit

www.amillionmilesfromanywhere.net

THANKS

Big thanks as always to those of you who provided help and encouragement. My editors and proofreaders Kim, Nick, Jenny, Hazel, Kathryn and Lisa get a special mention, as does as always, my muse, Jenny Twist.

In addition, extra thanks goes to my Patreon supporters, in particular to Amaranth Dawe, Janet Hodgson, Leigh McEwan, James Edward Lee, Catherine Crispin, Alan MacDonald, Eda Ridgeway, Nancy, and Norma.

You guys are awesome.

Printed in Great Britain
by Amazon